MAP of the GOLD REGION of CALIFORNIA

GOLD IS WHERE YOU FIND IT

TELLER'S CAMP

DIRECTOR'S CHOICE
BEST WESTERN DRAMA FEATURE
The Wild Bunch Film Festival
2023

PLATINUM REMI
WorldFest-Houston International Film Festival
2023

2024 WILL ROGERS MEDALLION AWARD WINNER

WATCH THE TRAILER AT WWW.TELLERSCAMP.COM

SADDLEBAG DISPATCHES

EST. 2014

Our mission at *Saddlebag Dispatches* is to keep the spirit of the frontier alive by fostering interest, discussion, and writing in the history and legacy of the American West.

WINTER 2024 • VOLUME 10, ISSUE #2

For advertising rates and schedules or business-related questions, contact Business Manager Amy Cowan
amy@saddlebagdispatches.com

CONTACT INFORMATION
Saddlebag Dispatches, LLC
2401 Beth Lane, Bentonville, AR 72712
479.657.3894

WEBSITE
www.saddlebagdispatches.com

Dedicated to the memory of our late co-founder, Dusty Richards, and our dear departed friends and partners, Velda Brotherton and Bob Giel.

GOLD RUSH COUNTRY FEATURES

SHORT FICTION

WESTERN POETRY

PERSPECTIVES

BEHIND THE CHUTES

Dennis Doty
PUBLISHER

Striking Gold in the Wild West

Celebrating Stories and Winners from the Frontier

Welcome to the Winter issue of *Saddlebag Dispatches* magazine. This issue dives deep into the California Gold Rush, exploring its rich history and captivating stories.

We also celebrate the success of the 2nd Annual Longhorn Award. This year's winning story, Bob Armstrong's "Clay Allison's Girl," is featured in this issue. Special congratulations to last year's winner, Michael Norman, whose story "A Death of Crows" went on to win gold in the Western Short Fiction category at the Will Rogers Medallion Awards. Another frequent contributor and celebrated author, W. Michael Farmer, earned silver for his story, "Finding Fortune," a compelling modern western set along the southern border.

The Will Rogers Medallion Awards spotlighted even more talent in the western genre. Bob Boze Bell, publisher of *True West*, took home the coveted Golden Lariat Award for service to the Western genre, and Jane Kirkpatrick was awarded a richly-deserved Lifetime Achievement Award.

In the Western Traditional Fiction category, W. Michael Farmer's *Desperate Warrior: Days of War, Days of Peace, Chato's Chiricahua Apache Legacy Book One* tied for Silver with Pegg Thomas' *Silver Prairies,* while Paul Colt earned Bronze for *Lunger: The Doc Holliday Story*. Reavis Z. Wortham claimed Bronze in Western Mystery for *Hard Country,* Chris Enss won Silver in Western Non-Fiction for *An Open Secret: The Story of Deadwood's Most Notorious Bordellos*, and Sherry Monahan's *Signature Dishes of America* took Silver in the Western Cookbook category.

Bringing Home the Hardware: A bevy of terrific Western writers show off their Will Rogers Medallions during the WRMA Awards Banquet in Fort Worth, Tx. in October. From left: *New York Times* Bestseller Reavis Z. Wortham, Michael Norman, Joni Franks, *New York Times* Bestseller Chris Enss, and Sherry Monahan.

Hard Work Pays Off: Managing Editor Anthony Wood (left) proudly displays the medallions awarded to Michael Norman and W. Michael Farmer for their Short Fiction stories, both published in *Saddlebag Dispatches,* while author Barbara L. Clouse (center) and Young Dragons Publisher Amy Cowan (right) celebrate Barbara's Gold Medal win in the Western Illustrated Children's Fiction category.

In the Illustrated Western Young Readers category, Joni Franks' *Corky Tails: Holly Berry & Mistletoe* won Silver, and she was also named Illustrator of the Year. Finally, our very own *Saddlebag Dispatches* Research Director, Barbara Clouse, earned Gold for her book, *The Healing Lodge.* Congratulations to all these remarkable western authors!

Hearty congratulations are also in order for *New York Times* bestselling author Chris Enss, who also recently won Women Writing the West's prestigous Downing Journalism Award for her article, "The Attorney Teacher: Sarah Herring Sorin," which appeared in the *Tombstone Epitaph.* Her remarkable work was joined by runners-up Kenyon Bennett for "Rowdy Cowboys, Outlaws, and a Blood Feud" in *True West* Magazine and Michael Gear and Kathleen O'Neal Gear for "Bison: A Barnyard Revolution? Or a Looming Disaster" in *Bison Review* Magazine. Well done to all of these outstanding journalists!

This issue offers even more treasures. Regina McLemore shares the incredible journey of a Cherokee wagon train to the goldfields, while Sherry Monahan's *Lively Libations* column adds a bright and flavorful touch. Terry Alexander delves into Hollywood's interpretation of the Gold Rush era, examining how it has been portrayed on the silver screen.

Among our features, Anthony Wood brings us a fascinating look at the true identity of the legendary Zorro, while Regina McLemore tells the inspiring story of Mary Ellen Pleasant, the first Black woman millionaire. Terry Alexander highlights the adventurous life of gambler Eleanor Dumont, and George "Clay" Mitchell shares an insightful profile of Reavis Z. Wortham.

Our short fiction selection for this issue is equally compelling, showcasing the work of five exceptional western authors, including Thom Brucie, Will Ames, Don Money, Benjamin Thomas, and James A Tweedie.

Last but not least, settle in for "Second Anniversary," Part 2 of our 3 part Western Time-Travel serial by *New York Times* bestseller Reavis Z. Wortham.

As we continue to celebrate *Saddlebag Dispatches'* 10th anniversary, we're thrilled to announce some exciting news. Starting in April, the magazine will expand to three issues per year, ensuring even more stories, columns, and features to delight western enthusiasts. Thank you for your continued support over the last decade, and we look forward to bringing you even more incredible content in the months and years to come.

So, pull up a log, pour yourself a steaming cup of coffee from the camp pot, and settle in to enjoy the very best in western storytelling.

Dennis Doty

WILD WOMEN

Chris Enss
ADVERTISING MANAGER

Sarah Royce's Journey West

Across a Wasteland of Dreams

The long shadows of a beleaguered wagon train stretched across the Carson River Route, a parched trail through Nevada. Pioneers traveling west used this unavoidable route to get to California. The long, dry crossing was one of the most dreaded ordeals of the entire emigrant experience. The sources of fresh, drinkable water were forty miles apart from one another. Thirty-year-old Sarah Royce had read about the desolate section of land in the fragments of a guidebook she'd found while on the journey to the Gold Country in 1849. By the time many of the sojourners had reached this part of the trek their wagons and livestock weren't fit to continue. Sarah, her husband, and their two-year-old daughter, Mary, stared in amazement at the abandoned vehicles and carcasses of ox and mule teams lying about. It seemed to the weary couple that they could walk over the remains of the animals for the duration of the trip and never touch the ground.

The grim markers were nothing Sarah envisioned she would see when she embarked on the six-month venture. Having left her home in Iowa to follow the hordes of other pilgrims hoping to find gold, she set her sights on a serene and profitable life in a country depicted as a utopia. The expedition had proved to be more difficult than she had expected. As she recalled in her diary: "While making our way over the desert we came upon a scene of a wreck that surpassed anything preceding it... As we neared it, we wondered at the size of the wagons which, in the dim light of the moon, looked tall as houses, against the sky... We turned to look at what lay round the monster wagons. It would be impossible to describe the motley collection of things of various sorts, strewed all about... There was only one thing, (besides the few pounds of bacon) that, in all these varied heaps of things, many of which, in civilized scenes, would have been valuable, I thought worth picking up. That was a little book, bound in cloth and illustrated with a number of small engravings. Its title was Little Ella. I thought it would please Mary, so I put it in my pocket. It was an easily carried souvenir of the desert; and more than one pair of eyes learned to read its pages in after years."

As a natural educator, Sarah was drawn to items that would teach children. Her parents encouraged that gift when she was very young and encouraged her to study a variety of subjects from religion to world cultures. She was born Sarah Eleanor Bayliss in Stratford upon Avon, England, in 1819. Her mother and father moved to America when she was six weeks old and settled in New York. She excelled in every area of school and was a voracious reader. She graduated from Phipps Union Female Seminary and became a schoolteacher in Rochester. After she met and married Josiah Royce Sr., the two relocated to the Midwest. Shortly after the birth of their first child, they traveled to Missouri and began preparing to head west.

Seated in a wagon filled with all her worldly possessions, Sarah, along with the other men, women, and children in their party, left Independence on April 30, 1849. The first day of the journey was uneventful. They stopped to eat a "pleasant lunch on the prairie" and when the trip resumed, she watched the afternoon "wear quietly away." The mundane beginning would not be sustained. The roads were rough, the weather either too cold or too hot, and unexpected problems, like the livestock wandering off, continually arose. "It soon became plain that the hard facts of this pilgrimage would require patience, energy, and courage fully equal to what I had anticipated when I had tried to stretch my imagination to the utmost," Sarah wrote in her journal.

At various stops along the way, the Royces met with other emigrants making the move—families with the same visions of happily-ever-after that Sarah possessed. When they reached a post well

Sarah Royce.

along the Missouri River, news of the grasslands between Kansas and Colorado having been eaten up by the stock from other wagon trains and of an outbreak of cholera made Sarah reconsider going any further. Josiah managed to persuade her to continue on.

On June 11, 1849, Sarah and her family reached Council Bluffs, Iowa. A week after their arrival a ferryboat transported their wagons, belongings, and pack-animals across the Missouri River. She wouldn't eat a meal or sleep a single night inside a house until she reached Fort Laramie, Wyoming. She wrote in her journal later that "outside of our wagons there were no homes or shelter anywhere along the vast wilderness we came." Among the difficulties that presented themselves to Sarah and her fellow travelers were the Plains Indians. Frustrated by the invasion of white settlers of their ancestral lands, the tribes sought restitution against the hordes of interlopers.

As Sarah recounted in her journal: *"As we drew nearer, to what was initially thought to be buffalo, they proved to be Indians, by hundreds. And soon they had arranged themselves along each side of the way. A group of them came forward, and at the Captain's command our company halted, while he with several others went to meet the Indians and hold a parley. It turned out they had gathered to demand payment of a certain sum per head for every emigrant passing through this part of the country, which they claimed as their own. The men of our company, after consultation, resolved that the demand was unreasonable! That the country we were traveling over belonged to the United States, and that the red men had no right to stop us. The Indians were then plainly informed that the company meant to proceed at once without paying a dollar. That if unmolested, they would not harm anything; but if the Indians attempted to stop them, they would open fire with all their rifles and revolvers. At the Captain's word of command all the men of the company then armed themselves with every weapon to be found in their wagons. Revolvers, knives, hatchets, glittered in their belts; rifles and guns bristled on their shoulders... we were at once moving between long, but not very compact rows of half-naked redskins... After a while they evidently made up their minds to let us pass, and we soon lost sight of them."*

Sarah and the other pioneers on the train formed close friendships. They helped each other through misgivings they had about the trip, shared food and supplies, nursed one another back to health, and gave proper burials to those who didn't recover. Whenever a sojourner was lost along the way, Sarah recalled the heavy gloom that surrounded the emigrants. *"We couldn't help but wonder who would go next,"* she wrote in her journal. *"What if my husband should be taken and leave us alone in the wilderness? What if I should be taken and leave my little Mary motherless? Or, still more distracting a thought—what if we both should be laid low, and she*

"The Covered Wagon," painting by W.H.D. Koerner (1921).

be left a destitute orphan, among strangers, in a land of savages? Such thoughts would rush into my mind, and for some hours these gloomy forebodings heavily oppressed me; but I poured out my heart to God in prayer, and He gave me comfort and rest."

At the end of each day the leader of the train would direct the company of wagons into a large circle. The cattle or oxen were unhitched and the tongue of each vehicle was laid at the end of the wagon in front. After the animals had a chance to graze and get water, they were led into the center of the circle for their protection and to keep them from running off. While the men tended to the livestock, Sarah and the other women were busy cooking, mending clothes, and caring for the children.

By July 4, Sarah's wagon train had made it to Chimney Rock in Nebraska. They stopped to celebrate Independence Day and to give thanks for making it as far as they had. Sarah used the sights and sounds experienced on the trek as lesson objects for her daughter. She climbed Independence Rock with her little girl, teaching her about landmarks and distances. *"Of course, I had to lift her from one projection to another most of the way,"* Sarah later wrote. *"But we went leisurely and her delight on reaching the top, our short rest there, and the view we enjoyed, fully paid for the labor."* After leaving Independence Rock, the teacher and her family pressed along the Mormon Trail to the Great Salt Lake Basin. On August 30, 1849, Sarah and her husband decided to set off on their own and cross the Salt Desert. The majority of the party they had traveled with wanted to use a new, virtually untried route into California.

The Royces did not trust the so-called "experimental guide" who had plans to start the venture in October. At a date so late in the year, Josiah believed the way would be impassable by snow. The Royces and a few other families took the usual trail to their destination. *"Our only guide from Salt Lake City consisted of two small sheets of note paper, sewed together and bearing on the outside in writing the title 'Best Guide to the Gold Mines, 816 Miles, by Ira J. Wiles, GSL City.'"*

Sarah and her family encountered more Native Americans on their journey. They would hide along the trail and ambush travelers as they passed. Josiah maintained a strong, businesslike stance against the Natives, refusing to give up any livestock or provisions. His resistance rattled them, and they eventually let the Royces' wagon train continue on.

The Salt Lake Desert and the Carson River Route were the most grueling parts of the journey for Sarah. Violent thunder—and windstorms halted travel and threatened to leave them stranded forever in the desolate locations. The intense heat of the sun forced them to make their way by night. They were thirsty, exhausted, and disoriented much of the time. Sarah remembered: *"It was moonlight, but the gray-white sand, with only here and there sagebrush, looked all so much alike that it required care to keep to the road. And now, for the first time in my life, I saw a mirage; or several repetitions of that optical illusion. Once it was an extended sheet of water lying calmly bright in the moonlight with here and there a tree on its shores; and our road seemed to tend directly towards it; then it was a small lake seen through openings in a row of trees, while the shadowy outlines of a forest appeared beyond it; all lying to our left. What a pity it seemed to be passing it by, when our poor animals had been so stinted of late. Again, we were traveling parallel with a placid river on our right; beyond which were trees; and from us to the water's edge the ground sloped so gently it appeared absurd not to turn aside to its brink and refresh ourselves and our oxen."*

Sarah, Josiah, and their daughter arrived on the other side of the desert on October 17, 1849, and faced the towering Sierra Nevada Mountains. Stormy weather had already deposited a heavy layer of snow over the rocky range. Following after her husband and their mules as they made their ascent, Sarah held her child closely with one arm and held tightly to the branches and bushes along the mountain wall with the other. At night they had no choice but to make camp near snow-covered bluffs. Their water supply turned to ice and campfires had to be constantly maintained to keep them from dying out and the wagon train from freezing to death.

On October 19, 1849, Sarah celebrated the progress they'd made climbing the mountains. She was closer to her new home and wrote in her journal that *"hope now sprang exultant." "We were to cross the highest ridge, view the promised land and begin our descent into warmth and safety,"* she recalled. *"So, without flinching I faced steps still steeper than the day before: I even laughed in my little one's upturned face, as she lay back against my arm, while I leaned forward almost to the neck of the mule, tugging up the hardest places."*

The Royces reached the growing gold-mining town of Weaverville in late October, pitched their tent, and *"began to gather about [them] little comforts and conveniences, which made [them] feel as though [they] once more had a home,"* Sarah remembered. While Josiah searched for gold, Sarah maintained their canvas home. Lonely miners on their way to and from their claims often stopped to watch Sarah and Mary. It had been such a long time since they'd seen a woman or toddler they couldn't help themselves from staring. The men bowed courteously to Sarah and made mention of how Mary reminded them of their children they left behind in the East. Josiah eventually abandoned min-

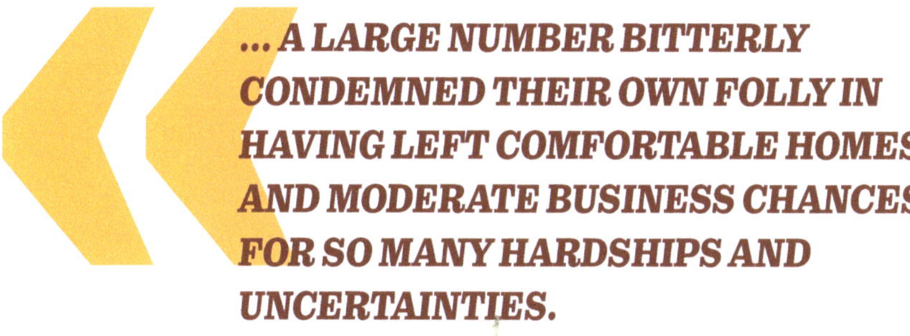

> **… A LARGE NUMBER BITTERLY CONDEMNED THEIR OWN FOLLY IN HAVING LEFT COMFORTABLE HOMES AND MODERATE BUSINESS CHANCES FOR SO MANY HARDSHIPS AND UNCERTAINTIES.**
>
> **SARAH ROYCE**
> *On the Prospectors of the California Gold Rush*

ing and went into business with a pair of investors seeking to open a mercantile in town.

Sarah and Mary accompanied him to Sacramento to purchase supplies. When they returned, a crude store had been constructed. The Royces lived in the back half of the building and managed the buying and selling of goods in the front half. Sarah would overhear prospectors lamenting their decisions to come to California with the Gold Rush. Finding riches was not as easy as they dreamed it would be. *"They had to toil for days before finding gold,"* Sarah wrote in her journal, *"and when they found it, had to work hard in order to wash out their 'ounce a day,' and then discovered that the necessaries of life were so scarce it took much of their proceeds to pay their way, they murmured; and some of them cursed the country, calling it a 'God forsaken land,' while a larger number bitterly condemned their own folly in having left comfortable homes and moderate business chances, for so many hardships and uncertainties."*

After Sarah and her family suffered through an attack of the cholera-morbus (acute gastroenteritis), Sarah, her husband, and child moved to Sacramento to avoid other more serious illnesses that were circulating around Weaverville. From January 1850 to 1854, the Royces lived in a variety of thriving northern California towns. Among them were Folsom, San Francisco, and Martinez. In the spring of 1854, Sarah, Josiah, and their growing family of three moved to Grass Valley, a popular mining location in the high Sierra Nevadas.

They moved into a small house along the main thoroughfare down to a ravine where prospectors were hunting gold. Shortly after their arrival Sarah gave birth to the couple's fourth child, Josiah Royce, Jr. Sarah devoted a great deal of time to educating her children. She taught them how to read using the Bible as a textbook. Astronomical charts, histories, and an encyclopedia of common and scientific knowledge were used as well to train the youngsters. Periodically, the children of other camp followers were sent to study with Sarah. The need was so great for a teacher in Grass Valley that she decided to open a school for young ladies and misses. Despite the fact that the main objective was to reach girls, it was co-educational, and the boys she taught included her own son, who went on to become a distinguished professor of philosophy at Harvard University.

Josiah, Jr. fondly recalled his mother's classroom influence in his own memoirs published in the early 1900s: *"My earliest teacher in philosophy was my mother, whose private school, held for some years in our own house, I attended, and my sisters, who were all older than myself, and one of whom taught me to read. I very greatly enjoyed my mother's reading of the Bible stories."*

In 1857, Josiah Sr. went into business with a friend and purchased several acres of farmland outside of Grass Valley. He named the large spread Avon Farm after Sarah's birthplace. Sarah continued to teach while her husband raised a variety of crops and supplied the community with apples, peaches, and dairy products. More than nine years after they had moved to the mining town, the Royces returned to San Francisco.

Sarah's son called his mother an "effective teacher" and her journal, entitled the Pilgrimage Diary (which was published later in a volume entitled A Frontier Lady), has been used for centuries to educate students. Studying her memoirs educates readers about the sights, terrain, and hardships of traveling over the plains.

Chris Enss *is a* New York Times *bestselling author who has written about women of the Old West for more than thirty years. She's penned more than fifty books on the subject and been honored with nine Will Rogers Medallion Awards, two Elmer Kelton Book Awards, an Oklahoma Center for the Book Award, three* Foreword Review Magazine *Book Awards, and the Laura Downing Journalism Award.*

LIVELY LIBATIONS

Sherry Monahan
CULINARY EDITOR

Gold, Greed, and Whiskey

How a Teamster's Taste for Whiskey Uncorked the California Gold Rush.

In the early 1800s California remained largely unsettled—until James W. Marshall changed everything. While working to build a mill on the American River near Coloma, Marshall spotted something gold and shimmering in the water. A New Jersey native employed by entrepreneur John Sutter, Marshall later appeared rain-soaked at Sutter's home, carrying a small item wrapped in cloth. When Sutter unwrapped the bundle, revealing gold nuggets found on his land, he unwittingly set off a chain of events that would become one of history's most famous gold rushes.

Sutter, understandably, wanted to keep the discovery a secret, but fate—or perhaps whiskey—intervened. A Swiss teamster working for Sutter, with a known fondness for drink, may have been responsible for leaking the news. Tasked with gathering supplies in Coloma, the teamster encountered men offering gold dust and boasting of its source. After completing his errands, he stopped at Smith & Brannan's mercantile for a well-earned drink, paying with some of the dust. The storekeeper, curious about the unusual payment, pressed the teamster for details. According to historian Hubert Howe Bancroft, the teamster explained, "Gold," prompting the storekeeper to inform Sutter. Around the same time, Sutter's schooner carried samples of the gold downstream, and word quickly spread.

Marshall made his discovery in January 1848, and within weeks, the California Gold Rush was underway. Within four short years, the boom would subside, leaving Sutter bankrupt. During the rush's height, thousands flocked to towns like Coloma and Hangtown (now Placerville), all hoping to strike it rich. By day, miners toiled in the cold waters of the American River, panning and sluicing for nuggets and dust. By night, they spent their hard-earned findings on gambling, drinking, and other indulgences. Gold, whether in nuggets or dust sacks, was the currency of choice. Bancroft observed that miners *"drank to get cool, if cold, to get warm, if wet, to get dry—and some were always dry—to keep out the wet."*

The isolated mining camps created opportunities for merchants to charge exorbitant prices. In early 1848, flour cost $4 for 200 pounds, while beef went for $2 for the same weight. Miners earned anywhere from $1 to $128 worth of gold per day, with gold selling for $12 to $16 per ounce.

Sacramento, then known as "Embarcadero," quickly grew into a bustling hub. A gold rush pioneer from Panama recalled arriving in 1849: *"At the time of our arrival... there was not a frame building in the town, except a small one-story structure, where Sam Brannan kept a store.... There was a rush from the mines, coming after stores, or to have a grand carouse. All had gold dust, and nearly all drank whiskey. It was no uncommon occurrence to see a miner call up every person around and spend an ounce or two in treating."*

The drinking culture extended to Sutter's Mill, as gold rush pioneer Heinrich Lienhard noted: *"The impudence and boldness of the gold prospectors of that day was unbelievable. Strong liquor was popular, and the miners drank greedily. Whiskey bottles ceased to be a curiosity, being found everywhere.... Enormous piles of them accumulated inside the fort... where men who had mined hundreds or thousands of dollars' worth of gold congregated and attempted to atone for recent hardships by enormous quantities of alcohol."*

Sherry Monahan *is an award-winning culinary historian who enjoys researching the genealogy of food and spirits. While there's still plenty to explore about frontier food, she's expanding her culinary repertoire to include places and foods from all over America and beyond. She holds memberships in the James Beard Foundation, the Author's Guild, Single Action Shooting Society, and the Wild West History Association. She is also a professional genealogist, and an honorary Dodge City marshal. One of her latest titles,* Signature Dishes of America, *won the 2024 Will Rogers Medallion Award Silver Medal in the Best Western Cookbook category.*

Whiskey Toddy

1/2 teaspoon sugar
1 teaspoon water
1–2 ice cubes
1 wine glass of whiskey (6 ounces)

Place the sugar in a whiskey glass and add the water. Stir to dissolve and then add the ice. Pour the whiskey into the glass and stir. Note: The original recipe instructions read, *"The most proper way for the bartender is to dissolve the sugar into the water only, and leave a spoon in the glass, hand out the bottle of whiskey to the customer to help himself."*

Source: Adapted from *Harry Johnson's New and Improved Illustrated Bartender's Manual*, 1882.

THE BOOK WAGON

Doug Osgood
BOOK REVIEWER

Golden Frontiers

The Social and Personal Costs of California's Gold Rush.

Tensions Run Gold Deep

On a California emigrant's wagon along the Truckee River, Cherokee Bill stumbles upon a grim scene: a man and a young boy dead from cholera, leaving only the wife, Maggie Magee, as the sole survivor. After looting the wagon, Bill abducts Maggie and later sells her to Smiling Jack, the keeper of a saloon in a bustling gold town. In John Rose Putnam's ***Hangtown Creek*** (Published by by John Rose Putnam, 2016) the story follows three converging groups whose lives become dangerously intertwined in the chaos of California's gold rush. Meanwhile, Pa Marsh, forced by debt to sell the family farm, packs up his three sons and heads west to the goldfields near Sutter's Mill. At the same time, Eban Snyder and Joshua Stone, fresh from their army service in the Mexican-American War, muster out at Sutter's Fort and stake a claim in the same region.

As these three groups converge, their fates become dangerously intertwined. Maggie sneaks away from Smiling Jack to beg Eban and Joshua for help, asking them to take her far from her captors. Enraged, Jack and Cherokee Bill vow to punish Maggie and kill anyone who dares to aid her.

Putnam masterfully weaves these storylines together, shifting between the groups while building tension and delivering strong action sequences. The characters are well-drawn, making readers care deeply about their struggles, and the plot's twists and turns keep the stakes high. Will Jack and Bill exact their revenge, or will Maggie find the freedom she seeks?

While not quite reaching the heights of the genre's finest offerings, *Hangtown Creek* stands out as one of the best self-published frontier westerns. With its compelling characters, tightly crafted plot, and engaging writing, it's a fast-paced and enjoyable read.

Rating: 4 Nuggets out of 5.

Gold Camp Nightlife

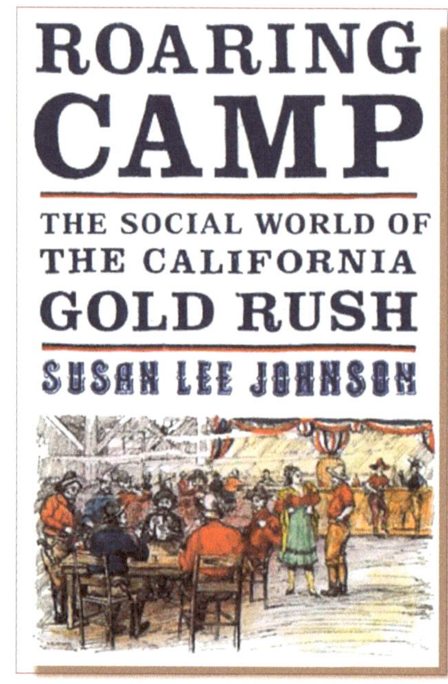

Susan Lee Johnson's ***Roaring Camp: The Social World of the California Gold Rush*** (Published by W.W. Norton & Co., 2000) explores the intricate social dynamics of the California mining camps during the Gold Rush. The events that set the stage for this transformation occurred within eight days in early 1848. On January 24, James Marshall discovered gold in the western Sierra Nevada foothills near present-day Sacramento. Just over a week later, on February 2, the Treaty of Guadalupe Hidalgo ended the Mexican-American War, ceding California to the United States. These two events forever altered the region. News of the gold discovery at Sutter's Mill quickly spread worldwide, drawing an influx of fortune seekers to the area. In Tuolumne County, south of the more established mining operations along the American River, a racially diverse population formed, including indigenous Miwoks, Mexicans, Chileans, and emigrants from other nations. Their interactions created a vibrant social world, rich with cultural exchanges through fandangos, bull-and-bear fights, and religious ceremonies.

Women played a pivotal role in shaping this social life. Indigenous Miwok and Mexican women were already present in the region, with Mexican wives often joining their husbands. However, women from other ethnic groups were scarce, leading entrepreneurs to bring in women to work in dance halls and brothels. These establishments, alongside saloons offering gambling and drinking, became the central hubs of social activity in the mining camps.

Originally written as a dissertation, *Roaring Camp* examines not only the lively social life of miners but also the dominance of white male perspectives in shaping the area's long-term development and its retelling in history. While the book's academic tone and occasional moralistic undertones may challenge casual readers, it remains an insightful and thought-provoking study of the cultural complexities of the Gold Rush era. For those interested in the nuanced social fabric of California's mining camps, Johnson's work offers a compelling and richly detailed exploration.

Rating: 3.5 Nuggets out of 5.

Survival & Stamina

It's 1852, and fourteen-year-old Jeremy Ash and his grandfather, Harry, embark on a journey westward from their Indiana farm to the Sierra Nevada gold fields in Peter Grant's ***Wood, Iron, & Blood*** (Published by Sedgefield Press, 2022). Near St. Joseph, Missouri, they join a wagon train led by seasoned guide Mike Jarrod and his scout, Rod Willis. Their journey is fraught with challenges: thieves seek to rob them, storms and scorching heat test their resolve, and the rugged terrain pushes them to their limits. Internal strife from dissatisfied tinhorns, prairie fires, and the ever-present threat of hostile natives add to the peril. Jeremy and Harry must rely on their wits, strength, and determination to navigate this treacherous crossing.

Peter Grant has crafted a well-researched novel with vividly drawn characters. The detailed descriptions of supplies, animals, and weapons offer a fascinating glimpse into the logistical demands of a cross-continental journey. The methods for overcoming natural obstacles—fording rivers, scaling rocky trails, and crossing canyons—are presented with precision. However, the story suffers from a missed opportunity to deepen its tension. While errors in judgment can make main characters' struggles more compelling, Grant instead reserves such mistakes for supporting characters, limiting the story's emotional stakes and suspense.

At times, *Wood, Iron, & Blood* reads more like a survival guide for wagon train travel than a gripping adventure novel. While the rich detail adds realism, it occasionally overshadows the narrative drive. A stronger focus on character flaws and moments of vulnerability, something more akin to Zebulon Pike's dramatic exploits than the pragmatic style of The Prairie Traveler—would have elevated the story. Though enjoyable for a single read, the novel could have benefited from a more balanced approach to its blend of survivalism and storytelling.

Rating: 3.5 Nugget out of 5.

Doug Osgood

MARLEEN BUSSMA

SADDLEBAG DISPATCHES POET LAUREATE

GUNS, GARTERS, & GOLD

Loud cackling laughter ricochets through dingy smell and smoke.
Unsteady miners at the bar will drink until they're broke.
Stray bullet holes around the room are part of mayhem's mix.
The door has been unlocked since new, in 1856.

Gold blasts the quiet from the dozing hills like dynamite.
The miners spread through California's turf, a bawdy blight.
They come from many countries as they dig and grub for gold.
In just four years the population goes up sixteen-fold.

A constant noisy clatter cries as dirt and stones are hurled.
The hunger for this metal eats the hills as flakes are squirreled
away, then used as legal tender for a whiskey meal.
His distant shabby tent lays bare his squalid life's ordeal.

Most towns are just an eyesore shaped by canvas and some wood.
They spring up overnight like mushrooms, vulnerable, and could
expire by raging fire, then turn to dust from which they've sprung.
Like footloose men who come here, towns live fast and can die young.

A Forty-Niner greenhorn ripens quickly on a claim.
When facing bleak starvation, he might wonder why he came.
A bear may want to share his tent. The wolves will end his life.
His dreams are a remote escape to hearth, safe home, and wife.

The presence of a woman is a rare sight in these hills.
She sparkles like a diamond in their dim lives where she fills
the primal need. Grim circumstances keep her options lean
and withered like dried apples in this life that's hard and mean.

The miners' roots are shallow as a harlot's hardened heart.
When high-grade ore tails off, they pack up ready to depart.
Another town will spring up on some undisturbed terrain
where men will dig like gophers for that now elusive vein.

SADDLEBAG
DISPATCHES
PROUDLY PRESENTS THE WINNER OF OUR 2024
LONGHORN
PRIZE
FOR WESTERN SHORT STORIES
BOB
ARMSTRONG
"CLAY ALLISON'S GIRL"

BOB ARMSTRONG

CLAY ALLISON'S GIRL

A SHORT STORY

Winner of the 2024 *Saddlebag Dispatches* Longhorn Prize for Western Short Fiction

Abigail Bartlett honored her father's exhortations to turn the other cheek long after she had abandoned many of his other teachings, but now, as Bull Turnbull's blood soaked into the floorboards, the homily in her mind ran more along the lines of "if you don't want somebody sticking you with an Arkansas toothpick, keep your damn hands to yourself."

Truth to tell, it was hard to form any kind of thought, what with Abigail's struggle to keep her balance over the twitching bulk of the dying man, her vision blurred by whatever caused her head to pound like the devil's own hammermill and by a spray of hot, viscous liquid she wiped from her eyes. It didn't help that a murder of crows seemed to have roosted in the cramped bedroom, though a blink of Abigail's eyes revealed that the dry, croaking sounds were in fact emerging from the throat of poor, little Effie Hutchins, kneeling on the floor beside Bull and frozen in place with her mouth agape.

Abigail lowered herself to Effie's bed to collect her breath and assemble her thoughts. Head throbbing. Salt on the tongue. From her own blood, thank god, judging by the raw flesh on her lower lip. Effie's eyes wide in terror and bulging unnaturally. A pair of hands, scarred and calloused. The inhuman sounds of a beast, unleashed by cheap whiskey and whatever drove men to hate the women they bought.

It was all coming together.

Effie's screams had reached Abigail in the private parlor adjacent to Dan Harmon's Rivoli Garden Saloon and Dance Hall, where she was entertaining a pair of commercial travellers with a rendition of Beethoven's Moonlight Sonata. As the men enjoyed drinks and cigars and waited to select their company for the evening, Abigail's fingers were halted by sounds of distress. She abandoned the sonata in the midst of the delicate adagio sostenuto and rushed up the stairs, noting with alarm the ominous percussion of heavy blows landing on soft flesh. By the time she threw open Effie's door, the blows had ceased and Bull's hands encircled Effie's throat.

Without waiting for Dan Harmon's bruiser, she flew at the big trail hand.

"Let her go! You're killing her!"

Bull, well over six feet tall and broad-chested as the creatures that inspired his name, shrugged her off like a bothersome fly. When she hauled back her right arm and landed a windmill blow on his ear, he released Effie and turned his full attention to Abigail. Eyes shining, face scarlet with rage and rotgut, he operated the mighty bellows of his lungs for two deep breaths, during which Abigail hoped he would come to his senses, or Dan's man would come to her rescue.

Neither came to pass.

Moving with surprising speed for a man of his bulk, he grasped Abigail in his meaty paws, lifted her to his own height, and slammed her head against the wall, hard enough to dislodge a gilt-framed mirror.

In Abigail's mind, events immediately after her head hit the wall were jumbled. A series of images in uncertain order flashed in her head like a magic lantern show. She conjured a picture of Bull Turnbull kneeling over Effie, hands on her neck, Effie's face empurpled with blood. Another image depicted Effie, her mouth open with a scream choked off by terror and damaged vocal chords, her face and her torso gleaming in a spray of blood. The final tableau offered up Bull face-down on the floor, a gaping wound in the side of his neck, a crimson halo around his head.

It was that image that made her recall the Reverend Horace Bartlett's admonitions, drawn from the Sermon on the Mount, to meet violence with meek forgiveness.

Well, the Reverend Horace Bartlett, in addition to being a social-climbing hypocrite who had tried to marry his eldest daughter off to a desiccated corpse in the guise of an Episcopalian bishop, knew nothing of managing a stable of girls in a Kansas cowtown.

A heavy weight in Abigail's hand brought her back to the present. It was the pig-sticker Bull had had on his belt when he arrived with the crew from the Bar Lazy S earlier that evening, the once-shining blade now dark with the same liquid that coated Abigail's hand and forearm.

The sight of Bull's knife spurred her to action. First, she had to shut the door, still wide open from when she'd burst in a few minutes before. Turnbull's men were scattered around Harmon's saloon, drinking or gambling away their wages or being serviced by girls in the other bedrooms. One of them could saunter by at any moment. Abigail and Effie were likely to end up decorating a cottonwood down by the Arkansas River if the Lazy Bar S men discovered what had happened to their outfit's trail boss.

Before she could reach the door, a man appeared there. Abigail jumped, then realized who it was and pulled him into the room, placing a hand against his mouth. This was no cowboy, just scrawny, big-eared Harold Farlinger. He'd dropped by the parlor earlier, bringing flowers for her and a pig's ear for her Gordon setter, Princess, but had shaken his head when Abigail had offered to introduce him to one of the girls. "I just love to hear you play piano, Miss Abigail," he'd said.

Attracting admirers was a hazard of the business, especially given that Abigail no longer worked in its direct customer-service side. Well, not unless the customer was especially well-heeled, clean and discreet. Harold could only lay claim to the latter two virtues. As a telegraph operator, he practised discretion daily at work. Abigail hoped she could count on that from him now. With his pencil arms and delicate fingers, he wasn't going to be much good keeping the Bar Lazy S men at bay, but he could at least make himself useful.

"Harold. I need your help. Run and get the marshal now. But act natural."

Abigail ushered him out and closed the door and turned her attention to Effie. She lifted the girl up from the floor and moved her into the lamplight to inspect the marks on her neck and the swelling around her mouth, nose and eyes. She handed Effie a glass of water from the pitcher on the nightstand.

"It might hurt to swallow, but you probably need a drink."

She removed a handkerchief from her sleeve, moistened it and held it against Effie's nose, wiping her clean and smoothing her hair with calming gestures. She might need a witness who could testify to Bull's murderous rage and an incoherent Effie would be no good to either of them.

She assessed the scene of carnage. A thorough clean-up would have to wait until closing time, but she had to do something. The blood was likely to drip through the floorboards onto whatever lay below.

This was not the first time a girl had been hurt at the saloon, nor was it the first time a man had died violently. But it was the first time a man's violent death had been caused by one of the women in the establishment. Abigail expected no sympathy from the Lazy Bar S men toward the kind of women politely referred to as "soiled doves."

She heard a heavy pounding at the door.

"Bull! You still in there? What's keepin' you?"

She placed a hand over Effie's mouth and whispered: "Stall them."

Effie gaped with incomprehension, still too stunned to speak. Abigail would have to improvise.

"Again, Bull?" Abigail said. "Oh, you know how to please a gal."

That brought a chorus of guffaws from the men outside the door.

"We got a high-stakes game startin' downstairs. You said to tell you when the playing got interesting."

"It's getting interesting here," Abigail replied, to additional hoots.

Abigail heard footsteps withdrawing and assessed the feasibility of dragging Bull's body into a corner, rearranging the furniture to block it from view. She slid the bed to the side to create a path, grasped an arm and tugged. After some coaxing, Effie took hold of the other arm. The exertion muffled the sound of returning footsteps.

Abigail had a wrist in her hands when the door opened. With a roar of outrage, the Bar Lazy S men swarmed in. One man slammed into Abigail with such force that she was knocked to the floor, an elbow absorbing just enough of the force when she hit the floor that she retained consciousness. She strained to breathe with the man's weight on her chest and his rotten, yeasty breath in her face. More noise: pounding feet, drunken shouts, a slap, a woman's cry.

"The whore killed him!"

"No, the madam killed him!"

Another slap. This one louder because it was Abigail's cheek that stung.

A cry went out to string them up. Fingers tightened around Abigail's hair and a cowboy hoisted her to her feet. She pulled back an arm and raked somebody's face with her nails, then felt her arm twisted back and a pain in her shoulder as it nearly popped out of the socket. As she was dragged from the room, Abigail felt the crook of an elbow around her throat. Hands ran up and down her body and she heard her dress rip and feared the men might take their vengeful, brutal, pleasure with her before the lynching. But the probing hands withdrew as the two biggest men carried her down the stairs, like a rolled-up carpet, one at her feet, one at her shoulders. Small mercies, at least.

Dan Harmon and his muscle man watched from the bar but made no move to intervene. She caught Dan's apologetic shrug, a gesture that meant perhaps: "Sorry, but what can I do?"

That's the protection she paid half her earnings for? She spat in disgust.

Outside the saloon it was the same story. By the light of a gas lamp she saw the marshal, a lone armed man with no hope of winning a gun battle against the gathering mob of cowboys. Beside the marshal, Harold Farlinger shouted in his ear and pointed at the scene. You didn't have to be a lip reader to know Harold was imploring the lawman to take action.

The men turned away from the saloon and toward the cottonwoods lining the river. Somebody was sent to get a rope, then told to make it two. Abigail realized the men didn't even care which of the two women stabbed Turnbull. The crowd swelled with onlookers. They had no particular attachment to the Bar Lazy S or to its dead foreman, but they knew a good show when they saw one.

When they reached the trees, the rabble had to wait for the arrival of the ropes. Abigail chose this moment of relative calm to speak up.

"Let Effie go!" she cried. "Bull was strangling her and I stabbed him. Look at her face! Look at her throat!"

She was silenced by an open-handed blow.

"We'll start with this one!"

A cheer followed.

One thin, reedy voice rose in opposition.

"She's telling the truth! Look at them both!"

Despite herself, Abigail had to smile. Brave little Harold Farlinger: the only man who would stand up against the mob. If only she had a gunman defending her instead of a Western Union telegraph operator.

The word "telegraph" brought another smile to her lips. This one, a smile of hope.

"You hurt me and you'll answer to Clay Allison!"

A wave of whispered questions swept the crowd. "Did she say Clay Allison?" "What's that about Clay Allison?" "Does that girl know Clay Allison?"

Abigail turned and saw the fist of the man holding her, frozen in place by the name she'd invoked.

"I'm Clay Allison's girl!"

"Bullshit!"

"Tell them, Harold!"

Abigail prayed that Harold's mind worked as fast as his key-tapping fingers. The young man stepped forward and pointed one at Abigail.

"Miss Abigail is Clay Allison's girl. I've seen the telegrams."

The cowboys holding Abigail relaxed their grip. She saw them look at each other, at her, at Harold, expressions of doubt and fear meandering across their faces.

"I work at the Western Union, so I see messages coming into town. And I tell you, Clay Allison is sweet on Miss Abigail. If you want her punished, you'd best leave it up to the law."

That cooled the fire enough to allow the marshal to exert his authority.

"Boys, I'm taking these women into custody pending a coroner's inquest. If a murder charge is warranted, you'll see justice done."

The marshal placed one hand on Abigail's arm and another on Effie's and led the two women away from the dissipating mob. Removed from immediate peril, Abigail felt her muscles release and saw the horizon tilt sideways. When she looked up at the stars, she saw the marshal, Effie and Harold looking down at her as scrawny Harold struggled to hold her limp body above the mud.

"Clay Allison?" Harold said.

"A girl could do worse."

The marshal, accompanied by Harold, took Abigail and Effie to the lockup for the night to await the coroner. In the marshal's office, she asked for a pen and paper to write out a message, folded it around the key to her apartment and handed the package to

Harold. Harold could think on his feet and he was resourceful. He'd understand the message.

Knowing she would need to be rested for the coming events, Abigail pushed thoughts of the last hour from her mind and willed herself to sleep.

By the light of morning, she was relieved to see that Effie's face bore signs of Bull's abuse, one eye nearly swollen shut and her fat lower lip jutting far out from her upper. Better still, from the point of keeping the two women above ground, was the ring of bruises around the girl's throat. If the coroner's jury proved to be motivated by truth, they would certainly rule this a case of self-defense. That was a Texas-sized if.

Abigail and Effie were led over to Dan Harmon's saloon under guard for the beginning of the inquest. The marshal, now assisted by two deputies, led the women past the Bar Lazy S men, who snarled and cried "murder!" and "justice for Bull Turnbull!" Inside the saloon, reconfigured as a courtroom, Abigail examined the jurors, noting nervous tics and beads of sweat. These men knew how the vengeful cowboys would respond to a self-defense ruling. They knew the Lazy Bar S men were fighters who had grown up amid the Comanche wars and now defended their herds against every rustler in Texas and the Indian Territory. Without some special intervention, it was obvious that the terrified jurors would recommend a murder trial and that the trial would be equally tainted by fear of vigilantes.

Looking down the row of seats toward the press box, Abigail saw the Western Union man who represented the intervention she needed. She nodded in his direction and, as spectators crowded the room and their excited speculations created a rhubarb, he produced two slips of paper from an envelope, stepped forward, and handed them to the nearest juror.

Abigail watched for the words to create the hoped-for effect. The juror read. His face blanched and he passed the papers on to a colleague, who had the same reaction. A flurry of whispers engulfed the citizens as they prepared to carry out their public duty. Doc Henderson, acting as coroner, looked on in consternation until a juror passed the papers to him. Now he joined the others in urgent consultation. The jury foreman spoke up moments later and announced that the inquest would reconvene on Monday. The foreman beckoned the marshal forward. More urgent debate ensued.

As the spectators' disappointment at missing out on a show grew louder, the marshal returned to the prisoners' bench and handed her the two sheets of paper with the Western Union insignia on top.

How's my dark-haired beauty?
Clay Allison.

Arriving noon train Friday to see my special girl, Clay Allison.

"Never pictured you as the type to associate with a mankiller like Allison," the marshal said. "I hope you know what you're getting into."

Abigail had heard stories of Clay Allison's murderous exploits, in Texas, in the New Mexico Territory, riding in the war with Bedford Forrest's cavalry. She'd heard of the speed and accuracy of his shooting, his skill with a knife, his ruthlessness. She knew not even the Bar Lazy S men would want him for an enemy. But Abigail, who had met Allison months before when he visited the Rivoli Garden, knew there was another side to the killer.

The jurors may have had their doubts about the telegrams. Faced with the choice between recommending a murder charge, and possibly placing themselves in front of Allison's pistol, or letting Abigail go free and enraging the Lazy Bar S men, pausing the inquest until Monday gave them the chance to render a decision in safety. If Allison hadn't taken her away by then, Abigail knew they'd give Bull's cowboys what they wanted.

Abigail remained on bail in her apartment, the front window of which provided a view of the railway station. On Friday, she bundled a few of her most expensive dresses into the suitcase, along with her jewelry and her favorite sheet music. Not Moonlight Sonata, though. She didn't think she ever wanted to hear it again. She reached into her wardrobe and put on a travelling cloaktoo warm for Kansas in this season but the gold pieces sewn into the lining would come in handy.

As noon approached, she stood by the window, packed and ready to go, and watched the train huff its way toward the station. She noticed watchers on the street, also waiting for one particular passenger.

At 12:05 the station doors opened and a handful of passengers emerged. She could group them by their dress and the luggage they carried: homesteaders, commercial travellers, soldiers. And one man she identified by his dark, wavy hair, elegant Van Dyke beard, and deep, smoldering eyes.

It was Clay Allison.

"Let's go, Princess," she said, and heard the tapping of three sets of paws.

Lifting her travelling bag, she held the door open for Princess and her remaining puppies and began to put her Dodge City life behind her. Walking toward the station, she knew she was being watched, but knew as well that the watchers were aware of Allison's presence.

"Good morning Mr. Allison. You received my telegram?"

"Surely did. Surprised to hear you're pulling up stakes so suddenly."

The smiling killer looked less lonely than he had when he'd visited the Rivoli Garden some months before. Of course, it likely was a lonely life, travelling the West, being feared by all. For such a man, perhaps no human companionship would be possible. That might explain why his eyes had lighted up so suddenly on that visit when Princess, her teats swollen with the litter she was expecting any day, waddled into the room.

"The train resumes its journey in five minutes," said Harold Farlinger, approaching the human and canine gathering. Harold held out two train tickets and handed one to Abigail. "I decided it would be best for my health if I left town as well."

The train was bound for Denver. Tomorrow she would start a new life there, as would the quick-thinking young man beside her.

Allison removed a billfold from his jacket.

"You sure I don't owe you anything?"

"Absolutely not, Mr. Allison. Just provide a good home for Princess's baby."

The train whistle sounded. The conductor called all aboard.

"Don't you worry at all about that, Miss Abigail," he said, kneeling and running a hand through the dark coat of the largest of the puppies. "You're my special girl, aren't you, huh? You're my special dark-haired beauty."

THE AUTHOR

Bob Armstrong *is a novelist and freelance writer from Winnipeg. His novel* Prodigies *(Five Star/Gale), focusing on three uncannily gifted teens in 1877 Deadwood, won the 2022 Margaret Laurence Prize for Fiction in the Manitoba Book Awards and his writing has appeared in literary magazines on both sides of the Medicine Line and in anthologies of comedy, speculative fiction, travel writing and drama. An avid hiker and history buff, he has wandered western trails from south of Tombstone, Arizona, to north of the Yukon Territory's Tombstone Mountains. His travel misadventures and musings can be found on Substack @wanderingwriterbobarmstrong and at www.bobarmstrong.ca.*

Mary Ellen Pleasant

SAINT OR SINNER?

Mary Ellen Pleasant, a bold entrepreneur and abolitionist, rose from humble beginnings to become a millionaire and a powerful advocate for civil rights in 19th-century San Francisco.

STORY BY

REGINA MCLEMORE

Not everyone who came to California during the Gold Rush was looking for gold. Some came intending to become rich by providing services to the gold seekers. Such was the case of the Black entrepreneur, Mary Ellen Pleasant. Author Herbert Asbury in *The Barbary Coast,* described her appearance and arrival in San Francisco in early 1850 as "a gigantic Negress from New Orleans, black as the inside of a coal-pit, but with no Negroid features whatever, whose culinary exploits were famous." Asbury related that she was met by a crowd of men, all anxious to hire her as a cook. She finally sold her services at auction for five hundred dollars a month, with the stipulation that she would do no washing, including dishwashing.

In her autobiography, published in 1902, just two years before her death, Pleasant said, "Some people have reported that I was born a slave, but as a matter of fact, I was born in Philadelphia." She described her father as a gigantic native Hawaiian and her mother as a tall, full-blooded Louisiana Negress, both contributing to Mary's considerable height. Mary was taken from Philadelphia at a young age to be raised on the island of Nantucket as an indentured servant to a Quaker family. She was soon put to work as a clerk at their store and gained the reputation of being "a girl full of smartness and quick at coming back at people when they tried to have a little fun talking with me."

According to author Lynn M. Hudson in *The Making of Mammy Pleasant, A Black Entrepreneur in Nineteenth-Century San Francisco,* Nantucket proved to be the perfect training ground for young Mary. The town was made-up of shops, ran by independent women whose husbands or other male relatives, were away at sea. When she left the island in her twenties, she carried with her considerable business skills and strong political convictions.

After moving to Boston, Pleasant worked in a tailor's shop where she likely met her first husband, James Smith, a wealthy man and a strong abolitionist. When he died in the 1840s, he left her a considerable sum to carry on his work.

Between his death and her arrival in San Francisco, she married John Pleasants, who later dropped the s in his name, and had a daughter. It is believed Pleasant traveled to San Francisco in 1849 alone and was joined by her husband and daughter at a later date. They often lived separately as John's work as a ship's cook took him away for long periods of time.

Besides the opportunity to become rich, California's free status before and after becoming a state in 1850 drew African Americans to settle there. Dark skin seemingly was no restriction to obtaining wealth or power. Pleasant arrived in California with some money and a strategy for success. "I divided this money between Fred Langford, William West of West & Harper... They put out my money at ten per cent interest and I did an exchange business, sending down gold and having it exchanged for silver... Most of this business was done through Wells Fargo..." She wisely operated simultaneously as an investor, a business owner, and a laborer. Like many black abolitionists, she made a living while she worked for freedom.

While working as a cook for some of the most elite families and bachelors in San Francisco, Pleasant purchased laundries. By the time the Chinese largely took over the laundry business in the 1860s, she had sold her laundries and bought boarding houses. It has been reported that at least one of these boarding houses was a secret safe house for runaway slaves.

Pleasant didn't squander the wealth she accumulated. She contributed funding to open the Athenaeum Institute, containing a library and a saloon, which served as a meeting place for African Americans. She is also believed to have been a founding member of the Franchise League, organized by black San Franciscans in 1852. Its purpose was to combat slavery and protect the rights of black men and women.

Although California was admitted as a free state in 1850, it passed its own Fugitive Slave Law in 1852. Slave captures and slave sales were not unheard of in the first decade of statehood. Pleasant had a reputation for helping out black citizens who found themselves in dangerous situations. One case involved George Mitchell, who had been brought as a slave to California in 1849. The owner was trying to hold George under the 1852 Fugitive Slave Act. While the owner and his lawyer were building their case, Pleasant and her friends hid George away until April 1855 when the California Fugitive Slave Law had truly expired.

John and Mary Ellen Pleasant traveled to Chatham, Canada, in 1858, a center of black abolitionist activity. One purpose of their visit was to join with other black abolitionists to offer their support to famous abolitionist, John Brown. In May 1858, Brown held a convention in Chatham to bring together some of black America's best known leaders, such as Martin Delaney, Mary Ann Shadd Cary, William Howard Day, and the Pleasants. Chatham was a perfect place for Brown's activities, mainly because it was beyond the reach of United States law enforcement.

Mary Pleasant was very proud of her role in supporting John Brown's raid on Harper Ferry in 1859. After interviewing her in 1901, writer Sam Davis included her story in his journal, *The Pandex of the Press,* in the article, *"How a Colored Woman Aided John Brown."* She told Davis, *"...before I pass away I wish to clear the identity of the party who furnished John Brown with most of his money to start the fight at Harpers Ferry and who signed the letter found on him when he was arrested."*

Davis checked out her story and found two of John Brown's children who confirmed that their father *"met a colored woman in Chatham and received considerable money from her."* Their father never disclosed his benefactor's name, but it was widely believed it was Mary Pleasant. Davis also found proof that Mary had taken a large sum of money from New York and had it converted to Canadian currency in the spring of 1858.

Illustration of John Brown during his ill-fated raid on Harper's Ferry, Virginia in 1859.

1870's San Francisco Streetcar.

Pleasant also claimed to have ridden around the South, in advance of the raid in the fall of 1859, dressed as a jockey, to incite an uprising of the slaves. They were to rise up when Brown made a stand at the ferry. *"...Our plans were knocked all to pieces by Brown himself. He started the raid on Harper's Ferry before the time was ripe. I was astounded when I heard that he had started in and was beaten and captured and that the affair upon which I had staked my money and built so much hope was a fiasco."*

A letter was found among Brown's papers, which read, *"The axe is laid at the root of the tree. When the first blow is struck, there will be more money and help."* Pleasant said that the letter, signed W.E.P., was written by her, and that she was lucky to have escaped to New York during Brown's hanging and his co-conspirators' executions.

Mary Ellen Pleasant's request that the words, *"She was a friend of John Brown,"* be printed on her gravestone was finally honored in 1965 when the San Francisco Historical and Cultural Society placed a marker bearing the phrase on her grave in Napa, California.

Although she was reportedly well-off, Pleasant continued to work as a domestic servant to wealthy families in the 1860s. Researchers have speculated that in her guise as "mammy," Pleasant had access to the political and financial workings of San Francisco's wealthy elite. Some have said she had a hold on some of them because she knew their secrets.

The 1860s also marked the beginning of numerous legal litigations by Mary Pleasant. Nearly a century before Rosa Parks made her stand on a Montgomery bus, Mary Pleasant sued streetcar companies in San Francisco. She testified that on September 27, 1866, she was waiting for a streetcar to take her downtown. When she hailed the streetcar, the driver did not stop, even though there was room on the car, and she had her tickets. Pleasant appealed to the conductor, who was riding at the back of the streetcar and was told, "We don't take colored people in the cars."

Riding in the car was one of Pleasant's former employers, Lisette Woodworth. She saw what was happening and told the conductor, "Stop this car; there is a woman who wants to get in."

He took no notice of her, and Woodworth demanded to be let off the streetcar.

No doubt Woodworth's testimony helped Pleasant's case, and she was awarded $500 in punitive damages.

However, the company appealed the case to the

Pleasant/Bell Mansion, also known as the "House of Mystery."

California Supreme Court in 1867, and the judgment was reversed. The supreme court ruled that there was no evidence of special damage or willful injury so damages weren't measurable and shouldn't have compensation.

Because of this suit and others that she brought before the courts of San Francisco, Mary Ellen Pleasant has been called the Mother of the California Civil Rights Movement. She continuously fought for the right to equal treatment under the law for all black people.

In 1869, Mary Ellen Pleasant moved to 920 Washington Street where she established an elaborate boarding house. Her new place catered to white men who were leaders in state government and commerce, and Pleasant took advantage of the information they revealed to increase her own wealth and status. Some said she provided prostitutes for her guests, and she gained the reputation of being San Francisco's black madam. Whether this was true or not has not been proven, but records do exist showing her charitable and fund-raising activities.

In the 1870s, Pleasant moved into a multi-story Victorian mansion which encompassed two city blocks. Valued at $100,000 at the time of its construction, the press soon dubbed the house as a "House of Mystery." Some claimed that Pleasant practiced voodoo there. During this time, she became linked to Thomas Bell, the Vice President of the Bank of California. He became her financial partner and moved into her house, and it appeared they shared ownership of the property and ongoing expenses. Bell later moved his wife and children into the mansion.

She continued going to court either as a plaintiff or a witness on a regular basis for much of her life. In two of the most sensational of these cases, *Sharon vs Sharon* (1884) and *Sharon vs Hill* (1885), Pleasant was a key witness. These cases, involving a secret marriage, voyeurism, voodoo, and several other scandalous activities, provided sensational press releases and entertainment for San Francisco and national audiences.

In 1892, Thomas Bell fell over a railing in the house he shared with Pleasant and died of injuries. He left most of his fortune to his widow, Teresa Bell, and his children. Teresa Bell continued to live with Mary Pleasant both at the mansion and at a ranch that Pleasant had bought in 1891.

Bell's son, Fred, accused Pleasant of stealing jewelry, giving money from the big house to "colored people," and tricking her mistress, Teresa Bell. Bell defended Mary Pleasant against her son until 1899 when she reversed her position. She wrote, *"Mary Pleasant and the 23 years of frauds she has worked on me will last me for the rest of my life..."* Bell evicted Pleasant from their ranch home and the House of Mystery.

Mary Ellen Pleasant Memorial Plaque in San Francisco.

By the end of Pleasant's life, she had lost most of her property and money to lawyers, creditors, bad investments, and competitors, and was relegated to living with friends in a cottage. Sam Davis said, "Since she landed in San Francisco... she has made and checked out through the local banks over a million dollars."

At her death, though, her estate was valued at a mere $10,000.

Mary Ellen Pleasant's unique life proved fascinating to reporters, writers, and playwrights. She has appeared as a central character in at least seven novels, two plays, one television drama, and several films between 1922 and modern times. In early plays and films, the part of Pleasant was played by a white actress, sometimes in black face. In the 1920's her story inspired a novel, a play, and a silent film. In 1984, Pleasant was featured as a character in Frank Derby's novel, *Devilseed.* In the novel, Pleasant tells one character, "I like you. You're all I've always wanted to be—and failed. Mistress of yourself. And of—the world."

Regina McLemore *is a Will Rogers Medallion Award-winning author and retired educator of Cherokee heritage. Her great, great grand-mother, Susie Christie Clay, survived the Trail of Tears in 1839. Regina's Young Adult Trilogy, Cherokee Passages, is a fictional retelling of her family's history from the Trail of Tears down through the modern day.*

SHERRY MONAHAN

Sherry Monahan is a multiple Will Rogers Medallion award-winning Culinary Historian with over sixteen books. She's a member of the James Beard Foundation and the Authors Guild. She enjoys sharing the history behind food and drink because tasting history is better than just reading about it.

Victorian Recipes with a Side of Scandal is Sherry's latest book. Monahan creatively weaves Victorian-era recipes with the true, and sometimes scandalous life of an English socialite named Ethel Barry. Discover how this young woman grew up in a proper English home and attended all the right schools but found salvation in a kitchen—a place she wasn't supposed to be. She was expected to find a suitable husband in her class, get married, manage a household staff, and have children. But that's not exactly how her life turned out because she broke Victorian protocol.

Cooking, which she never learned because her parents had staff for that, turned out to be her escape when she was "exiled" in America. She turned to food to sustain them in California as she quickly discovered that her life didn't turn out the way she expected. Learn about Ethel's life through over seventy-five Victorian-era recipes she either made or enjoyed. It's served with a side of scandal, like when she went skinny-dipping and when her divorce appeared in multiple U.S. newspapers with wild accusations.

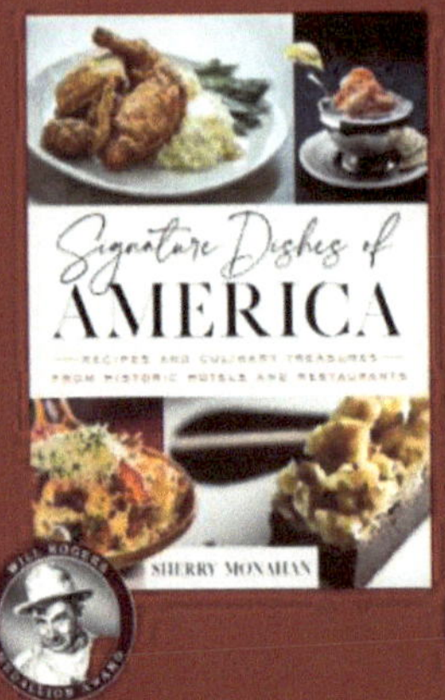

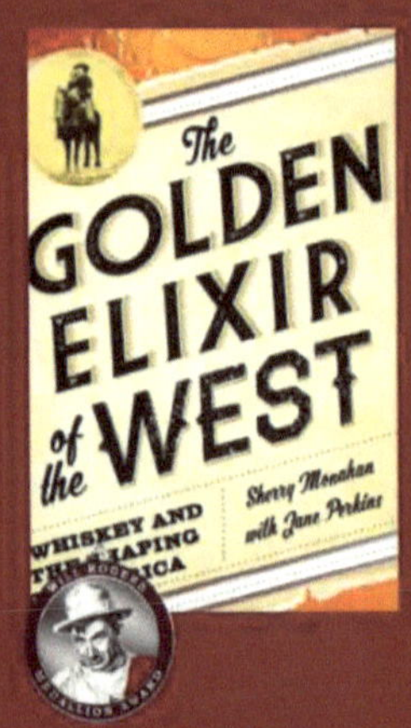

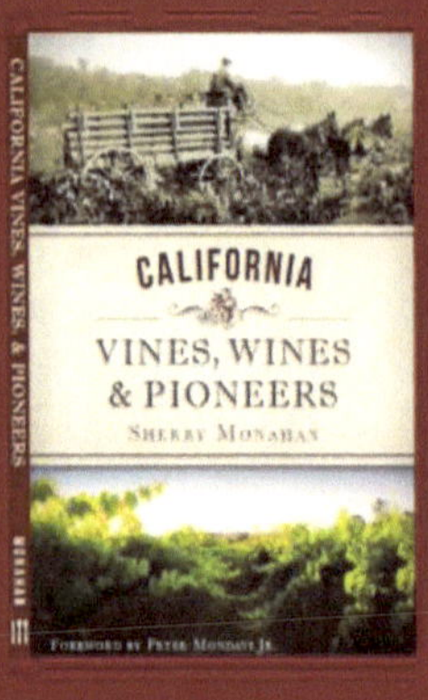

Visit sherrymonahan.com to learn more about Sherry and over sixteen of her books. You can aslo scan this code now.

VELDA BROTHERTON

PARTNERSHIP

A SHORT STORY

Squatted on her haunches, Isabella swirled water and gravel in the battered pan. Nothing gleamed, glistened, or winked.

"Damnation," she muttered, stood, and spread fingers over her aching back.

Just too danged old to be out here squatted like some hillbilly, getting her butt wet. And for what?

Nothing.

The river chattered over its rocky bed, paying her no mind at all. If she didn't get a strike soon, she'd likely starve and no one would even miss her.

She emptied the pan with a shake, tossed it on the ground beside her pack, and stomped off into the woods. Finding a likely spot surrounded by shrubs, she unfastened the galluses of her overalls. Just as she started to shove them down, there came a crashing through the woods that had to be a danged bear.

And her with her rifle and the Colt back at camp. Even as she slipped the straps over her shoulders and turned to run, a voice shouted something she couldn't make out.

A man. Men being like they was around women, this could be worse than any bear.

She crammed her sloppy hat down on the wad of hair stuck up under it and said in as low a voice as she could manage, "Couldn't hear ye."

"I said, having any luck?"

Gangly birch and full willow trees cast deep shadows so she could barely make out his face. A black beard, teeth showing between smiling lips, long dark hair sticking out from under a hat that looked worse than hers, old pants long in the crotch, and a dirty shirt stuffed into their waistband.

Not much to tell him apart from all the men swarming the creek to pan for gold. A typical gold seeker. Starting with rotten luck and it getting worse with every pan he worked. Except for gender, a lot like her, if she'd admit it. Well, she wasn't about to make friends with this one. Two losers hooking up didn't make a winner.

Now he needed to allow her some privacy, but it didn't look likely.

"You been over to Alder Gulch?" he hollered. "Hear they're hitting pay dirt there. Figger with my luck, time I get over there, it'll all be panned out."

Didn't want no danged conversation with this one, or any other. Still he was looking funny at her and she had to say something. Something that would require no reply, or make him want to talk some more or worst of all, reveal her sex.

"Guess I'll head out that way then." She started off through the brush like she'd had enough of this lip flapping. Which she had.

You'd think coming west to Montana would give a feller space to be alone, but there was always someone butting in.

"Oh, yeah?" He was right on her like a wolf running a rabbit. "Well, maybe I'll tag along. Ain't no sense anyone going it alone in such dangerous times. Men killing men over a chunk of gold."

First you have to get that chunk of gold, fool. Now what? Did she just outright tell him she'd rather go alone? If he came along, sooner or later he'd guess she was a woman, and she'd had enough of living in this country as a female. Only two things a man expected from a woman, and the second one was doing his danged laundry. She wasn't up for either. Maybe she ought to shoot him and be done with it.

Instead she kept walking, hoping he'd get the message, but he loped to catch up, long legs bringing him to her side right quick.

"You got you a mule or something?" He kept pace with her, though she trotted as fast as she could, considering the underbrush tugging at her pant legs.

Maybe if she ignored him, he'd disappear. But he didn't. Just kept right on yakking and walking. "A stout little Jenny could carry all our gear, and if I struck it rich, I'd give you a share for the use of the animal." He paused when together they burst from the thicket onto the river bank then added, "Mine died."

When she fetched the burro she'd come across in Virginia City and began to pack her things, he raced to grab up an old blanket already folded and tied around his scant belongings.

"Name's Rand Tolbert." He smiled in a goofy way that annoyed her. But he did have nice teeth. Something unexpected in these parts.

"Sorry," she muttered. "No room. Too heavy." Short sentences were easier to keep gruff sounding. With a grunt, she tied her bundles securely on Clem's back. "Gotta go."

She drew a sigh of relief when he didn't follow her toward the trail that wound through the woods to the south. That was it. She was well rid of him. She began to hum to the little burro, that would follow her anywhere if she sang to her. Especially her favorite song, "Clementine." A good tune for an afternoon walk.

Too soon. The thought she'd be shed of him came too soon, for he chased after her yelling, "Hey, hey." And he didn't stop the infernal hollering till he'd caught up with her. "You going the wrong way for Alder Gulch. Better let me go along and guide you. I know this country like the back of my own hand."

Maybe she'd have to kill him, after all. Serve him right, too. Being so nosy. A real meddler. Inside the overalls, over top of her pantaloons, a leather belt held her holstered Navy Colt. Loaded. Along the banks of the river, men were lined shoulder to shoulder panning for the elusive gold. But a gunshot would most surely grab their attention.

"Well, are you coming or what?" He waited patiently behind her.

"If I keep going this way, you gonna follow me?" She was so exasperated she forgot to work on the quality of her "man voice."

He stared at her, yanked off his dirty hat, and hit his thigh a couple of times with it, sending out a fog of dust. "Why danged if you ain't a woman. What you doing out here by yourself, being a woman and all?"

In the silence that followed a gust of wind caught his long hair, blew it across her his face. She reached inside the overalls, slipped the Colt out in one swift motion. "And you'd better not have anything in mind, or I'll let those men bury you right here." She made a couple of gestures with the gun then trained it on him.

His hands popped into the air, the hat went flying, and he danced backward a couple of steps. "Whoa, Nellie. I ain't fixing to hurt you. Just being friendly. See why that might bother you, but I gotta say, ain't no one gonna look twice at you the way you're got up."

Little did he know, but she kept her lips tight. No sense in showing him what she really was. A killer. "You stay here now. Leave me be" She slid the gun back into its holster. If she threw a rock at this one, he'd be gone.

"This just means one thing, far as I can see."

"What might that be?"

"Why, you need you a man to come along and keep off the lechers."

"I what? I just offered to shoot you 'cause I thought you were a lecherous old coot."

"You can go to jail for shooting a man. Now if I was to rough him up a bit on your part and send him on his way, there'd be ought to pay."

"You know something? You're crazy as a danged loon. Now go on and leave me be. I don't need a protector. I don't need a man. All I need is to be left alone."

He leaned down, fetched his hat by its floppy brim, and backed off. "I'm gone. Gone." And he was.

She made sure of that by watching him go plumb out of sight, then went on up the hill leading Clem. She had no intention of going to Alder Gulch. That was too close to Virginia City and all her old troubles. He was right about one thing. She could go to jail for killing a man. She could also break out of jail, but probably not twice in a row.

That night she dry-camped to make sure if he was trailing her, there'd be no smoke. She fed Clem then hobbled her in a patch of sweet, green grass. The burro was such a pet, she didn't wander, but some wild critter could startle her into running. She rubbed the soft furry nose, whispered a few words of endearment, and opened up the pack. Jerky and hardtack wasn't her idea of a full meal after trudging all afternoon, especially without coffee, but it'd have to do. After a while she stretched out on her blanket and lay back on double-folded hands to gaze at the stars strewn like lit paths across the heavens. No matter where she looked she saw his face, and there he was, right in the middle of the Milky Way.

In her memory, he came at her, fist raised to hit her again. One hand slipped the Colt from under her pillow, aimed it, and pulled the trigger. The ball split his nasty grin, stem to stern. And then she sat there waiting for someone to call the law, for the sheriff to come and haul her off to jail. Over the past few months, she'd lost count of how many times she killed the man who once told her she was his love, his life, his reason for being, for God's sake. And still, every time, she shed tears.

Dear God, weren't women fools?

The sun wasn't up good when Clem squealed her funny call, almost as if she'd been trained to awaken a person like some crazy rooster. Isabella crawled out from under her blanket and there sat the man called Rand, a small fire spitting sap into licking flames.

In the crisp morning air hung the aroma of coffee, fresh ground and fixing. And damn his hide, he had the audacity to smile at her as if they were long lost buddies. Sure had kind eyes to go with those durned purty teeth.

"What the thunder you think you're doing?" She huffed and pulled the blanket over her chest. An involuntary gesture, since her breasts were bound and invisible beneath the white long johns. Men always looked there first when they met a woman, so it was a natural protective gesture.

"Made coffee. Figgered you'd want some, seeing as how you suffered through a dry camp last night."

"Not exactly what I mean by the question. Why are you trailing after me like an un-weaned pup."

That brought a different sort of grin to his face, and she immediately regretted the reference.

Dang, how she hated the thought of killing again, not being natural born to it, but forced to once by a brutal man. This one trod a dangerous path, and somehow, she had to get shut of him. He poured a tin cup full of black, strong coffee and held it up to her, watching her like a rat on cheese. Despite everything, she couldn't resist the offer and took the cup by its handle, placed it on a rock near the fire, and settled herself.

Even as she enjoyed the bitter brew, she had to face the mistake she'd made. Yet, the one thing worse than unwanted company was having no coffee to start the day. He chattered on about the dangers of hunting gold, the worse dangers of finding it. While she finished her coffee, he tied his pack on Clem, then began to pack her stuff into the blanket, laying aside the rifle after studying it with some interest.

"Take your hands off my belongings." She leaped to her feet, tossed the dregs toward the fire, and headed for him. "And get your pack off Clem. You think sharing a cup of coffee gives you the right to just settle in with me? If you ain't the dangdest man I ever met."

Hands out, palms down, he turned from the burro. "Sorry. Damned if I ain't. You are some touchy female. I ain't gonna hurt you."

"Didn't say you were. I just don't like company."

He sucked air between his teeth, then untied his pack from Clem's back and headed toward the creek. "Put out the fire before you leave."

"Well, hell!" she shouted. "I know that. See, that's what I don't like. Someone assuming 'cause I'm female I'm ignorant."

He whirled to face her. "The last thing in this world you are is ignorant. You ain't gonna shoot me in the back are you?"

A chuckle burst out before she could stop it. "'Course not, you danged fool."

He stood there, pack hanging from one hand, watching her with a baleful look, and she sighed. "Oh, all right. You can come with me. But one wrong move and you're gone. You understand?"

Packed up, she moved off leading Clem. Rand trudged along behind. Yakking.

"I'll just bring up the rear, keep an eye out," he called. "How come you to change your mind?"

She mulled that over for a good long while, and he waited for her answer. "Not sure. Ask me in a week, or a month. If this partnership lasts that long."

He remained quiet most of the next day. And the next. Late one night he stirred at the fire with a stick, sending bright sparks into the crisp night air. Spoke in a voice soft with grief.

"My wife Annie passed near a year ago. The cholera took her." He could say no more.

She laid her hand on his arm for a moment, then pulled away, fearful of what a man could do to a woman.

Across the fire, his sorrowful eyes reflected the flames. "I surely do miss her, you know?"

Tears hot on her cheeks, she turned away, unable to allow his grief to touch her heart.

As summer wore on into fall, he continued to follow along, never raising his voice nor fist to her.

At last she related her private tale of a man driven to brutality and a woman driven to kill, and how the law hunted her like a wild animal. She held her breath for fear of his reaction.

What would he think of a woman who could kill?

Why should she care, anyway?

Maybe now he'd be on his way.

No.

The idea sickened her heart.

Dark eyes shimmering, he watched her for a long while. "Well, I reckon it might be time we moved on west, then. What do you think about California? That is... well, if you still are of a mind to continue this partnership."

She nodded, and without speaking, shook out her blanket, spread it on the ground near the fire, and lay down, turning her back to him.

"We'd best get some sleep, then. It's a long trek."

THE AUTHOR

Velda Brotherton *wrote for decades from her home perched on the side of a mountain against the Ozark National Forest. Branded as Sexy, Dark and Gritty, her work embraces the lives of gutsy women and heroes who are strong enough to deserve them. After a stint writing for a New York publisher in the late '80s and early '90s, she settled comfortably in with small publishers to produce novels in several genres.*

While known for her successful series work–the Twist of Poe romantic mysteries, as well as her signature Western Historical Romances–her publishing resume includes numerous stand-alone novels, including Once There Were Sad Songs, Wolf Song, Stoneheart's Woman, Remembrance, *and her magnum opus,* Beyond the Moon.

Following the tragic passing of her longtime writing partner, legendary Western author Dusty Richards, in early 2018, she took up her pen to finish several of his outstanding works, including the standalone novel Blue Roan Colt *and the* Texas Badge *Mystery Series. Sadly, Velda herself passed away in early 2023, leaving behind scores of up-and-coming writers she'd mentored through the years.*

WILL THE REAL ZORRO PLEASE STAND UP?

Beneath the swashbuckling hero immortalized in films and novels lies the shadowy legacy of Joaquin Murrieta, whose life of vengeance and rebellion in Gold Rush California inspired one of the most enduring icons of justice.

STORY BY

ANTHONY WOOD

As a boy, I enjoyed watching the 1950s reruns of the classic television game show, *To Tell the Truth,* whose weekly episodes spanned several decades and had but one goal—unmasking the truth-teller. Three contestant challengers, each claiming to be the main character whose unusual life experience was read aloud by the moderator, were then asked their names and a series of questions. Four celebrity panelists voted as to which challenger was, in fact, the "real" person. The moderator then asked, "Will the real [person's name] please stand up?" With a bit of hem-hawing around and false starts feigned by the challengers, the great reveal came when the real character finally made his or her identity known by standing up. The winner then was declared, after which the imposters shared their true names and occupations.

Like the game show, the true historical identity of the man who inspired a beloved fictional western character draped in black and wielding a rapier, and whose heroic antics captured my heart as a child more than any other, has been elusive at best—the masked swordsman, Zorro. Though the dramatis personae of Zorro has enjoyed a rich history in Hollywood and literature, discovering the factual hombre from which the character of Zorro sprang has been like a gold miner trying to find water in a "dry as dust" summer in the rugged Great Basin Desert of California.

Growing up in the '60s, I also religiously listened to Herb Alpert and The Tijuana Brass Band's instrumental, "A Taste of Honey," on my mother's album, *Whipped Cream* (1965), as I played with plastic toy cowboys, one of whom was dubbed as Zorro. While enjoying Alpert's peppy jazz tunes and dramatic toy soldier shootouts at age nine, I also sneaked glances at the seemingly nude beauty, Dolores Erickson, sitting in a huge mound of whipped cream graced with a generous dollop resembling a flower on top of her head. Though not of Latino descent, Herb's mariachi-inflamed instrumentals

Whipped Cream & Other Delights by Herb Alpert & The Tijuana Brass, 1965.

Zorro's first appearance in the August, 1919 issue of *The All-Story Weekly.*

drew me into appreciating Mexican culture early on and musically inspired my bit of obsession for the masked TV hero played by actor Guy Williams. Even then, I wondered, who was the true Zorro of myth and legend?

POPULARIZING THE LEGEND OF ZORRO

The character of the sword, bullwhip, and pistol wielding vigilante bent on defending the indigenous and common people of California against tyrannical villains was based on Johnston McCulley's (1919) novella. First serialized in the story, *The Curse of Capistrano,* in the pulp magazine, *All-Story Weekly*, and later in *Argosy* magazine—*The Further Adventures of Zorro* (1922), *Zorro Rides Again* (1931), and *The Sign of Zorro* (1941)—the character of Zorro grew with each new release.

Republic Pictures Corporation produced the well-received *Zorro's Fighting Legion* (1939), but it was *The Mark of Zorro* (1940), starring Tyrone Powers and Linda Darnell, that brought the character of Zorro to fame and inspired a host of short story adventures and other characters similar to the masked crusader, notably Batman and the Lone Ranger. Walt Disney's *Zorro* television series, starring Guy Williams, ultimately sealed the legendary status of Zorro as a classic national American western character hero who fought for justice as a *bandito* against an oppressive Mexican government in the years before the California Gold Rush.

Although Disney's *Zorro* was set in 1820s California, while still under Mexican control, the inspiration for the true character steps from the foggy past of another time period. And though Guy William's rendition of Zorro had always been my favorite, when Antonio Banderas sprang onto the big screen to replace Anthony Hopkins as the aging Don Diego de la Vega and accompanied by the lovely Elena Montero played by Catherine Zeta-Jones in *The Mask of Zorro* (1998), I was first in line to get a movie ticket. Bandera's version stands as the most historically accurate big screen presentation of the actual outlaw that inspired the swashbuckler dressed in black.

Much like Baroness Orczy's *Scarlet Pimpernel* character Sir Percy, Don Diego (Banderas) cloaks his pursuit of justice under the guise of an effete dandy wearing lace and writing poetry, living in luxury and leisure, and shunning all forms of violence until he

secrets away wearing his black mask to flash his lightning-fast sword.

So you may be asking, just who was this masked bandit? Who was this caped crusader wandering the countryside seeking justice against an unjust government and leaving the unmistakable mark of Zorro, the famous "Z", on walls and the backsides of Mexican soldiers? Was it Douglas Fairbanks's character in the silent movie, *The Mark of Zorro?* Maybe Guy Williams's Robin Hood-like character who robbed the rich to help the poor in the action packed TV serial? Or Antonio Banderas's Don Diego who defeats wicked men bent on getting rich from the labor of the poor? In the spirit of the game show *To Tell the Truth,* "Will the real Zorro please stand up?"

Television and cinema have popularized the legend of Zorro over the decades. While entertaining, though, they often play fast and loose with historical accuracy.

Discovering the historical inspiration for the incredibly acrobatic bullwhip-carrying savior donned in black portrayed in movies, comic books, and a TV series has been evasive as the Zorro character himself. Yet, one figure lurking in the shadows of myth and legend steps into the light as a suspected candidate. He was not the rugged doer of right hiding behind the façade of a fancy and dandy gentleman. No, the man who inspired the mythical Zorro whom we've all come to know and cheer, was nearly that himself—the stuff of legend. Although finding the truth about the real Zorro can be as tricky as a bandit escaping a posse into the wilderness of the Sierra Nevada Mountains, one outlaw of old seems

Purported photo of Joaquin Murrieta, ca. 1850.

Artist's depiction of Capt. Harry Love, the California State Ranger who killed or captured most of the Five Joaquins Gang in 1853.

to have been the inspiration. All trails lead back to none other than Joaquin Murrieta, sometimes known as the Mexican Robin Hood or the Robin Hood of the West.

WILL THE REAL ZORRO PLEASE STAND UP?

Historian Susan Lee Johnson wrote, "So many tales have grown up around Murrieta that it is hard to disentangle the fabulous from the factual." She goes on to say that the consensus of historical fact is that Murrieta was driven by Anglos from a rich mining claim and "his wife was raped, his half-brother lynched, and Murrieta himself horsewhipped." Although historical fact regarding a notorious bandito whose popularity rose during the California Gold Rush is scarce as hen's teeth, much has been written about the outlaw of Mexican descent who wreaked vengeful havoc on his Anglo oppressors.

Sketchy facts form a puzzle with several missing pieces to form a picture of a man desiring to start a new life of mining with his wife, only to have his pure intentions dashed in changes made by the American government after California came into possession of the U.S. following the Mexican War (1846-48).

Like thousands of gold seeking Americans and immigrants from other nations, legend has it that Murrieta, a *vaquero* from Sonora, Mexico, came to California as a forty-niner. One version attests that, with nothing more than peaceful intentions, Murrieta and his brother were accused of stealing a mule. Though untrue, his Anglo pursuers horsewhipped Murrieta, hanged his brother, Alejandro, and his wife died in his arms after having been brutally raped. He embarked in savage revenge to find and kill the Anglos responsible for violating and murdering his wife.

Another version claims that Murrieta was forced off his gold claim because of the Foreign Miners' Tax of the 1850s, designed to protect American miners from immigrants who might challenge their claims. Dispossessed of a mining claim by the American government due to his immigrant status, Murrieta and other former miners erupted in a spree of banditry that led to a series of thefts, robberies, and murders, mostly targeting those who had stolen their claims. Soon, nearly every crime committed in Northern California was attributed to Murrieta and his gang.

According to an ancestor's report on Find-a-Grave, Joaquin Murrieta, born around 1830, and his wife, Rosita Feliz, were lured to the gold rich fields in Stanislaus County in Northern California. Five drunken Anglo miners, who didn't like sharing mining claims with Mexicans, broke into Murrieta's cabin and commenced their dastardly deeds. Murrieta and his elder brother went seeking retribution for the crimes, but he was horse-whipped and his brother hanged. The Five Joaquins Gang soon emerged and in 1853, Captain Harry Love and his Rangers killed or captured most of the outlaws, including Three Fingered Jack. Murrieta was taken to jail in Mariposa and subsequently hanged, his head being severed afterwards. The relic was sent to Stockton and on July 28, 1853, the California State Legislature verified its authenticity, and was later confirmed by Father Dominic Blaine on August 11, 1853.

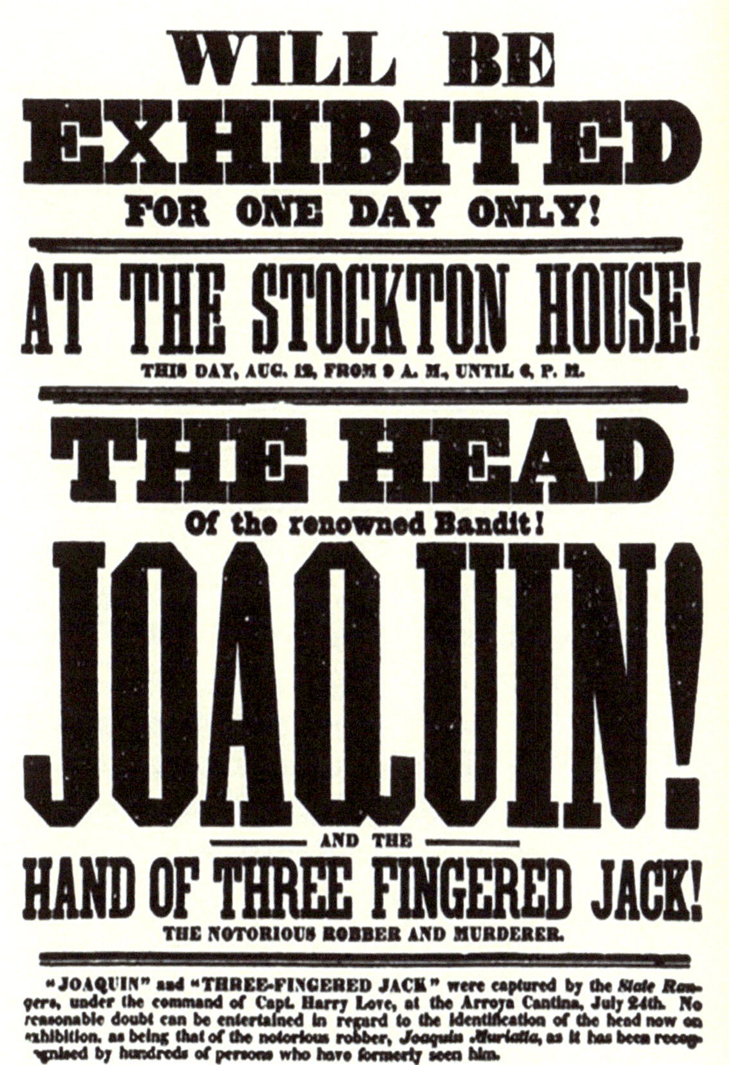

Soon after the confirmation of his death, Murrieta's life was first popularized as a historical figure in Native American (Cherokee) John Rollin Ridge's novel, *The Life and Adventures of Joaquin Murieta: The Celebrated California Bandit* (1854), the State of California's first published novel. Portrayed as a victim of ethnic discrimination, Murrieta turned to crime only after the evil events that disrupted his life. He announced that he would, from that moment, "live on for revenge, and that his path would be marked with blood."

As a member of the Five Joaquin's Gang, Murrieta was known to have had a number of companions who engaged in his outlawry, most notably, Three Fingered Jack. Legend has it that between 1850 and 1853, the Five Joaquin Gang's rampage of destruction was responsible for the theft of $100,000 in gold and over one hundred horses, and the death of nineteen people while evading three armed posses, but not before killing at least three lawmen. They were accused of killing at least thirteen Anglos and twenty-eight Chinese immigrants.

The intensity of Murrieta's short-lived career drew enough attention to warrant Governor of California, John Biglar, to enact the organization of the California State Rangers on May 11, 1853, to be led by former Texas Ranger Harry Love. Being paid $150 a month and a chance to split a $5000 reward, the Ranger's sole mission was to capture Joaquin Murrieta, "dead or alive." On July 25, 1853, near Pancho Pass in San Benito County, Ranger Love and his men shot it out with men believed to be the Five Joaquins Gang. Two Mexicans thought to be Murrieta and Three Fingered Jack were killed. As proof

Thomas Armstrong's depiction of "Joaquin the Mountain Robber" as published in the *Sacramento Union Steamer Edition* on April 22, 1853.

A drawing of Joaquin Murrieta's severed head.

John Rollin Ridge, one of the authors who made Murrietta famous in his novel, *The Life and Adventures of Joaquin Murrietta.*

of their identities, the Rangers removed Murrieta's head from his body and Three Fingered Jack's hand. Both were placed in an alcohol-filled jar to secure the reward and then placed on public display in a number of mining towns throughout the Mother Lode country as well as Stockton and San Francisco. Though never proven it was the actual head of Murrieta, and despite the fact that seventeen people, one of which was a Catholic priest, signed affidavits testifying to the truth that it was actually Murrieta's head, patrons still lined up to pay one dollar each to view the two outlaw's ghoulish remains. Though the facts of Murrieta's demise are sketchy at best, and setting controversy aside, the gang broke up and outlaw activity attributed to them ceased.

Much like other outlaws thought to have survived an alleged demise, like Billy the Kid and Jesse James, witnesses claimed to have seen Murrieta around California in a number of places. A young woman, professing to be Murrieta's sister, after having viewed the head, testified that the relic did not have the prominent head scar her brother had. The great San Francisco earthquake of 1906 destroyed Murrieta's displayed head in a fire.

What we can definitively know about the man who inspired the character of Zorro is captured in this report found in a January, 1853 issue of the San Joaquin Republican—"a band of Mexican marauders have infested Calaveras County, and weekly we receive the details of dreadful murders and outrages... the band is led by a robber, named Joaquin, a very desperate man."

MURRIETA AS ZORRO? OR ZORRO AS MURRIETA?

John Rollin Ridge's dime novel fictional account of Murrieta reprinted in the *California Police Gazette* (1858) became the impetus for the mythical hero we now know as Zorro. Translated into several European languages and later into Spanish by Roberto Hyenne, who subsequently exchanged every reference to "Mexican" for "Chilean," brought more fame to Murrieta. When Johnston McCulley (1919) based his fictional Don Diego de la Vega on Ridge's novel on Murrieta, the legend of Zorro was born.

The image of an aggrieved avenging widower against Anglo aggression emerged due to Ridge's version in his *The Life and Adventures of Joaquin*

Murrieta, and later retellings. This in part could have been inspired by Ridge's own killing of a Cherokee judge, David Kell, who supported those who murdered Ridge's father. Though exonerated, Ridge fled the Indian Territory the same year he claimed Joaquin Murrieta arrived in the California gold fields. Ridge was noted as saying that he would amass enough wealth to enable him to return to the Indian Territory and exact revenge on those who murdered his father. Writing in a letter to his cousin, Ridge expressed that he possessed "a deep seated principle of Revenge." Ridge's own life experiences certainly influenced his account of Murrieta's life.

But it was Walter Noble Burn's, *The Robin Hood of El Dorado: the Saga of Joaquín Murrieta, Famous Outlaw of California's Age of Gold* (1932), and later made into the motion picture, *The Robin Hood of El Dorado* (1936) by director William Wellman, that cast the vengeful outlaw into a righteous seeker of justice.

The life and outlawry of Joaquin Murrieta as a historical social icon unquestionably inspired a rich gold strike of popular literature, movies, and even a number of pieces written in the genre of corrido. Most notable is an English language ballad written by Jack Hanna, sung by the family trio Sons of the San Joaquin and released on their album, *Way Out Yonder* (2005). Similar to Marty Robbin's number one hit, "El Paso" (1960), the traditional *vaquero* style ballad, graced with mariachi horns and Spanish guitars, incorporated into the lyrics the facts and legend of Murrieta's life. The ballad continues to solidify Murrieta's place as a social icon. That standing was also true when Murrieta became a resistance symbol for the Chicano Movement in the 1960s, complete with a dormitory and cultural center near UC Berkeley's campus named *Casa* Joaquin Murrieta.

Joaquin Murrieta would have never guessed that one day he would be the inspiration for such characters as the vigilantes Batman and Lone Ranger, the demon-cursed *El Diablo* of DC Comics' fame, or the pulp hero El Coyote who protected the original Mexican landowners from land grabbing Anglo-Americans after the Mexican War. The guitar wielding alter-ego Zorro-like character El Kabong of *Quick Draw McGraw* cartoon, Texas Tech University's mascot nicknamed the Masked Rider, and the tongue-in-cheek version, *Zorro, The Gay Blade,*

The comic book character El Diablo debuted in *All-Star Western* #2 (October 1970).

Warner Brother's El Kabong swinging to the rescue as a Zorro type character in *Quick Draw McGraw.* The cartoon was nominated for an Emmy Award in 1960.

The Amazon Studios 8 episode TV series, *The Head of Joaquin Murrieta* (2023), is both fiery and gripping.

were all, or at least in part, influenced by the character of Zorro, and in turn, Murrieta.

The History Channel's excellent documentary, *Behind the Mask of Zorro* (2010), may prove to be the latest word on how the historical Joaquin Murrieta inspired the character of Zorro, but it is John J. Valadez's eight-part dramatized version series, *The Head of Joaquin Murrieta* (2023), that brought back to the screen a fresh look at the Robin Hood of the West, offering the best of both worlds of fact and historical fiction. One writer captured the mood and essence of the effort to re-popularize the myth of the man behind the legend of Zorro, describing it as "a dissenting view of American history from a decidedly Chicano perspective. Deeply personal, irreverent and entertaining, the film tears open a painful and long ignored historical trauma that has never been explored on American television: the lynching of Mexican Americans in the west."

Not bad for a little known Mexican bandit who still evades the net of historical fact as one seines the rivers of research and who now lives primarily in the annals of myth and legend. And though these are the latest attempts at getting at the truth of the man behind the mask, I am certain that they will not be the last.

CA Historical Marker #344, about nine miles from Coalinga.

Anthony Wood *grew up in historic Natchez, Mississippi, fueling a life-long love of history. He is the author of A Tale of Two Colors, a series of Civil War historical novels based on the real-life wartime journey of his ancestor, Columbus Nathan "Lummy" Tullos. His writing has won a number of awards, including a Will Rogers Medallion for his Western short story "Not So Long in the Tooth." He serves as Managing Editor of* Saddlebag Dispatches *and was inducted into the Arkansas Writers' Hall of Fame in 2024.*

The legend continues....

MIMI SIMMONS

Team Simmons

The minute you meet Mimi, you feel her passion for real estate and her community. A 5th generation Native of Nevada County, Mimi has been in real estate 40 years and loves every moment of it! In 1992 Mimi co-founded Cornerstone Realty Group. Starting with 6 agents and built the company to 4 offices and 65 agents before selling the Company in 2006. During this time, Mimi served two years as President of Nevada City Chamber of Commerce and on the Board for 18 years. She is also former President of Big Brothers Big Sisters, Nevada County Board of Realtors and has received numerous awards for her community service and involvement. Mimi is also involved with Nevada City 49er Rotary Breakfast Club and Board Member of Bright Futures. Every Escrow that Mimi closes benefits these non-profit organizations.

She created Team Simmons with *Holli Navo* and *Tammy Andreozzi*, who have been with her over 23 years, and welcomed Kaetlyn Lientz to the team 2 years ago. Team Simmons has been the top producing team in Nevada County for over 14 years and is currently 3rd in California and 17th Nationally with Century 21 Global. Mimi is an avid water and snow skier, and married to her only love, Phil Ruble for 26 years. Hop up into the saddle with Mimi Simmons and her team!

CENTURY 21®
Cornerstone Realty

Mimi Simmons
Team Simmons
DRE 00871435
www.MimiSimmons.com
530.265.7940

DON MONEY

GOLD IN HAND, BLOOD IN THE WATER

A SHORT STORY

The first gunshot sent the pan falling from Cain Marke's hands, landing with a splash in the Mokelumne River. A second round landed in the water just ahead of him, causing the man to lose his balance and fall backwards into the shallow water near the bank. The third shot landed somewhere away from Cain, and the respite sent him scrambling on his hands and knees for the riverbank and cover in the dense brush.

Cain Marke was no stranger to gunfire. He had felt the closeness of death whispering in his ear dozens of times serving with the Seventh Infantry in the Mexican-American War. First, at the Siege of Fort Texas and later when he had killed men for the first time at the Battle of Monterey. The killings had left a scar on his mind that he hoped never to have to live through again.

A cry of anguish escaped Cain's lips as he looked down the riverbank and caught sight of his father slumped over the rocker box he had been faithfully working at just minutes before. His father, Enverst Marke, had heard the siren call of the rush for gold in California all the way down in Texas and convinced Cain to accompany him on the adventure. He had told his son as they set out, "Those gold nuggets would be the life of this family or the death of him."

Glancing through the brush, Cain could see on the embankment above their camp three men with rifles looking around trying to locate where he had scrambled off to hide. All the men wore long dusters and had their cowardly faces hidden behind bandannas pulled up over their noses. These men must be claim jumpers. His father had gone into town the day before to purchase supplies, and despite Cain warning him not to, had bragged about the gold they were beginning to find in the river along their campsite.

From his vantage point, Cain saw that his father was not moving. He had to find some way to get to him and escape together if he still lived. Despite the possible dangers he might face, Cain had chosen to avoid the demons of the past and not gone to California heeled. A choice he now questioned seeing his father laying fifty feet from and perhaps growing closer to death with every minute Cain wasted trying to get to him.

"Listen up down there." The gruff voice of one of the men on the ridge called out. "Just throw down your gun and come out. We'll let you get the old man and clear out."

Cain could see the big man in the middle was the one doing the talking, and as he finished, he motioned for the man on each side of him to make their way down to the camp. These vultures did not intend to let him or his father go. Cain lost sight of the men coming down and knew any minute now he would be caught in the open with them at the riverside on his level.

Just then, a moan came from his father and his body stirred somewhat. "Father!" Cain jumped to his feet and ran toward where the body lay.

From the bottom of the hillside near where his father was, one of the bandits appeared and fired off a shot at Cain. The bullet came close and Cain ducked behind a large rock.

"I thought you said you would let us go," Cain yelled.

The man at the top of the hill laughed. "That was

before we knew where you were. You are caught between a rock and a hard place now."

Behind him, the final man who had come down the hill walked out from behind the shack his father and he had built. Cain would be dead in the man's eyesight as soon as he turned his head. His hand scrambled around and found purchase on a smooth rock that filled his palm. He closed on it, picked it up, and with all his might heaved it at the man twenty feet away.

The claim jumper had begun to turn toward Cain just as the airborne rock connected with his chin. An awful snap sounded as the rock broke the outlaw's jaw. Springing from behind the cover of the rock, Cain charged to where the man fell. Gunshots rang out behind him and flecks of rock and dirt kicked up where the bullets impacted along his escape path.

The shack walls provided a new cover from the view of both the man on the ridge and the other man along the river. Cain prepared to overpower the man he had hit with the rock and take his weapon, but as soon as he saw the body, he knew there was no need. The rock's impact had sent the man falling backwards and his head had hit the ground striking a larger rock. Blood from the damage of the thrown rock ran down to join the blood seeping from the back of his head.

Cain felt a darkness close in around him. Despite the braggadocio tales from men around the saloons who plied their stories to impress or intimidate, old soldiers like Cain felt no kinship for death. Even though the claim jumper intended to take Cain's life, he was sorry that the man was dead. Cain pulled back the man's duster and tugged the Colt revolver from the holster on the man's hip. He slipped the revolver into his pants waistband and scooped up the Winchester rifle that had moments before been intended to take his own life.

Armed now, Cain worked out a plan to get to his father. He leaned the rifle around the corner of the shack, firing off a wayward shot to discourage the river outlaw from charging freely at his position. If he could keep the two outlaws ducking long enough, maybe he could get out of this with his father safe and only one death on his conscience.

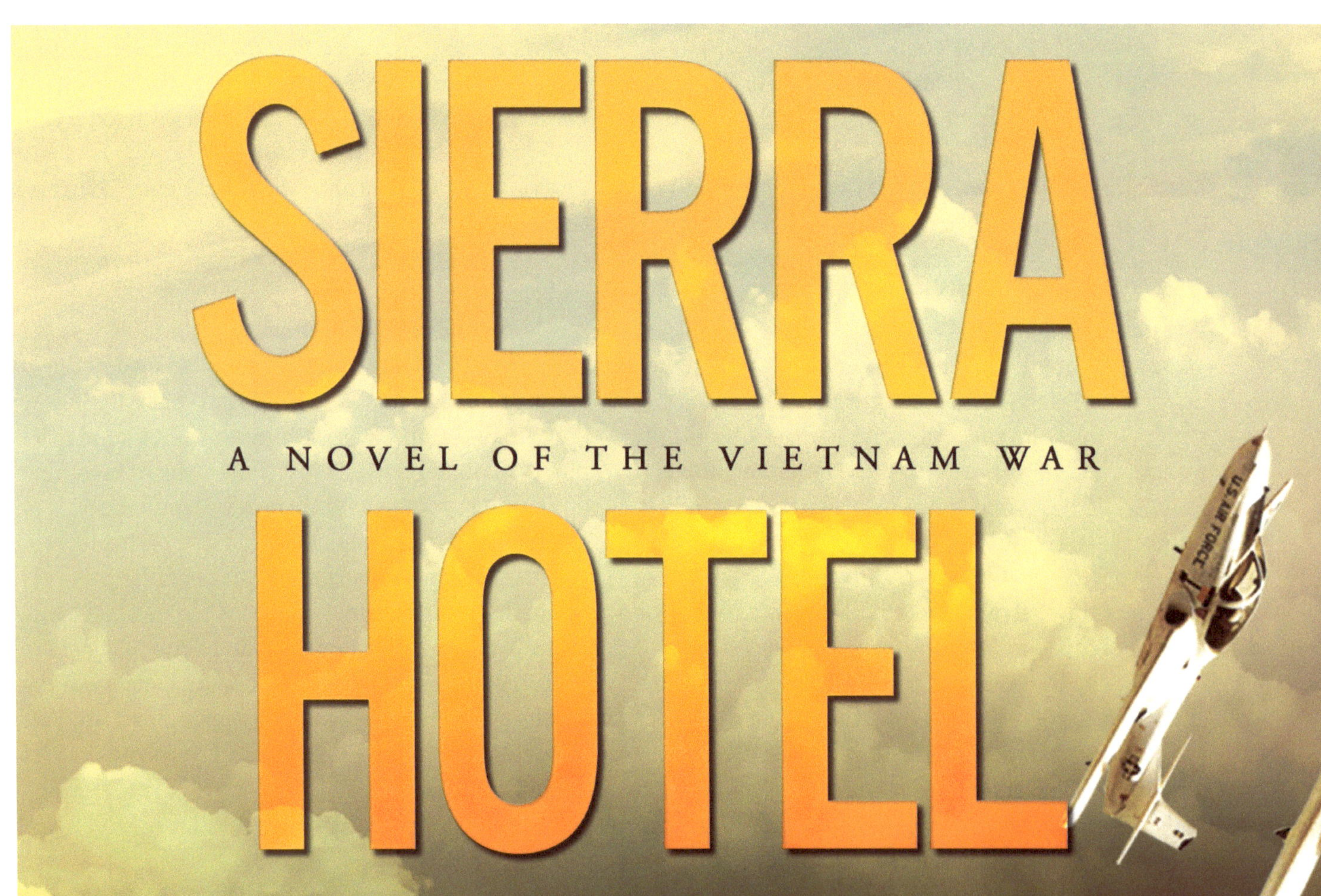

"Amos!" The man up on the ridge yelled down toward the shack. "You ok?"

"Your man is dead," Cain, answered back.

A withering number of rounds struck the top of the shack in response. "You killed my brother!"

"I didn't kill him directly, he fell and hit his head. My father and I did not ask for this. You are the ones who brought this hell to us."

A yell and more shots from the ridge thudded into the wood that obscured Cain's position. Cain could hear the man on the ridge giving more instructions. "You two get down there with Clete. I'll draw him out and the three of you finish him off."

More men complicated the plan to get his father out alive with no further death. Not knowing where the man already at the river had gotten off to, his absence worried Cain. He decided to risk peeking around to check on his father. As his face came around the side it nearly collided with a rifle barrel snaking its way silently along the wall of the shack. The man behind the rifle was just as surprised as Cain was to see his enemy this close.

Cain pushed the rifle barrel into the wall with his left arm as he swung up the Winchester with his right hand. The rifle came flush with the man's stomach as Cain pulled the trigger. The shot being so close propelled the man violently backwards, his grip released on his own rifle and he wind milled to the ground.

A ragged yell came from behind him. "The bastard just gut shot Clete." A pistol shot from the man behind Cain creased along his right thigh, stinging, but not dropping him. Cain brought the weapon up to his shoulder with practiced efficiency and sent a shot rifling down the barrel and into the skull of his attacker.

The man on the ridge with the rifle had moved down its edge until he found a place along the precipice to have a chance at Cain. The first rifle shot missed, and Cain turned back toward the safety of the shack. Just as he reached the corner a shot from above hit the corner of the wood wall and sent a shower of splinters driving into Cain's face. Dropping the rifle, he swiped his hand across the side of his face to wipe away the blood but felt the sting of the dozens of wood fragments embedded there.

The man on the ridge called down to the last claim jumper along the river. "Murt, he went back to the shack. I think I got him though."

Cain pulled the Colt from his waistband and lay on the ground holding his eyes open a tiny slit. With the bloody condition of his face, he hoped it would sell to the man coming his way that he was out of commission. Scraping sounds along the rocks came closer as the man emerged from the brush to the side of Cain. A double-barreled shotgun held out in vanguard to the outlaw's approach to the downed gold miner.

The man prodded Cain with the shotgun and relaxed as a toothy grin appeared on his face. "You got him, Brannon. You tore the hell out of his face. The boss will be sure to reward us for this one."

As the shotgun barrel moved away, Cain's eyes shot fully open and he brought the Colt up and fired a round into the man's chest followed by a second one. The shotgun clattered to the ground.

"Murt." A call came from the ridge. "You finish him off?"

The life taking that Cain pledged to himself to stop at the end of the war had been washed away in a deluge, as the four bodies of the men lay scattered along the Mokelumne River. He angrily called to the man on the ridge. "This was not what I wanted. You brought this on me. Damn you! They are all dead, and for what, a little gold in your hand and our blood in the water."

An uneasy quiet settled along the claim site. Cain

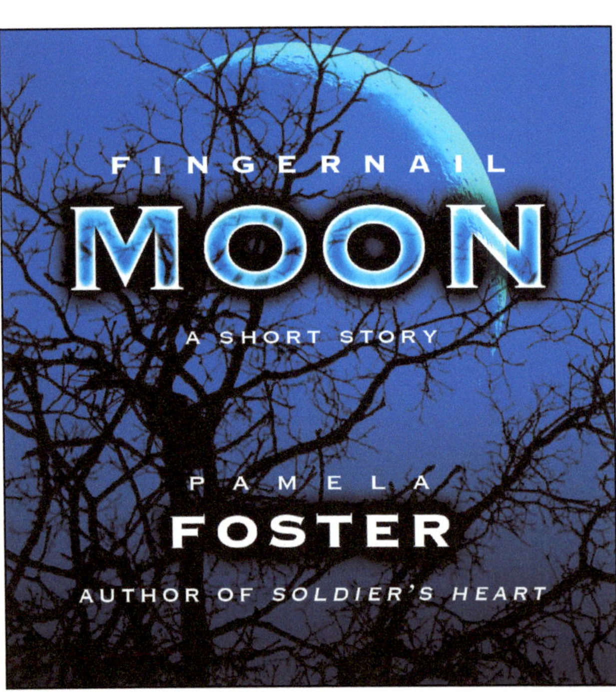

gripped the Colt in his hand as he stood back up. The sounds of sliding rock caught his attention and he realized too late that the man on the ridge had forged a new path down the hillside.

An angry growl came from behind him. "You killed all of my brothers." The man fired a shot from his revolver that struck the Colt in Cain's hand. The pistol broke apart and Cain felt the shock run up his arm. A second shot passed through Cain's left shoulder and sent him tumbling to the ground.

The man walked closer to stand right over Cain's prone form. Anger boiled across his outlaw's face. The rage had blinded him as he aimed his pistol at the gold miners face. Cain through gritted teeth worked his right hand until he found the shotgun that lay next to him. He swiveled it the best he could and aimed upward. His finger snaked into the guard and pulled the trigger.

An explosion sounded as the full brunt of shot caught the outlaw directly in the left knee and severed the leg. A scream echoed along the river as the man fell. Cain pulled himself over to the man's dying body and yelled in his face. "All of this death is on your hands. Damn you for what you made me do."

Cain stood and left the man to slowly bleed out. He stumbled toward where his father lay. He pulled his father's body back from the shaker box and knew right away with all the blood around soaking into the sand he was dead. Cain cried as he cradled the body thinking back on the prophetic words his father had said before they had set out on this journey.

The scars of death scabbed over in Cain's mind as he lay his father back on the ground. He walked back to the dying man.

"Help me," the man said. "I don't want to die. You can save me, tie off my leg and get me to town."

A coldness came from Cain's voice. "Who sent you? Who is the boss you work for?"

"I'll tell you, just promise you will get me to help."

Cain nodded.

"Taylor. Mr. Taylor the bank manager. He is collecting up all the claim sites that find gold and putting in his own people to run them."

Cain turned to walk back to where his father lay.

"You promised to help me," the man whispered from where he lay bleeding.

"That is the second promise I've broken today," Cain replied as he walked away to bury his father and tend to his injuries.

The bookish teller opened the door to the bank manager's office. "Mr. Taylor, there is a customer here asking for you."

"Tell him I'm occupied," Harrison Taylor replied.

"He asked me to mention he has a claim on the Mokelumne River and has made an interesting find."

Taylor smiled as he stood up from behind his desk. "Send him in. Send him in."

The teller stepped aside as the man walked into the bank manager's office then closed the door and returned to his station.

"How can I be of service, Mister...." The banker extended his hand already greedily thinking of what this man might tell him.

"Cain," the customer replied.

"Well, Mr. Cain, what can I do to help?"

"It's just Cain." He left the man's hand hanging in the air. "I know about the men you send to jump claims for you."

"I don't have any idea what you are referring to." Sweat began to trickle from the banker's brow.

Cain pulled the revolver that he had taken from the last man he killed and aimed it at Taylor.

"Now wait a minute. Those men may have worked for me, but I didn't tell them to do any killing to get the claim." The banker babbled as he tried to spin his story

"I don't believe you. They killed my father. I am here to end this with you."

"No, no, no." The banker stammered. "You can't do this. You shoot me now you will be killing me in cold blood. You kill me and you will be marked, Cain."

"I can live with that." Cain extended his arm and pulled the trigger. Afterward, he walked back through the bank and out the door to his horse. He rode his mount out of town with the banker's last words on his mind.

THE AUTHOR

Don Money *was born and raised in rural Arkansas. He spent the majority of his youth exploring the woods around their family farm or with his face buried in a Western novel. After graduating high school he joined the United States Air Force and traveled the globe as a Nuclear, Biological, Chemical Weapons Defense Specialist. After ten years in the service, Don returned to his roots in Arkansas and now teaches Language Arts to sixth graders. He holds Masters and Bachelors degrees in Education from Arkansas State University. Don is an active member of the White County Creative Writers group and enjoys writing fiction across multiple genres. He has sixty short stories published in a variety of anthologies and magazines. Don resides in Beebe, Arkansas with his wife Sarah where they are the proud parents of five children.*

REAVIS Z. WORTHAM

SECOND ANNIVERSARY

PART TWO OF THE EXCLUSIVE SERIAL NOVELLA

A SHORT STORY

It was raining and had been for hours, the type of cold, steady shower that seems to fall endlessly, whispering onto the cracked pavement. The saturated ground could hold no more. The runoff in front of the Alamo filled the gutter, curb deep.

Ambrose B. Hollis watched a familiar young lady step out of a black Suburban. Sandy Anderson held a folded newspaper overhead as an impromptu umbrella as the Uber pulled away and looked down at the damp guidebook in her hand. She glanced up at the squat gray structure across the busy street.

She was a mature woman now, but he remembered her as the young lady he'd met amid a storm of horror and death, however briefly, on a grassy Montana hillside five years before.

Ambrose B. Hollis wasn't an average man. He was a dwarf and wasn't particularly offended by the word, but he preferred to be called Ambrose, or Mr. Hollis. He didn't look upon his unusual size as an affliction, it was merely an obstacle occasionally presenting minor challenges.

Long blonde hair hung damp and limp against Sandy's face, falling in strands across her shoulders. She hunched her shoulders against the cold rain running off the paper that trickled down the neck of her blue cotton shirt.

Tucking a rogue strand of hair behind her left ear, she sighed and smiled to herself. Even though it had been raining from the moment she landed at the airport, things had been going fairly well. Her first vacation in five years was a well-deserved three-week break.

Sandy peered through the gray curtain of falling weather and studied the Alamo before her, comparing the tired old chapel to the movie images she'd seen on television. She was surprised to find that instead of the vast emptiness she expected to see surrounding the old San Antonio mission, it sat huddled small, dwarfed amid buildings towering like a man-made forest above its weathered facade. Behind her, a garish display of tourist traps hawked cheap Texas souvenirs made in China.

Sandy started across the wet street, its gutters running full and fast. The heavy traffic momentarily held her at bay while she looked both ways as her mother had taught her, then darted through an opening.

Her sneakered foot slipped off the curb and into the small, cold current, just before reaching the safety of the sidewalk. Water filled her sneaker and she grimaced and shook her foot, standing like a stork on the other.

Hollis watched her through the milling swarm of people from under his wide-brimmed hat. Rainwater dripped from the ancient oak tree above him, steadily plopping onto his already soaked hat to funnel off the back of the brim. The tree was a leaky shelter at best, but it would do until he got his gabbling tour group inside the old mission where it was dry and comfortable.

Hollis was still a tour guide, a profession he'd loved for more than fifteen years. He began his career at the Custer National Battlefield in Montana and had been guiding tours there when he first saw Sandy and her husband, James. Their acquaintance had been brief, less than an hour, but it had drastically changed the lives of Hollis and Sandy forever.

And had killed her husband.

He surveyed the group of tourists. Colorful umbrellas created a constantly shifting roof over the crowd as they packed closer to hear his lecture. Thunder rumbled across the sky and lightning pulsed in the gray clouds overhead.

Removing the ever-present cigar from its accustomed position in the corner his mouth, Hollis cleared his throat and pointed toward the Alamo behind him. "We're standing in what was the southern fortification in 1836." He leaned heavily on his black cane; the lead-colored head grasped firmly in a stubby fist.

"This area is a small corner of the overall fortification. The common misconception is the chapel behind me was the entire fort. But if that had been the case, I doubt that the Alamo would have ever fallen.

"But the sad truth is the outnumbered defenders had too large an area to cover. It's testimony to their fighting skills that they held out as long as they did." He puffed in vain on his soggy cigar. "Behind you is the plaza which was then a dirt parade field. Legend has it that Colonel Travis scratched his line there in the dirt for his defenders to cross when he asked for volunteers to stay and fight."

Sandy frowned at the dense cluster of people blocking the sidewalk.

Another tour group. *It seems like everywhere I go there's a tour of some kind blocking the traffic. Loud, slow, and in the way*

She dropped the wet newspaper in a nearby trash can as the unseen tour guide's voice traveled clearly over the wet swish of the traffic in the street behind her. He sounded vaguely familiar. She felt uneasy for some unknown reason.

Probably the tone of his voice. Sometimes a person's voice grates on my nerves like fingernails on a blackboard

Sandy dismissed him and looked to her left toward a cream-colored marble statue dedicated to the Alamo's doomed defenders.

James would have liked it here.

The unconscious thought caught her completely unaware and for a moment she again felt the familiar sharp ache of his loss. It didn't hurt as much as it used to. Five years had passed since James died, and time had softened the raw edges a little more with each passing year.

The deepest grief had passed, and she could think back on her incredibly short marriage without the heart-wrenching anguish that had plagued her for the first two years without him.

The tour director's lecture again filtered through her thoughts, and she strained to find the source of the familiar sound.

"It seems to be getting a little damp out here." Hollis' weak joke was rewarded with a courteous chuckle from the crowd gathered around him. "Let's get inside for a while until the rain quits. We'll tour the museum and then re-form after you leave the visitor's center."

Hollis pointed with his cane toward the wall of the long barracks. "Remember, for those of you who still carry cameras, no photography is allowed inside. I'll see you all in about fifteen minutes."

The cluster of tourists dissipated and flowed around the water puddles toward the Texas shrine. Hollis tugged his hat lower and puffed on the stub of his cigar. Several diehards stayed with him instead of going inside, forcing him to answer their questions. He sighed, fielded as many as possible, and kept one eye on Sandy through the crush of bodies behind his group. Putting his answers on autopilot, he considered the best way to approach her, one which would cause as little shock as possible. Time and circumstances betrayed him though, and when the last of his people began to move away, Hollis knew the exact second Sandy saw him.

With a suddenness that took her breath away, the crowd broke and through a tangle of umbrellas, arms, and cameras, Sandy caught a glimpse of Hollis. He saw the pain and terror in her eyes as recognition flooded in. Five years hadn't changed him at all, other than adding a touch of distinguished gray to his temples.

She saw a ghost from the past. In shock, she took a defensive step back into the busy street just as a city bus roared past. The driver abruptly jerked the wheel to the left, barely missing the young woman suddenly appearing in the street. He hit the horn and splashed by scant inches away. A sheet of water rose from the huge tires and soaked the back of Sandy's jeans.

She looked up in time to realize what she'd done, but only the bus driver's quick reaction saved her from being struck down. With her legs soaked with cold water, she stumbled back onto the sidewalk.

Without moving a muscle, Hollis watched Sandy's near accident with the same impassive attitude he demonstrated the day her husband had kicked out his life on the grassy Montana hillside.

That's what he did in Montana. He just leaned on his cane and watched,

But just as soon as she felt the flash of anger, it seeped away and was gone.

Let the past stay in the past. We're probably both different people now. Besides what could he have done, stop James from dying, or stopped the bus?

Hollis puffed his cigar, shifted his weight and repositioned his cane. Before either could make a move one way or another, a member of Hollis' tour stepped between. Sandy cautiously walked to Hollis' side and waited, half listening to his discussion.

He still looked the same. The only difference was the clothing he now wore. In Montana he was dressed in buckskins like one of Custer's scouts. Here it was jeans, boots, a leather vest, and large-brimmed hat. Hollis handled the glossy black cane as if were an extension of his body.

The oddly shaped lead-colored head seemed to be molded to fit Hollis' stubby fist. He again shifted his weight on the thick prop to rest his bad leg. The gray metal tip scraped the ground and left a water-filled indention that vanished like a breath.

The tourist moved away and Hollis turned toward Sandy. "That was a close one. You're lucky the driver had such good reactions." He tilted his head upward and looked into her eyes. "It's been a long time."

She nodded, not trusting her voice.

"You look good. Been taking care of yourself I see," he tried again.

"I work out twice a week. I don't think you've changed much at all, of course I saw you only that one time."

"I'm surprised you remember anything..." Hollis stopped. "Look, Sandy, isn't it, I'm sorry."

She realized his dilemma and helped him out. "It's all right. I've come to terms with James' death."

Hollis sighed with relief. "On vacation?"

"Yeah, this is the first one I've had since I last saw you," she said, looking at the familiar chapel over Hollis' head.

The small talk became more and more difficult to maintain.

"This is a good town for sight-seeing," Hollis said. They stopped, finding themselves locked into the uncomfortable silence.

Hollis followed her gaze and on impulse turned back to Susan.

"Hey, would you like for me to take you on a tour?"

Sandy brightened. "That would be great!" she said. "You still owe me one anyway." A relieved smile smoothed the worry lines on her forehead.

He grinned up at her. "Fine. And if you're up to it later, I'll take you to dinner on Riverwalk tonight." He paused, fearing he'd again stepped over some unseen limit.

Sandy nodded and then shivered as a drop cold of rain ran down her neck. Her wet jeans felt cold and clammy against her legs. "When do we start?"

"As soon as I've discharged my duties with this bunch. I'll make you an honorary member of my tour group," he laughed. They made small talk for the next half hour, neither mentioning how they'd watched her husband James die at the Little Bighorn, one last victim of that battle way back in 1876.

A few tourists slowly made their way back to where the two of them stood under the ancient old oak tree. She moved away and stepped back toward the street to allow the returning members of the group better access to the lecture. They crowded around, laughing, talking, and opening umbrellas.

Hollis waved a hand for attention. "We all know the Alamo fell on March 6, 1836, and the Texans repelled attack after attack for thirteen days of siege, but the information you've learned from television and recent movies is a little different from the actual facts of the battle." Hollis gestured toward the grassy section of the Alamo Plaza beside them. "If you'll follow me, I'll try to correct what Hollywood may have misconstrued."

Limping slightly, Hollis led them closer to the front entrance of the ancient shrine. "As I stated earlier, this tiny area you see here was not the entire fortress. It extended to a point across the street where those markers are standing, past the drugstore there and then stretched several hundred yards to the north." With his cane, Hollis pointed down the street, past the monument to the defenders, to a cluster of new buildings. "The street in front of us, and those buildings across and down from here, all sit upon what was the makeshift fort...."

A young man in his early twenties brushed past Sandy and slowly maneuvered through the crowd to get closer to the speaker. Ben Carter was also enjoying the first vacation he'd taken in several years. A native from Tennessee, Ben had never been to Texas before. But from the moment he stepped off the bus to follow the little tour guide he felt a strange sense of deja vu. The instant he set eyes on the Alamo, Ben couldn't get over the feeling he'd been there before.

Ben stepped between Sandy and Hollis to better hear the lecture. He had an uncanny feeling that he knew exactly what Hollis was about to say. It seemed to him the events of the battle were sitting on the edge of his mind and the split-second Hollis made a statement, Ben knew what he was going to say. The feeling was almost like trying to mime a speaker and say the same words, only a microsecond later.

"On the right-hand side of the chapel, our right facing the Alamo, stood several yards of earthen breastworks. These were defended by Davy Crockett, who preferred to be called David by the way. He and his Tennessee sharpshooters were positioned at this most vulnerable spot in the fortifications and held it until the last minutes of the battle. This section was one of the weakest links in the fort's defenses and it was felt that Crockett's men were the only ones capable of repelling attacks here.

"From what we've been able to find out from old letters and piecemeal correspondence from the surviving Mexican soldiers that participated in the assault, legend is accurate when it says the area where we now stand was the last section to succumb to the attack. Crockett was reported to have fallen here in one of two places," Hollis pointed with his cane. "In front of the chapel doors, or there," he turned toward the long barracks wall to their left. "Some reports say that he fell against that wall, the long barracks, where one would assume he and his men made their final stand."

Thunder rumbled suddenly and a terrific crack

made them all jump. Lightning struck somewhere dangerously close, filling the humid air with the smell of ozone. Sandy looked up in surprise at the low menacing clouds she would have sworn weren't so dark and ominous five minutes before.

Hollis rested his weight on the cane once again. "New evidence tells us that Crockett and a few other defenders actually survived the initial assault and surrendered, to be executed a short time later. There are two factions of historians who argue this point, though, because legend and honor have become intertwined with the facts."

Carter felt his hair prickle with static electricity. He glanced uneasily toward the sky.

"Crockett wasn't the only famous person to die here that day," Hollis continued. "Along with 185 to 215 other men, depending on what sources you choose to believe, were William B. Travis, the commander, and James Bowie, inventor of the famous Bowie knife and co-commander of the Alamo. He relinquished his portion of command after becoming ill, and some say injured, at the beginning of the battle. He was placed in the chapel where he suffered in severe pain for days. Mexican records indicate that Bowie was killed at approximately the same time Crockett died, as the soldiers poured into his room on the south side of the chapel."

Static electricity made Ben's skin tingle. Rubbing his arm, he looked around at the others beside him, wondering if they were affected by all the electricity in the air. He'd heard that prior to being struck by lightning, survivors said they felt the hair rise on their bodies. No one else seemed to notice though. Just in case, he again shifted his position closer to the weathered, pockmarked doors.

"Travis fell dead across a cannon with a bullet through the brain somewhere along the northern fortifications." Hollis pointed his cigar down the street, in the direction of the flow of traffic. He puffed again, but the smoke once again refused to re-light. He turned toward the crumbling chapel and directed their attention to an imaginary emplacement on the other side of Ben. "The fortifications here...."

Ben turned from his examination of the chapel to find himself looking down the length of black ebony cane in Hollis' hand. For a nerve-shattering instant, he saw a blue bolt jump from the metal endcap of the walking stick.

He barely had time to wonder what it was when the light snapped his head back with the force that only he could see and feel. With a stifled scream Ben clutched at his temples and dropped to his knees on the wet concrete.

Everyone froze. Tourists passing by on their way in and out of the chapel stopped to watch the young man who crouched on his knees before them in a puddle of muddy water. A blonde woman circled warily around the crowd of people and came to a stop beside the guide.

As she placed her hand on the little man's shoulder, Ben folded completely over, clutching his temples. His long hair brushed the puddle in front of him. With a groan he raised his head, dripping water in his eyes, and looked through the odd couple staring at him.

"Tell the Colonel they've almost breached the south wall again! I think this is it!" The stranger shouted at the stunned couple before him.

An icy chill went down Sandy's back. "What's he doing, Hollis?" She whispered and turned in sudden fury toward the little guide, her face twisted in anger. "Is this something you've set up?"

"What are you talking about?" Hollis asked in shock, not understanding her sudden outburst.

"This person!" She spat down at him. "Do you think it's funny for him to act this way? What kind of evil joke is this?"

Understanding finally dawned on him and he raised a defensive hand. "I don't know who this man is and if you think I had something to do with the way he's acting you'd better think again. This is as much of a surprise to me as it is to you. Good lord woman, I haven't thought about you since you stepped off the street a few minutes ago!"

The man lurched toward the sidewalk that was once the earth and log breastworks guarding the southeastern defenses of the Alamo. Eyes wide, the stranger shambled several steps away from the group, hands clutched his unopened umbrella as if were a rifle. He stared into the distance at something only he could see, and stopped suddenly, squinting as if he were peering into the sun.

The skies above darkened and thunder rumbled again. Streetlights up and down the street flickered to life as a cold gloom settled upon the city. A gray curtain of rain drew itself over the crowd gathering around the three figures in front of the old mission.

Ben looked over the earthen breastworks only he could see and stared into the bare, rolling hills surrounding the Alamo. The eastern skies were beginning to lighten with a false dawn as the sun rose toward the horizon. Mist drifted up from the nearby river, obscuring the sage and cactus before him. The Mexican encampment began to define itself in the distance and the advancing army became more and more distinct.

Shaking off the early morning chill, he looked to his right, over the line of defenders beside him. Instead of the tourists and businesses surrounding him, Ben saw grimy, sleep-deprived men staring grimly over the adobe walls.

The Tennessee volunteers settled themselves behind the barricade, adjusting weapons, checking their knives and preparing for the next wave of attackers. To his left, the remaining members of his party rose to peer over the breastworks.

In the darkness, a horde of soldiers abruptly appeared out of the ground mist and advanced bearing ladders and fixed bayonets. The mournful melody of the "Duegello" followed a shouted command from a Mexican officer.

"Adelante!"

The screams of the charging attackers were drowned by the roar of exploding charges.

Ben didn't speak Spanish, but the shouted order was clear. "Here they come!" he shouted. He shouldered his long flintlock rifle and shot the first clear target he saw. A snap followed the pull of the trigger, a puff of white smoke, and then the sharp crack of the firing rifle was lost among hundreds of other rifles and muskets following the same pattern and firing against each other. The brightly dressed soldier in his sights clutched his chest and fell, dropping the ladder he helped carry.

Gunsmoke immediately obscured the attackers and Ben hurriedly reloaded his rifle. A young man dressed in homespun clothes rushed up behind him and stopped, panting.

"Colonel Crockett! They've breached the north wall and Colonel Travis is dead!" He cried. Tears washed clean trails across his grimy cheeks.

Ben turned. "You go back, son, and tell them to hold their positions as best they can," he said calmly. Crockett was no stranger to violence, or violent men. "If things start falling apart, you boys move back here to the chapel and the long barracks. We'll hold them here if we can."

"Yessir."

Crockett turned back and checked his fortifications again. "All right, boys, let's show Santa Anna how we can shoot!"

Hollis instantly knew what was going on and this time he wasn't about to be cheated out of the knowledge that was before him. Five years ago in Montana, he'd been so shocked that rational thought was beyond his reach. Here and now there would be no indecision.

"Sandy! It's happening again." He turned to the crowd of tourists. "You people get back!"

The horror she'd pushed back into the dusty corners of her mind resurfaced and threatened to engulf her. "I've got to get out of here. I can't go through this again!" She turned to escape through the gathering ring of people.

Hollis reached up and grabbed her wrist with the speed of a striking snake. "No! You have to stay here. We've got to find out what's making this happen again."

"I can't!"

"You have to." He held tight and she tried to jerk away. "Maybe we can understand what transpired with your husband."

The tourists melted away from the arguing couple and the strange young man standing alone in a puddle of water, talking to himself. Rain made small explosions in those same puddles that stretched across the flagstones around them.

"Watch that bunch over there!" Ben called to a crowd of people beside him, but he saw nothing that stood with him. His mind saw the charging Mexican army on the morning of March 6, 1836.

As the Mexican soldiers waited for men to climb hand to heels, the rest could do nothing but huddle beneath the Alamo's fortifications and shoot at anything they saw above. The Tennessee marksman leaned over to fire into the mass below, but this subjected them to the Mexican muskets. It proved too costly, and they concentrated their fire on the next wave that advanced at a distance.

It was chaos against the walls. The soldiers below were to scale the walls or die by their own men. No one was allowed to stop or retreat. Taking fire from the defenders above and by their own officers from the rear, the Mexican troops had no alternative but to scale the crumbling adobe. Desperate soldiers leaned newly arrived ladders into position and they soon overwhelmed the defenders with sheer numbers.

"They've broken through!" Someone shouted from Crockett's right.

He spun around and with the butt of his rifle, clubbed a Mexican soldier boosted by his fellow soldiers over the makeshift barricade. "Hang on till I get back!" he shouted over his shoulder and ran toward the parade ground and the northern battery of eight pounders. Gunsmoke obscured the entire plaza area.

Crockett raced past men with fear-tightened faces and continued through the confusion almost halfway to the northern section of the fortress. He stopped in shock. In the firelight, brightly dressed Mexican soldiers swarmed over the walls like ants and engaged the defending Texans in hand-to-hand fighting.

Overwhelmed by sheer numbers, the Texas volunteers slowly retreated toward the chapel, bowing to overpowering superior numbers.

"Pull back!" Crockett waved a buckskin clad arm.

Those hearing over the screams of the horrified defenders and scores of dying men slowly retreated from their positions around the parapets. The defenders that hadn't heard succumbed to the pressure of the attacking army swarming over the walls. They fell back also, teaming up in twos and threes and slowly fighting their way to the long barracks.

The sun was still not high enough to peek over the horizon and illuminate the fortress directly, but the diffused glow from the sky and increasing numbers of fires were enough to allow Crockett to see the defenders shoot one last time before releasing their hold on the defenses.

The roar of war pounded on already dampened eardrums, nearly deafening attackers and defenders alike. The Mexicans poured like a red and white tidal wave over the walls. It was here that Travis' last orders were carried out. Several Texans swung a cannon loaded with scraps of iron, chopped horseshoes and rocks toward the attackers. They strafed the walls with murderous fire and scores of Mexicans fell wounded and dying.

Seeing they understood, Crockett turned and ran back to his Tennessee volunteers. Behind him more Mexicans filled the plaza, pressing the defenders even harder. Other Texans still manning the remaining cannon along the north, west and south walls also turned their weapons into the open area where they too razed the enemy with deadly results. With each shot more men fell, but replacements clambered over the walls.

The tactic was a costly one for the Texans and Mexicans alike. With the defensive pressure of the cannon removed, the multitude of attackers outside the walls had nothing to stop them. In minutes they scrabbled up rough ladders and were over the walls. The surviving Texans were soon forced back against the long barracks.

The Mexican army possessed the Alamo.

Hollis stood beside Sandy, watching the young man rush into the street and stop amidst diesel buses and horse-drawn carriages. Tires shrieked as drivers slammed on their brakes. Almost tentatively he put one sneakered foot forward, and then another until he stopped and looked.

"What is he doing?" Sandy asked, beginning to gain a tenuous hold on her panic.

Hollis clutched his cane with a white knuckled grip, not realizing the head was warmer than usual. "My guess would be that he's evaluating the enemies' position."

Neither realized they were alone with the possessed man in front of the mission. The remainder of Hollis' tour group had retreated to the street in front of the Alamo, blocking traffic with their mass. Horns honked as traffic stacked up.

An angry bus driver slammed open the doors of his bus with a pneumatic hiss. "What the hell are you people doing? Get out of the street! You trying to get killed or what?"

No one acted as if the driver existed. Their attention was riveted on the events unfolding before them as a forest of arms rose with phones in their hands, recording the incident.

A group of young Mexican-Americans appeared at the edges of the crowd and circled the curious onlookers like a requiem of sharks. Ignoring the rain, they wove their way through the crowd and up onto the

sidewalk. The oldest, a seventeen-year-old, stopped and gathered his entourage beside him. He knew Hollis well from his many visits to the Texas shrine.

"Hey, Ambrose! What's happenin', man? This dude freaked or what?"

Hollis turned at the sound of a familiar voice. "Arturo! Stay right there. I may need you in a minute." A disturbing thought crossed his mind. What if Ben could see the people around them? Would the sight of a Mexican startle him? He decided it would be best if the boys stayed out of the way. "Arturo! You boys back up to the street over there and stay out of the way. This man could get dangerous."

"Hey man," Arturo ordered his followers back to the street. "Your boy really trippin' out, man."

Not very many people could tell the hardened street kid what to do, but he liked the odd little dwarf and his curious ways. They again mixed with the rapidly growing crowd of gawkers. Traffic was now at a complete standstill up and down the street as far as the eye could see.

Sandy gasped and clutched Hollis' shoulder. Ben turned toward them. Hollis involuntarily stepped back, pulling Sandy with him. Ben aimed his umbrella, sighted and squeezed his index finger on nothing but air. He lowered his arms and with a sudden vicious snarl he swung the shaft in a short arc that stopped abruptly. He turned and raced past, directly through the spot where the two had been standing moments before and hurried almost to the street. He stopped suddenly within sight of the monument to the Texas defenders.

"Pull back!" He shouted and waved his short-sleeved arm. He looked through the ring of observers.

"What...?" Sandy started.

"He's calling in the defenders." Hollis' voice was full of wonder, his eyes darting from side to side as if seeing into the past. "I assume the Mexican army has breached the northern defenses. He's seeing them pour over the wall."

Ben wheeled and ran back to his original position in front of Hollis and Sandy, mimicking the actions required to charge a muzzleloader rife.

"God, I wish I knew what he was thinking."

"Who is he?" Sandy asked, finally getting a meager grasp of her emotions.

"I don't know his name. He's one of my tourists."

Thunder rumbled around them, shaking the ground beneath their feet. Lighting cracked nearby.

The ominous clouds swirled above. Hollis looked up at the Alamo's pockmarked doors and saw them slam suddenly. A thrown bolt rattled on the inside.

"Here we go again," Ben shouted.

Rain fell harder, soaking everyone not protected by an umbrella.

Crockett knew the Alamo was lost. He looked over his shoulder at the seething mass of fighting men and watched the plaza succumb to the Mexican horde. It would only be a matter of time before his position was overrun. He hurried to the barricades and looked down the line at his Tennessee volunteers.

Each man carefully picked off the screaming attackers as they rushed across the open landscape before them. Dozens of Mexicans fell before their deadly rifles. As soon as the defender fired his weapon, he leaned it against the breastworks and picked up another loaded weapon from the stack of several rifles before him. Defenders too wounded to fight reloaded the blistering hot rifles with desperate speed.

Dozens of Mexican soldiers reached the wall but there were too many men and too few crude ladders.

"Pour it on 'em!" Crockett shouted and shot the first man he saw coming over battlements. He reloaded and fired over and over again until he reached into his shot bag and closed a fist on nothing. He was out of ammunition. He wasn't the only one. Most of the defenders were soon resorting to hand-to-hand fighting.

Their fight was on two fronts now. They'd successfully defended their portion of the wall, but once the defense collapsed at the walls, the soldiers swarmed the interior.

A bloodied volunteer stumbled in and collapsed against the chapel wall. Crockett recognized James Bonham who shook his head in sorrow. "I told Travis we didn't have enough men for a fort this size!" He rose and staggered toward the long barracks.

"This is it!" Crockett shouted to a doomed friend beside him, turned his rife around to use as a club, and slammed an attacker off the wall. The Texan fighting beside him was killed almost instantly by a bayonet thrust. Before the Mexican could free his weapon Crockett smashed him in the face with the butt of his gore-splattered rifle, knocking the soldier off the wall and down onto the picket fence of Mexican bayonets strapped across the backs of those waiting to climb the ladders.

"Pour it on 'em!" Face white with very real fear, Ben aimed and silently fired his weapon at the trees and stucco walkway leading south from the chapel. He wiped a hand across his eyes, lowered his arms, and continued to make strange motions with his hands.

"What's he doing now?" Sandy asked.

"He's reloading." Hollis paced and chewed his cigar in frustration. A siren sounded in the distance. He cocked an ear and listened. "I wonder how much longer we'll have before they get here?"

A little blue haired lady rushed up to Hollis. "Ambrose, the police will be here momentarily," she said bursting with excitement and importance.

"Who told you to do anything?" Hollis shouted up at her in frustration. He threw his cigar into a puddle and bashed the end of his cane on top of the soggy mass. "Get out of here before I do something we'll both regret."

"Well!" The blue haired lady huffed away.

"That just tears it," Hollis growled to Sandy. "They'll be here in a minute and they'll try to take him away. I need time to evaluate these developments."

Ben Carter aimed and fired his umbrella again. Each time his index finger pulled an invisible trigger, his shoulder jerked backwards with the recoil of an unseen rifle. What they were seeing couldn't have been acting, for it was physics that jerked the man's body in response to the gun's blast.

The surrounding crowd around them tittered and moved forward.

Hollis turned and vented his anger at everyone around him. "Don't any of you move any closer to this man!" He pointed his cane like a saber. "I'm warning you, you'll get a taste of my cane if...."

He stopped and looked at the cane grasped in his tiny fist. "My cane. It's hot, and it tingles. Sandy, do you feel anything?"

She shrugged and looked at Ben. "No, all I feel is rain and the thunder."

"This is it!" Ben shouted in Hollis' direction, but his stare continued into another dimension. The water-soaked apparition looked up. With a shocked expression on his face Ben swung as if his umbrella was a baseball bat.

Ambrose involuntarily recoiled from the swinging umbrella. "They're over the wall!" he shouted and looked around as if to see hordes of Santa Anna's men converging on his position on the almost empty plaza.

His cane grew warmer. Lighting slashed overhead and struck the spreading live oak tree inside the courtyard. The explosion destroyed the tree, sending chunks of wood flying in all directions.

Ben fell to his knees and Hollis was thrown to the ground from the concussion. Screams pierced the sodden air and the crowd recoiled and rushed away.

A cannonball crashed through the earthen breastworks, knocking the defenders to the ground in front of the church, killing several. Rising from his knees and reeling from the concussion, Crockett bashed his rifle onto the side of a Mexican's head.

Shrapnel whizzed through the air. A piece of rifle barrel, sharp as a razor, flew past and sliced through Crockett's eyebrow. He staggered and clutched at the wound. The explosion was so close that both attackers and defenders paused for a stunned moment before pressing the attack.

The young messenger of no more than seventeen with a multitude of minor bleeding wounds covering his own smoke-blackened body hurried to Crockett's side and grabbed his arm. "You're hurt bad, Colonel! Get inside!"

"Naw, I ain't. This ain't nothing compared to what it's going to be like in a little while and don't call me Colonel, boy, the name's Crockett."

Lying on the ground and holding himself upright with one elbow, Hollis pointed as if the others weren't already looking at the animated young man. "Crockett! Crockett! By the Gods, this man is a reincarnate of Davy Crockett!"

The concussion from the lightning blast had hurled his tiny frame onto the wet grassy area in front of the chapel. Hollis struggled to his feet, wiping the rain from his eyes and peering up at Carter.

Clothing clinging to her shivering body, Sandy also crawled through the mud and leaned on one hand. "You all right, Hollis?"

"I'm fine!" His voice was full of elation. "Look! That's Davy Crockett and we're witnessing the final minutes of the Battle of the Alamo. How did... Why has something so—so amazing happening to the two of us again?"

"I don't know, Ambrose," she said quietly, trembling. "But I wish it hadn't."

"But it did, and it's just like the afternoon your husband died. Look, the same type stigmata from the wound over his eye. The storm. You and me." He felt for his cane and retrieved it from the mud. The lead-colored handle on the end was glowing with a pale blue phosphorescence. Pieces of the puzzle fell into place in Hollis' excited mind.

He looked at Ben, and back to the cane. "This is it!" He exclaimed. "This is what I was saying, Sandy, this is the catalyst. Somehow when you and I get together it finishes some kind of...cosmic circuit that has been incomplete all our lives. The two of us and this cane causes a person, a susceptible person, to go back in time within their mind. That's what happened in Montana, and it's happening here."

Ben swung his umbrella from side to side as he backed one slow step at a time toward where the long barracks once stood. In its place a stucco wall and metal gate guarded the entrance to the Convent Garden and Wishing Well. The gate had been twisted off its hinges from the lightning blast only minutes before.

Sirens grew closer.

"That's impossible." She shook her head. "We're just two people and that old cane...."

Hollis talked faster in his excitement. "This old cane was given to me by my grandfather when I was a very young man when he saw that I would need to help support my legs. It has been passed down in my family for generations. He told me that the head of this cane was worked from a piece of meteorite his grandfather found in the Appalachian Mountains after he watched if fall through the sky."

"Oh, come on Hollis," Sandy snapped, almost at the end of her rope. "If you think I believe in UFOs and crap like that you're crazy."

"Crazy, huh?" Hollis struggled up and planted his feet. Water cascaded from the brim of his hat. "Look at that man there, remember your dead husband and tell me if that's crazy."

The rain came harder, lashing at them in fury. He thrust the glowing cane into Sandy's hands.

Lighting sizzled overhead, again smashing into the smoking remains of the same ancient oak tree behind them. Sandy jerked at the explosion and stifled a scream as electricity flowed through her body.

Then she, too, saw the Mexican attackers. They were all around her. The harsh smell of gunsmoke and blood and excrement loosened from fear almost made her gag. She thrust the cane back toward Hollis, but he had already seen her expression, her eyes.

"You can see them, too!"

"Yes!" Sandy screamed.

Those nearby gasped. Hollis wheeled around and saw the blood spray in droplets from Ben's uninjured eyebrow.

The sirens were only moments away. "Arturo! You still here?" Hollis called.

"Si, amigo."

"Can you hold the police up for a few minutes?"

"No problem," Arturo laughed. "I need to get away from this crazy *gringo,* anyway." He gathered his entourage, and they disappeared.

"Sandy, I want you to hold this cane with me. Maybe we both can see what's happening inside that young man's mind."

"Are you nuts...?" she was interrupted by the deafening arrival of an ambulance. Rubberneckers hurried to get away from the shrieking siren atop the blue and white ambulance. The two paramedics jumped out and grabbed their gear.

"Stay away from this man," Hollis snapped, pointing his cane at the nearest paramedic.

Crockett and his remaining defenders fell back from the breastworks. Their only hope now was the safety of the long barracks that had been prepared for a last stand, but the intervening distance was a solid mass of fighting humanity.

He backed away toward the chapel wall, knowing if he and his men could get their backs to the thick adobe wall, they would stand a better chance of holding the Mexicans off for a little while longer.

Blood ran thick on the cold ground strewn with dead and dying men. Smoke blew around the soldiers and volunteers, sometimes obscuring them so much no one could tell who the enemy was until they were within grasping distance. The assault had deteriorated into a disorganized mass of desperate men fighting individual battles. Texan ammunition had long since run out and the continued press of the attack left no one time to reload.

Crockett's men formed a tight knot, using their

rifles as clubs, smashing one attacker after another and trying to avoid the long bayonets on the Mexican muskets. The Mexicans were like wolves, singling out a struggling individual, pressing him with sheer numbers until they quickly dispatched the Texan and then moved on to the next man.

The Mexican numbers kept the little group of defenders from moving more than a few feet. The fort's gates flung open, and with that, soldiers poured through the opening like sand through an hourglass.

Soon the only defenders left in front of the Alamo chapel were Crockett, a few of his men, and a handful of surviving Texans from the north wall. They knew death was near, and to a man they fought with the grim desperation that only comes from those completely outnumbered and with no hope.

Crockett was a whirling devil, swinging, slashing and moving, dodging in out of the bayonets forcing them inexorably toward the wall. Mexican bodies piled around combatants, forming a barricade of sorts the attackers had to climb.

The fresh soldiers pouring into the plaza had plenty of time to shoot and reload their weapons. Bullets zipped through the morning air, often as not hitting their own men in the process. The defenders dropped one by one.

Officers on horseback rode through the melee, swinging sabers indiscriminately. They intentionally spurred their mounts into clusters of men, riding down Mexican and Texan combatants alike.

Fatigue finally took its toll on the Texans. Two more detonations rocked the compound as the Mexica's turned the defender's own canons on the doors of the long barracks. The rattle of gunfire diminished as those inside ran out of ammunition and fought with blades and teeth.

Bodies around Crockett fell and minutes later he found himself left with only a handful of his Tennessee volunteers. The only sight in front of him was a red and white clad army and hundreds of bayonets pointing at them.

"Keep swinging, boys," he gasped. "We'll show these bastards how we fight back in Tennessee."

He realized with horror that he was talking to himself and several hundred men who couldn't understand a word he said.

He was suddenly and completely alone.

Crockett redoubled his defense and swung his shattered rifle like a madman. There was almost

nothing left of his beloved "Old Betsy" but the dented and bent barrel.

Still he fought, and step by bloody step retreated to the wall. The press of attackers continued almost halfheartedly. They both feared and admired the fighting outdoorsman.

Crockett kept backing until the heel of his moccasin bumped into what he thought was the long barracks behind him. Bullets continued to whiz past and smacked into the adobe only a few feet behind, showering him with dirt and debris.

One shot, whether accurate or accident, stuck him in the upper right arm. He gasped in pain and almost dropped the rifle barrel. Crockett knew the end was near. With an effort, he shifted his makeshift club to his left hand and reached with his right for the razor-sharp skinning knife he kept by his side.

A bayonet lunged for his eyes and only his instinctive jerk caused it to miss and slash a line across his forehead. He lunged, slashed the soldier's midsection, and danced back.

Blood ran down his arm and made the knife in his right hand slippery. Wounded more than a dozen times, Crockett was exhausted. Rest was impossible from the sheer volume of attackers. As if on a pre-arranged signal, the pressure suddenly slacked off. The soldiers halted in awe before the gore splattered frontiersman whose luck and determination kept them at bay.

Bloody and tired, Crockett slowly stopped fighting. Exhausted, and more scared than he'd ever been in his life, he stared at the picket fence of bayonets and waited for what might come.

But Crockett was no stranger to fear, and he knew that to show these warriors any shred of intimidation would be the end. Less than two yards apart, the combatants stared at each other with hollow eyes.

Shots and screams still echoed inside the fortifications, but the men before the tired outdoorsman were almost silent. Shoulders slumped with fatigue, Crockett warily lowered his hands and looked at the ring of grim soldiers surrounding him.

He wiped his tearing eyes. He'd passed that indefinable point in the human psyche where fear controlled a person's every move.

He was numb with pain and the horror of battle.

Nothing was left inside except an emptiness. When this point was reached by some individuals, the brain simply shut down. Crockett had seen it many times in the eyes of Indian captives. Dead eyes in a live body, eyes devoid of hope.

He fought against this very human emotion with the only thing he had left, the thing which had been his trademark throughout the Indian wars and his years in Congress. "Finally. You people give up?"

The Mexicans looked at each other in bewilderment, unable to understand the language of the strange, bloody warrior, but realizing that he was somehow laughing at them. They waited in awe of this man who defied his own death with a faint smile.

Ben Carter battled his way backwards step by step across the plaza. Blood mixed with the rain and ran down his snarling face, turning his shirt bright pink. Water from his plastered hair flowed with the blood into his eyes and gasping mouth. Droplets sprayed when he turned his head violently from side to side.

Carter backed himself to within three feet of the wall and slashed with his tattered umbrella at invisible opponents on either side of him. His right foot reached behind him and stopped suddenly, as if hitting an invisible obstacle.

"Everyone move!" shouted an authoritative voice from the rear of the astonished crowd of onlookers.

Hollis and Sandy turned from the stymied paramedics and watched as the crowd parted to allow a procession of police officers and handcuffed youngsters through.

"Lo siento, mi amigo," Arturo said apologetically and held up his arm which was manacled to the young man beside him.

Hollis chewed his newest cigar to shreds. *"No, yo lo siento."*

The youngster shrugged, not caring one way or the other.

"Would someone tell me what's going on here?" asked Lieutenant Scott Jackson. He looked over Hollis' head and gaped in surprise at the pantomiming, rain-soaked man with blood running down his face in front of the Alamo.

"What are we going to do?" Sandy whispered. She took a deep breath and watched Carter fight his invisible demons beside the wall. "What's happening now?"

"That's what I want to know?" Jackson answered. "What's going on here?

"He's alone, or he's one of the last survivors," Hollis began, and then caught himself. "We have to

hurry, Sandy. Take my cane again and hold my hand. I have to know what's happening. Maybe I can't see, but you can."

Her eyes widened in fear and she backed away from the offered cane. "No way, Hollis. What I saw a moment ago was enough."

Jackson stepped toward the desperate-looking individual swinging a broken umbrella in front of the Alamo chapel. "Take it easy, buddy. We'll help you."

Several women from the surrounding crowd screamed. Carter jerked violently, grunted and grasped at his right arm. Blood spurted through his sleeve, splattering everyone nearby.

"Gun!" Jackson shouted and fumbled under his yellow rain slicker for his weapon. His partner crouched and scanned the crowd, his pistol already drawn. "Get down!"

Sandy reeled away in revulsion, wiping the young man's blood from her face.

Hollis held his hand out toward the already reacting police officers. "No!" he exclaimed and limped closer to the officers as quickly as his legs would allow. "There is no gun, or any other weapon. This is a phenomenon I've seen before. It's some sort of stigmata. We can't fight anything here."

"That man has been shot," insisted Jackson, still not convinced.

"Yes, he's been shot. But by a rifle fired back in eighteen thirty-six."

"What?" Both officers asked in disbelief. They were joined by the paramedics who needed to get Carter on a gurney. In their experience, a bleeding man necessitated immediate medical treatment.

"Stay here, please." Hollis held up a pleading hand. The puzzled police and paramedics waited in disbelief as Hollis limped to within feet of Carter. Still more minor wounds appeared on his frenzied body and blood flowed profusely from each of them.

Sandy talked fast, trying to convince the officials to wait until Hollis called for them. In desperation she attempted to convince them that Hollis was a psychologist and Carter was his patient. Belied by the incongruity of his Hollis' felt hat, none of the city officials believed her story.

Ben Carter continued to swing and slash at invisible enemies. Exhaustion was rapidly slowing him down, but his eyes still contained the wild stare that saw into his deadly past.

"Sandy, come over here," Hollis demanded.

She hesitantly moved to his side, followed by the other officers and paramedics.

"Take this cane and hold my hand," he pleaded, holding out both. The huddled group watched as Sandy reluctantly took the warm, glowing cane in her right hand and touched Hollis' fingertips with her left. Before them, Carter gave no notice they existed.

Again, lighting sliced across the cloudy sky over the old mission, making everyone but Carter cringe. Sandy stiffened, then jerked away from Hollis.

"Did you see anything?"

"Yes," she answered in a barely audible whisper. Terror was evident in her eyes.

"We're going to have to restrain him." The nervous young paramedic never took his eyes off the man fighting his invisible devils. "He's going to hurt himself even more, or someone else."

"Wait," Hollis held his cane across the man's chest. "He'll quit in only a moment. Right, Sandy?"

She merely nodded, her tears mixed with the drizzle and ran down her white cheeks.

The youngest officer reached under his yellow slicker, unsnapped his handcuffs and removed them from his Sam Brown belt. More sirens gathered and grew louder in the distance. "What makes you think he's going to quit?"

"I know my history," Hollis replied flatly. He looked carefully at Sandy. "You all right?"

She shrugged. "Yeah. I'm just fine. Hollis is right. It's almost over."

Hollis watched Sandy and chewed his cigar thoughtfully.

"Do you know what's happening?" asked the second paramedic.

"Yes, he's experiencing the last moments of the battle of the Alamo," Sandy replied and then realized how ridiculous the explanation sounded.

She looked down at Hollis for help. He gave her a tight grin, knowing that nothing they could say would change anyone's mind, or would convince them that what they were saying was true.

Lieutenant Jackson snorted. "Right." He motioned for his partner to move forward. Talking in soothing tones, they slowly closed in on both sides of the grunting, frenzied Carter.

The senior paramedic slowly advanced also. "I've seen this before, and he's not coming down for a long, long time."

"That's your jaded opinion from the streets. I

know what I'm talking about, and he'll quit momentarily," Hollis snapped.

For the first time in twenty minutes Carter stopped dodging and fighting. He halted and dropped his hands to his sides, then wiped the rain and blood from his eyes. Exhaustion drained the color from his dripping face.

"Well, that's better" said Jackson, almost to himself. "He's quiet already. Come on mister, just take it easy."

Carter looked around him. He smiled slightly. "Finally. You people give up?" he asked.

The confused police officers exchanged uneasy glances and then frowned at Hollis.

"Sandy," Hollis said and held his cane towards her again.

Trembling, she closed her eyes and again reached out to touch the smooth black wood.

The Mexican soldiers surrounding Crockett were startled from their shock at the sounds of victory coming from behind them, the Alamo was almost theirs. Only one man stood between them and complete victory. A horse forced its way through the crowd of men, nearly trampling one underfoot. Several looked at a mounted officer for direction. They'd heard the explicit orders—no mercy, no survivors. Yet this man before them had earned his life. They would spare him.

But the officer knew that Santa Anna would enforce his orders to the letter. The musicians were still playing "El Deguello," the signal that the defenders of the garrison would receive no quarter.

No one was to be spared. If the defender before them was saved, it would be the officer's life given in exchange, then the buckskinned man would be executed. His life would be for naught. The officer shouted and almost as one they again renewed their attack on the exhausted Crockett, falling on him like a pack of ravenous wolves with a roar from a hundred throats.

Crockett shouted in desperation and launched himself forward in his own attack. He slashed with his long skinning knife and nearly decapitated the first Mexican who lunged within range. He lurched back from another bayonet thrust and once again backed against what he thought was the adobe wall protecting his rear.

Again and again he swung the rifle barrel and slashed with his bloody knife, so slick with blood that he nearly lost it several times. Writhing bodies stacked around him like cordwood. The press of attackers hindered the overall assault. So many men jammed forward they got in each other's way, and as they jostled for position, Crockett took a heavy toll.

But the safety from the adobe wall behind him was illusionary. Crockett had backed to within three feet of the wall, and against an upset wood cart which effectively kept him away from the protection he so desperately needed.

He never saw the cart, and he never saw the Mexican officer who slipped between it and the rubble strewn wall.

"Look out!" A woman screamed.

Crockett's head snapped toward the out-of-place voice as the officer aimed and carefully shot the former explorer and congressman in the back of the head. Crockett fell forward onto the forest of bayonets, and died.

The sun appeared over the horizon and lit the smoking carnage below.

The Alamo had fallen.

Sandy touched Hollis' cane once again and in that instant saw through the smoke of the dimly lit Alamo compound decades in the past. She watched Crockett back away, fighting with heart-wrenching desperation. She also saw the Mexican officer behind him.

"Look out!" She screamed over the sounds of slaughter. Several bloodied soldiers had turned in surprise to look for the source of the woman's voice in the carnage around them. Seeing only their own men, they resumed their attack.

Just as the officer pulled the trigger, Sandy released Hollis' cane and slumped to the wet pavement.

Both policemen jerked at her shouted warning. Carter's head snapped forward onto his chest and blood blossomed through the wet hair on the back of his head, splattering both officers. Experienced men, they knew the killing shot came from behind Carter, but the only thing there was a solid limestone wall.

Hollis ignored Carter's twitching body on the wet pavement and approached Sandy's kneeling form. "Are you all right?" he asked in genuine concern.

"Hollis, you won't believe what I saw." She broke down into hysterical sobbing.

Her position on the ground put her at Hollis' eye level. He awkwardly put his arms around her trembling shoulders and pulled her head to his chest as she cried in great, shuddering sobs for the stranger and for the husband she'd lost so long ago.

The police stood in wonder over Carter's body. They'd seen no gunmen, heard no bullets or their impact, yet a man was shot dead before their very eyes. He lay on the ground, blood seeping from a dozen places on his unblemished body. They looked upward at the bare wall and wondered.

The paramedics hurriedly turned Carter onto his back and efficiently checked for vital signs. Finding none, they examined every inch for a wound, but found only fresh blood. Baffled and not knowing what else to do, they covered the bloody corpse with a sheet and retreated to their ambulance to wait in stunned silence. This incident required a supervisor and they waited for instructions.

Hollis fumbled through his pockets and located a fresh, dry cigar. He scratched a match with his thumbnail and stood between Sandy and the now covered corpse. The overcast sky had nearly rained itself out. They moved toward the low walled seating area across the street from the Alamo, underneath a scattering of widespread live oak trees.

"What did you see?" he asked quietly.

Between trembling sobs, she told him of what she'd experienced. "You were there, you know," he informed her. "Somehow you were at the Alamo massacre."

She looked at him in disbelief. "Are you sure? When I screamed soldiers turned around and looked for me. But I wasn't really there. I saw it all in my mind."

"No, you were there," Hollis pointed at her feet. "Look at your shoes, and your hands."

He took her hands in his own fingers and held them out. Black gunpowder spotted her well-manicured fingers. Her once white sneakers were covered in mud and stained red with blood.

"There isn't any mud like this on the pavement, Sandy, nor that much blood. Especially not where we were standing. But the Alamo compound must have been ankle deep in gore that morning where we stand."

She groaned in revulsion and kicked off her shoes. Hollis dropped his hat over them to hide the reddish stains.

"How did it happen?" she asked. "Did I disappear?"

"No, you were still a physical presence here,

though you looked something less substantial than you do now. But somehow you exhibited the physical signs of the battle. I didn't notice, I wasn't watching you all the time, but I think the mud and gunpowder just appeared on your hands and feet. The same kind of stigmata we saw on your husband and poor man lying over there."

She stifled a gag and he gave her a pat.

"Sandy, we have a calling here to consider. We have to find out what caused this, and how."

"You want to kill someone else?" Her eyes flashed. "If we stay away from each other no one else will have to die, Hollis. I'm getting myself as far away from you as possible."

He puffed his cigar for a moment. The blue smoke quickly dissipated in the heavy, humid air. "We have a gift here that must be used. I want to know why this walking stick causes this phenomenon, and why it only works when you are present."

He frowned at the glowing end of the cigar and his face hardened as a thought came to him. "Don't you understand?" he said with an intensity that was almost frightening. "The two of us can see into history. We can solve the world's mysteries, the secrets of the pyramids, the Titanic, the crucifixion of Christ, or maybe we can discover the truth about evolution altogether with the right knowledge about how this phenomenon occurs."

"Yes, and people will die making these discoveries," she argued, eliciting curious stares from the police and paramedics who were anxiously trying to wrap things up. "Look at him. He died just like James."

"People often die in the course of dangerous research, but that may not happen again," Hollis countered. "Maybe without involving anyone else we can see what happened when the pyramids were built. The possibility exists that we can see into the past without a susceptible third person, now that we know you can use this cane."

Sandy simply stared up at the Alamo in silence without answering.

Another round of light showers came again as they huddled miserably under a tree across the street from the Alamo. The paramedics were gone with the body. The police had taken their statements and let them go, after sternly lecturing Sandy about lying to them concerning Hollis' alleged doctoral profession.

The boys had been forgotten in the excitement and then released when the officers were tied up with Carter's death.

Everything had returned to normal, temporarily.

Sandy finally made a decision and broke their silence. "All right, Ambrose. I still have two weeks of vacation left. We can try one more time."

Hollis almost leaped for joy. "You won't be sorry, Sandy. Let's go back to my apartment and make some plans. We can decide where we want to start."

"Maybe we can learn the mysteries of the Marie Celeste," she suggested, trying to find a non-lethal occurrence that might give them some insight into how the process worked. "That shouldn't involve anyone else."

"Right," Hollis said with enthusiasm. "Or we could go to Florida and find out the truth about the Bermuda triangle. Or better yet, we'll see if we can find out what happened to Sir Walter Raleigh's lost settlers in 1590. I've always wondered if they just moved away or were massacred."

"We could go to my home in Dallas and see who really shot Kennedy," Sandy added. "No one could get hurt doing that. We'll just stand in the crowd and watch for the assassin now that we know where to look. Only Kennedy was killed, though John Connelly was severely wounded."

Hollis smiled. "That's just what we'll do." The shower slacked off, and in true Texas form, the sun peeked through the diminishing cloud cover. They stood and prepared to leave. Hollis struggled off his perch on the low wall and left his cane leaning against the brick ledge.

Without thinking, Sandy picked it up and handed the walking stick to Hollis.

She felt nothing from the black ebony wood. Neither one of them realized the implications of that moment. An essential ingredient was missing. Hollis gripped the meteorite head in his small fist.

Twenty-four hours later they were on a plane bound for Dallas, and Dealey Plaza.

LOOK FOR
REAVIS Z. WORTHAM'S
"THIRD ANNIVERSARY"
ONLY IN THE APRIL ISSUE
OF *SADDLEBAG DISPATCHES*

THE AUTHOR

*New York Times bestselling author **Reavis Z. Wortham** is the recipient of numerous Will Rogers Medallion Awards, the Western Writers of America Spur Award, and the Independent Book Publishers Association's Benjamin Franklin Award. He has been a newspaper columnist and magazine contributor since 1988, penning over 2,000 columns and articles, and has been the Humor Editor for Texas Fish and Game Magazine for the past 26 years. When he's not writing, Reavis is also an avid outdoorsman, loves to travel, camp, canoe, backback, hunt, and fish. He and his wife, Shana, live in Northeast Texas.*

Photo by Shana Wortham

THE WRITER'S DESK

REAVIS Z. WORTHAM

THE ACCIDENTAL COLUMNIST: HOW ONE MAN DISCOVERED HIS VOICE... AND HIS DESTINY

With an evocative blend of gritty realism and spine-tingling suspense, Reavis brings the untamed landscapes of the West to life, crafting stories as haunting as they are unforgettable.

STORY BY
GEORGE "CLAY" MITCHELL
PHOTOS COURTESY OF REAVIS Z. WORTHAM

Reavis Wortham's path to becoming a celebrated author is a testament to perseverance, passion, and the power of storytelling. Wortham knew he wanted to write from a young age, inspired by a childhood filled with books and an elementary school librarian who nurtured his curiosity. His determination led him to pen countless stories, send manuscripts to magazines, and face rejection after rejection. Yet, each setback only fueled his resolve.

His career took a pivotal turn in the late 1980s with a bet during a mundane work session, sparking the creation of his first newspaper column. From that moment, Wortham's distinct voice resonated with readers, earning him a place as a beloved outdoor humor columnist and eventually paving the way for his acclaimed novels.

EARLY START

When he was 10, Reavis wanted to be a writer. He was a "voracious reader" in elementary school, and his librarian saw his interest in books and "just opened it up to me."

"When other kids could only check out one book. She let me check out two or maybe even three books," Reavis said. "All the time, I was constantly reading. At that age, an aunt asked me what I wanted to be when I grew up, and I wanted to be a writer. She told me to go do it."

He wrote for years in his youth and submitted to *Reader's Digest*. Reavis sent handwritten stories to adventure magazine and accumulated rejection letters. A junior high or middle school friend asked Reavis if he was making any money.

"I know a magazine that pays $2,000 for an article," the friend said.

"That's kind of cool. Where is it?"

"Come over to my house, and I'll show you."

Reavis went to his friend's house. His friend called out to an empty house.

"We go into his dad's bedroom, and my friend reached between the mattresses, and I got my first

Early Days: **Reavis has always worn boots and hats, and suspects it might have something to do with his love of the Old West and Roy Rogers on television. Left to right, ages 3 and 4 in Wortham's grandparents' farmhouse in Chicota, Texas. The photo sitting on the dresser of the man in the hat is Wortham's maternal grandfather, Constable Joe Armstrong, who became the foundation of Ned Parker in the Red River historical mystery series.**

close-up look at *Playboy* magazine," Reavis said. "After a while, he showed me where they offered $2,000. So I started corresponding with *Playboy.*"

He sent submissions and would get them back, telling him that his articles didn't meet their needs. His parents never questioned why their son was getting mail from *Playboy*. One day, he got his submission back (since the magazine required a self-addressed, stamped envelope). It was a manuscript he had submitted.

"But it had a coffee stain on it," Reavis said. "Which was the coolest thing for me because I knew some*body* looked at it. There was also a handwritten note: *'Keep going. Keep trying, but you need to learn how to type kid.'*"

He learned how to type the following year. He wrote and wrote. All through high school and college, but still didn't get published. He would start a manuscript and get in 20, 30, or 50 pages before the story he was writing bored him.

DIFFERENT CAREERS

Reavis spent two years at Eastfield Junior College in Mesquite, Texas (now Dallas Eastfield College). Two years later, he earned a B.S. in Industry Management from East Texas State University (now Texas A&M-Commerce). Instead of going into architecture as planned, he realized he had no interest in leaning over a drafting board for the rest of his life. He took another year's worth of courses and earned his teaching degree.

He landed at the Garland Independent School District in the Dallas suburb to teach middle and high school.

"We were paid once a month, and I received 10 times as many rejection notices during the same period from a wide range of state and national magazines," Reavis said. "Thinking I wanted to work my way up to the position of principal, I earned an M.Ed. from E.T.S.U. and a superintendent's certificate before deciding that wasn't where I wanted to spend the rest of my career."

REJECTION LETTERS DIDN'T DISCOURAGE ME—THEY ONLY FUELED MY RESOLVE TO BECOME A WRITER

THAT'S WHAT WRITERS HAVE TO DO. YOU HAVE TO READ, AND READING MAKES YOU A BETTER WRITER.

His best friend, Steve Knagg, was named Director of Communications in the Garland ISD in 1986, making Reavis the district's Communications Specialist.

"It's a nice title, but I'm sure someone made it off the cuff to satisfy the payroll department," said Reavis. "As the years passed, my title changed along with the duties required to keep a fast-growing district on track. I read voraciously then and discovered author after author who influenced my writing attempts."

INFLUENCES

Authors who have influenced Reavis over the years have been Robert Ruark ("the mentor I never met"), Fred Gipson, Louis L'Amour, Max Brand, Luke Short, and Clay Fisher (all the pulp Western writers). He later branched out and discovered Donald Westlake ("best mystery writer I've ever read"), Robert B. Parker, and David Morrell.

"David has been a huge inspiration for me. I read *First Blood* in 1972 when it came out. It was nothing like I've ever read before. I took that book, sat down, and tried to dissect it when I was 18 or 19," Reavis said. "I've even used it as a framework when writing some my stories. I've had the good fortune to become friends with David. I got into this business a little too late to meet those other guys and thank them for their help.

"I would try to emulate those old authors and figure out their style, not knowing their voice. Once I quit trying to write like them, I realized I could use those guys as a springboard to my works."

Reavis read other genres, including the works of Karl Edward Wagner, Philip José Farmer, Edgar Rice Burrows, Donald Hamilton, Robert Howard ("a couple of his stories still raise the hair on the back of my neck"), Raymond Chandler ("taught me how to write pretty tight"), and "a huge" Ray Bradbury fan. ("Those pulp writers knew how to crank out their stories.")

Other authors Reavis has enjoyed are Edward

Photo by Shana Wortham

Partner in Crime: **Reavis shares a moment with his wife–and permanent first reader–Shana.**

Abbey, John Gilstrap ("my running buddy"), Robert Crais, CJ Box, and Craig Johnson.

"That's what writers have to do. You have to read, and reading makes you a better writer. My problem is that I think I need to write while I'm reading. While I'm writing, I think I need to finish that book," said Reavis. "It's a catch-22, but that's what makes a good writer."

IT BEGAN WITH A BET

One day, he was sitting in the back of a room, attending one of those mandatory sessions you must attend for your job, which tend to last longer than the actual time expired. He was sitting next to a lady writing on a yellow legal pad.

"What are you writing? Because I know you're not taking notes on this."

"You're right. I'm writing an article for the *Dallas Morning News,"* she replied.

"I didn't know you were published. It's hard to do."

"I know it's not that hard with all that junk I see in newspapers. Anybody can write."

"I've been trying all these years, and it's not that easy."

"I bet I'll get published before you."

"No, you won't."

"I'll bet you $100 I'll get published before you."

"You're on."

Reavis got out his legal pad and began his first newspaper column.

"I realized that day that I didn't know what my writing was. I never really found my voice," said Reavis. "In the back of my mind, it was all those voices of other writers like Robert Ruark or Gene Hill. As I started to write on that legal pad, I decided that this was what I would do. I'm going to write a newspaper column."

He penned his first column longhand and typed it. He remembered that his hometown paper, *The Paris News,* ran articles and columns about outdoor sports. He sent the column to the sports editor. About three days later, Reavis received a phone call.

"Is this Reavis Wortham?"

"Yeah."

Butch & Sundance Ride Again: Reavis Z. Wortham (Sundance, on left) and Steve Knagg (Butch, on right), ca. 1988. *Photo by Landon McDowell.*

I CAN WRITE ANYWHERE—EVEN THE BACK OF A S.W.A.T. TRUCK.

Scan the QR code to listen to an exclusive audio interview with Reavis Z. Wortham, hosted by George Sirois on the *Excelsior Journeys* podcast. Dive deeper into the mind behind the stories and hear firsthand about his inspirations, process, and more!

"Well, I have your newspaper column in my hand, and I like it. We're going to publish it and pay you for it."

Reavis said he was estastic. He had been trying for 24 years to get published and paid. That was another shot.

"Here's the deal," the sports editor said. *"We'd like you to be our outdoor humor columnist for the* Paris News. *Can you write one of these every week?"*

Reavis was on the phone shaking his head no. But what he really said was, "Yes."

His first newspaper column appeared on Aug. 14, 1988. Since then, he has written over 2,000 newspaper and magazine articles. At the time, he

In the Zone: Reavis hard at work in his office on his next novel. His wife, Shana, knows he's nearing the finish line when AC/DC's "Thunderstruck" starts blaring on repeat at full volume. *Photo by* New York Times *Bestselling Author John Gilstrap.*

self-syndicated through 50 papers in Texas and southern Oklahoma, doing all the work to market his writing to other newspapers.

Then came the big time.

King Features Syndicate approached Reavis to represent him and offered to position him as the Dave Berry of outdoor writing and get him published nationwide.

"I'd finally made it. I told them it would be great, and I would love to do that," Reavis said. "Pretty soon everything was getting set up, and then about six weeks later, that little pesky thing called the internet came along, and it just killed newspaper columnists."

JUST PUT WORDS ON A PAGE

One day, Reavis came home from work. He needed to write a column but didn't have an idea that day. He remembered what his high school English teacher told them, "If you can't think of anything, just put words on the paper. Words will lead to more words, and you'll get an idea." So, he wrote about being "we're from up on the river." It's what his grandmother always used to say. She was born and raised near the Red River that separates Oklahoma and Texas.

As he wrote, he began a story about an old farmer finding a mutilated dog in his cornfield.

"I was so engrossed in that story, I didn't know where I was. My wife came up, put her hand on my shoulder, and told me it was time for supper. I almost went over the computer because she scared me so badly. When I was writing... I wasn't in my house. I was in the story... in that hot cornfield in 1964."

He ate dinner and did the dishes when his wife, Shana, sat at their only computer. Since he left the story up, she began to read it.

"When did you start this?"

"Tonight. I couldn't think of anything for my newspaper column."

"This is your novel. This is what you've been talking about. You need to finish this."

It became his first novel, *The Rock Hole,* which Kirkus listed as one of the Top 12 Mysteries of 2011.

"That's the long answer of how I got started," said Reavis. "The short answer? I tend to write what I want and the way I wonder."

WRITE ANYWHERE

Reavis has no set writing routine or ritual. He's written from his easy chair, deer stands, the backyard, and even the back of a SWAT truck.

"I was in Florida for a week's worth of training with my friend John Gilstrap. We were riding along on a bust at 3:30 in the morning. I remembered I had to get my column in that day," Reavis said. "All these guys are geared up, and they look like mon-

Photo by City of Garland

Work Hard, Play Hard: When he's not crafting his thrilling tales, Reavis enjoys traveling and cherishes spending time with his family–especially in the great outdoors. ***Top two photos by Steve Knagg, bottom photo by* New York Times *Bestselling Author John Gilstrap.***

sters. I have a helmet and a flak jacket. I pull out my laptop and hammer away on a column while all these guys are checking gear, and they're looking at me like I'm crazy.

"I don't have to have a quiet room, a big desk or window. I wrote my newspaper columns from anywhere. I can write my novels from anywhere. If I need to, sometimes I'll write like Mark Twain, lying on the bed. Sometimes, I have to sit at my desk in my office to hammer out a story or work on a manuscript. I don't outline, which drives other people crazy."

Reavis once tried an outline and gave up after the second page. He writes or puts his fingers on the keys and starts typing. He doesn't do bios on his characters. Reavis says his characters arrived fully realized, and they "walk onto the stage" when he needs them.

CHARACTERS TAKE OVER

"Sometimes they're a supporting character, and sometimes they take over. In the case of Tom Bell in my Red River series," Reavis said, sometimes they're so strong. "Tom Bell was supposed to be a walk-on character. Walk on, teach a young boy a lesson, and then walk off. He came on so strong that by the novel's end, he took on a presence I didn't expect."

SPOILER ALERT: Tom Bell was providing cov-

er for an escape for other characters and was left for dead. For the next two years, as Reavis met readers in public, they would give him grief about killing Tom Bell. A lady approached him at a signing, leaned over the table, and put her finger in his face.

"You bring Tom Bell back. He was my favorite character."

"You have to let him go. He's dead. He's not getting out of Mexico."

"No, he's not."

Reavis doesn't reread his work once it's published, but he had to reread Tom Bell's "death" scene.

"I didn't remember what happened to him. I knew he was shot up, but it never turned out I said he was dead. He was wounded providing coverage. So, I brought him back," said Reavis. "He's such a strong character that he threatened to take over the series again."

Reavis wrote a prequel that featured Tom Bell as a Texas Ranger, *The Texas Job*. It won gold at the Will Rogers Medallion Award in 2023. He's still debating if he will do a whole spinoff series with just Tom Bell.

"I don't plan. I don't think ahead. I just let my characters do what they want when they come on the stage, which has worked well for me. I know that drives plotters crazy. I can't follow an outline. It just doesn't work in my head. Even in my first novel, I didn't know who the killer was until the end of the book."

Reavis reviewed his manuscript, finding that he was writing about who would be the killer.

"My subconscious must have been planting the clues because I didn't notice them," said Reavis. "I was following the story. I cannot explain it. When I teach writing courses, I tell everybody I can't tell you how it works. Except my subconscious does the work."

John Hancock: **Reavis during a bookstore event, signing a copy of *Gold Dust* for one of his many fans.**

Hanging with Legends: Reavis poses with legendary Hollywood actor Barry Corbin at the Will Rogers Medallion Awards in Fort Worth, Texas, in October, 2024. *Photo by Shana Wortham.*

FINDING INSPIRATION

Reavis' forthcoming novel, the Western Horror crossover *Comancherria*, came to him in a dream—all the characters, plot points, and highlights. He got up at 3:30 a.m. and wrote until 9 a.m. Sometimes, his dreams become intense, and he wakes up tired or still captured by the dream until his wife puts her hand on him to let him know where he is.

"It has happened a couple of times a month. I'll be sitting in bed, but I would have felt like I had lived that story. In a dream, I was attacked by a mountain lion, and I came out fighting, and man… my heart was pounding. I had to lie awake until I calmed down," Reavis said. "There's always something going on inside my head, simmering in the pot, and it will find its way out.

"I don't believe in writer's block. I honestly never had a problem with it. I was working on my third or fourth novel once, and suddenly, I realized I was dead in the water. I remembered what David Morrell had told me. If your story stalls, it's not moving forward because you're making your characters do something they don't want or are not supposed to do. I went back and deleted that chapter, picked it up from the end of another chapter, and it flowed. I didn't have any more problems. That's the only time I've ever had an issue with the writing."

Reavis doesn't define himself by genre. He writes historical mysteries, historical mystery thrillers, thrillers, and pure Westerns and is looking to tackle Western horror.

"I never wanted to be just a mystery writer be-

Natural Habitat: **Reavis, an avid outdoorsman, finds joy in exploring nature and cherishes the time he spends at his country cabin.** ***Photos by Shana Wortham.***

cause I don't like boxes. I want to do what I want and do," said Reavis. "If you look at some great writers, they wrote in everything. I haven't tried science fiction yet. My second novel *Burrows* is horror. It's so claustrophobic that people tell me they couldn't finish it. That's exactly what I wanted. I wanted you to feel creepy. It's a book people love to hate, but at the same time, everybody talks about it, even if they can't finish it.

"That's what I want with my writing to stick with people and to stay there years and years from now."

George "Clay" Mitchell *is an award-winning reporter and photographer, a founding partner of* Saddlebag Dispatches, *and Executive Vice President and Publisher of its partner company, Roan & Weatherford Publishing Associates.He lives in Lavaca, Arkansas, with his wife and two daughters.*

(Opposite Page) Bringing Home the Hardware: **Reavis displays the Will Rogers Medallion Bronze Medal in the Western Mystery category for *Hard Country*. His fellow winners? Perennial bestsellers Craig Johnson (a buddy of his) and Anne Hillerman. Talk about stiff competition.** ***Photo by Casey W. Cowan.***

WILL ROGERS
MEDALLION AWARD

925-736-2280 | info@blackhawkmuseum.org | www.blackhawkmuseum.org

BLACKHAWK MUSEUM

DANVILLE'S HIDDEN GEM

5 Unique Exhibits

THE SPIRIT OF THE OLD WEST

The Spirit of the Old West Gallery weaves the story of the American West, depicting the challenges, successes, and failures of both Native Americans and American Settlers. Learn about the life of the Plains Indians and the settling of the Western Frontier, from Mountain Men and Settlers, to Outlaws and Lawmen.

WORLD OF NATURE

World of Nature is an incredible and expansive collection of carefully-curated animal species from all over the world. With more than 600 species on display, this gallery provides an exceptional learning experience for students and educators of all ages.

2025 SPRING SPEAKER SERIES

Join us for the 2025 Spring Speaker Series, featuring New York Times bestselling author Chris Enss on March 29 at 11:00 AM. Enss has written over fifty books about women of the Old West and has received numerous prestigious awards for her work. Don't miss this opportunity to hear her discuss her latest works and the remarkable women who shaped the frontier.

3700 Blackhawk Plaza Circle, Danville CA

JAMES A. TWEEDIE

MARIPOSA

A SHORT STORY

"I heerd Mackie hit a vein of gold four feet thick up at Mormon Bar and he's scoopin' it out with a spoon."

Jimmy Martin liked to talk more than he liked digging on his claim in Agua Fria. It was late January, 1850, and the day was sunny but biting cold.

"Hell," he added, "and Mackie's got water there in Mariposa Creek to wash what gold he can't pick up with his hands."

As Jimmy talked, his partner, Studs Kelly, leaned on a pickax and bit off a chaw of baccy

After chewing and savoring the juice, he spit out what he didn't swallow and started in on his usual complaint.

"So, Mackie's got the water and 'less'n we haul our dirt down to the spring we don't have nothing but rocks and dust. And now Fremont, what with his claim on the Rancho Las Mariposas, is sayin' that all the gold and water belong to him, and if'n he had his way I swear he'd pick our pockets and turn us out...."

"Now don't go bad-mouthin' General Fremont," Jimmy scowled. "He's a good man and you knows I owe him my life."

"Ha!" says Studs. "If you mean him givin' you a rifle and the pistol you're wearin' and then feedin' you enough grub to march you up and down the Sacramento in '46, and if you call that savin' your life, then you're the sorriest excuse for a soldier I ever saw."

Jimmy's face flushed red and hot.

"Now you listen to me. Afore Sutter found the gold two year ago, California wasn't good for nothin' 'cept for dry hills, flooded, marshy river bottoms, dirty Indians and mebbe some of them Mexicans. But the General had a plan. First off, we was goin' to get rid of the Indians....

Jimmy paused before adding, "But, Studs, you already know that story since I tell it near every day."

"Well," Studs answered, "you do like to tell it, and I don't mind listenin', but I can't say I much care for all the killin' you done."

"What's that you're sayin', Studs? Are you still feelin' sorry for them Indians? Well, don't waste your tears. The General he says to us, 'If you see a buck pick 'im off and don't bother to bury 'im. Leave 'im where he lies as a warnin' to the rest.'"

Studs went to swinging his pick again—blow after heavy blow—and took to talking while Jimmy scraped together the broken pieces of rock and searched them for color.

"The way I sees it," said Studs, "shootin' nine hundred Indians with their backs against the river up at Reading's Ranch wasn't 'pickin' 'em off.' It was a massacre. Women and children, too. That warn't a war. You executed them Indians as certain sure as if you'd strung 'em up on that tree in Hangtown. None of 'em had a chance. You even shot 'em up when they was tryin' to swim across...."

Now Jimmy was getting hotter than ever and cut his friend off in mid-sentence.

"Well, stop right there and listen up, 'cause you got it all wrong. The General stirs the pot by sayin' they was planning to attack us so we hit 'em first and good riddance. And anyways, there warn't nine hundred of 'em 'cause we didn't have that much lead anyhow. Mebbe two or three hundred at most and, sure, mebbe I do feel bad sometimes when I think

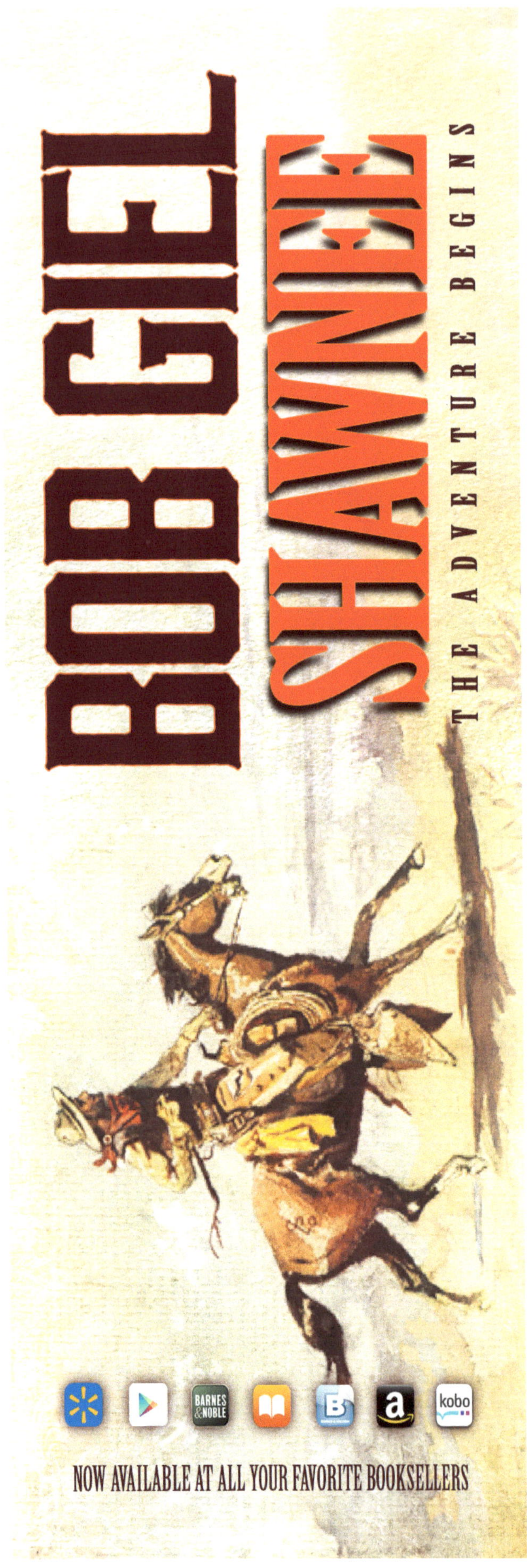

of the women and the babies, but later, when them Modoc picked off two of our boys, we took care of them on the shore of that lake up the Klamath. Made California safe so the Bear Flag could fly free and then kicked Mexico out so we can join the Union. And that's all because of General Fremont, so don't go sayin' nothin' agin' him."

Studs shot yet another stream of juice from his mouth. "I'll say what I want and who are you to tell me I can't spit on Fremont's boots if that's what I want to do? I'd say the hell with you, too, 'cept for this here claim. And as for Fremont, you're not all in with him yourself."

Without looking up, Jimmy continued to pick through the pieces of broken rock.

"You mean slavery? Well, even though we're both from Georgia, that's a point where the General and me don't see eye-to-eye. Because of the General, they're goin' to make California a free state. Well, God bless 'em, if that's what they want. But hear me out, 'cause no good's gonna come of it. Half the country's agin' the other half, and I know my folks would rather die than let them Northern boys take away their way of life."

"Well," Studs answered, "as far as I'm concerned, your ma and pa's way of life can roll over and die."

Jimmy's face turned red, again, as he rose up on one knee.

"Take it easy, there, Jimmy. I didn't say I want your ma and pa to roll over and die. It's all about the slaves. Someday—maybe not now, but soon—we'll all be free states, and them slaves of yours will...."

"Ain't got no slaves," Jimmy growled. "Ma and pa ain't got no slaves. They live off'n their own sweat, so what's that you're tellin' me? That you want all that hard work to come to nothin'?"

"Pay attention to what your doin' there, Jimmy!" Studs interrupted with a shout. "Unless my eyes are playin' tricks, that piece of quartz you just tossed aside's got color in it."

"No, it don't," Jimmy shouted back as he picked up the chipped crystal and held it up to vindicate himself.

"Yes, it does!" Studs yelled with even more enthusiasm than before. "We've hit a vein!"

After giving the rock a second look, Jimmy joined his partner on his hands and knees searching for the place the pick had clipped it off.

"Here!" Studs yelled again, as he pointed to a

spot where the vein of quartz ran across a granite shelf. "There's more!"

"Now, what do we do?" Jimmy asked. "We can't break up all that granite with a pick. Mebbe we can chip out some of the quartz, but if there's more underneath, we'll never get it out without dynamite."

"And that would probably blow the gold to kingdom come," Studs added with his enthusiasm beginning to fade like an ebbing tide.

The two men stopped talking and thought for a spell and then, when they were done, they thought some more.

It was Jimmy who finally broke the silence.

"I knows a man named Hyrum Booker who drills into rock and packs in just enough powder to split a piece off the wall in a mine or crack a boulder in half. I seen him do it up at Ophir Hill last September. Mebbe he'll do it for us."

"Why would he?" Studs asked. "Does he owe you a favor? Or what's it goin' to cost? We don't have any money—at least I don't—not near enough to throw it away on somethin' like that. And what if the vein runs dry? We'll be broke."

"Well," Jimmy said as he stood up and cast his long winter shadow across the granite shelf, sending a shiver through Studs as he suddenly found himself blocked from the sun. "If you don't have enough money to crack open this rock like one of them golden eggs, then I'll pay for it myself, and whatever I find after that will belong to me and you might as well call it quits and go back to Omaha."

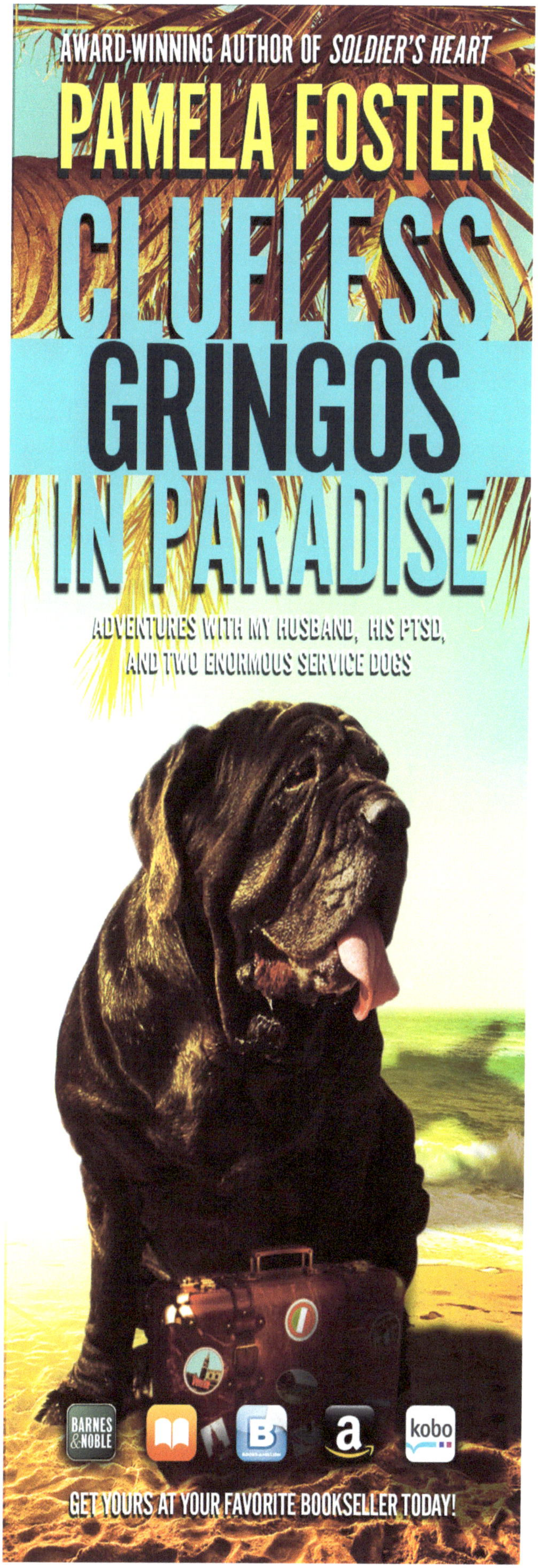

Studs slowly stood with the pick in his hands, holding it the way a man might hold it if he were planning to drill its point through the top of somebody's head.

"You'd cut me out of my stake?" he barked. "Just like that? After nigh onto a year pretending you were a partner and a friend? Then to hell with you, Jimmy. Go ahead and blow up the whole damn claim if you want. But I swear that I'll take my share of the gold if I have to take it over your dead body!"

Jimmy stepped back with his eyes fixed on Studs' pick, and after resting his hand on the pistol at his side, he snapped back at a man who, until a moment before, had been his best friend.

"What's this?" he demanded. "Did you just threaten to kill me? Over a claim? Well, I've got somthin' to tell you, Studs. No damn claim is worth getting' killed over. Not even for all the gold in the world. But if you come at me with that pick, I'll shoot you down like one of them bucks I sent to hell when I was on the march with Fremont!"

If pride goeth before a fall, then both Jimmy and Studs were set to throw each other into the abyss. Someone had to break the standoff, and it turned out to be Studs.

"The hell with it," he cursed as he threw his pick on the ground. "I ain't never killed a man yet, and I don't reckon I'm willing to trade away my neck just for the pleasure of breaking yours!"

With those words, Studs broke into a grin and extended his now empty hand toward Jimmy.

With an audible sigh of relief, Jimmy returned the grin as his hand left his pistol behind and joined with the hand of his friend.

As they reaffirmed their friendship, their eyes turned to the gold-flecked seam of quartz as they silently weighed the possibility of striking it rich against the more likely probability of going bust and losing everything.

And as they stared and pondered, the whisper of a winter breeze blew a small, thin, fragile scrap of orange and black across the rock shelf where it stopped inches away from the glint of gold.

Jimmy bent down and brought it up gently in his rough, calloused hands.

It was the wing of a Monarch butterfly, miraculously intact from the previous October when the old adults mated and died and the newly emergent

Monarchs spread their wings and began their winter migration to the coast.

"It's a Mariposa," Studs announced, though Jimmy already knew what it was.

"It's a sign," Jimmy replied.

"A sign for what?"

"If somethin' this fragile can survive, then so can we. I say we get Hyrum Booker and roll the dice. I'll pay, and you can pay me back from your share of the gold we're goin' to find when we break open this rock."

Later that afternoon, Jimmy tucked the butterfly wing between the pages of his bible, and it was still intact when his 10-year-old great-great-great-great-great grandson opened the book and found it 175 years later.

And for Jimmy and Studs—as luck would have it—the sign proved true.

Historical Footnote: *When the Spanish first visited the southern Sierra foothills, they saw so many Monarch/Mariposa butterflies that they named the local creek Mariposa. Later, the Rancho Las Mariposas took on the name, as did the town of Mariposa that grew up alongside it. Mariposa County claimed the name when California became a state on September 9, 1850, and later, the name was bestowed on the nearby Mariposa Grove of giant Sequoias, a grove now tucked inside the southwest corner of Yosemite National Park.*

THE AUTHOR

James A. Tweedie *has lived in California, Utah, Scotland, Australia, Hawaii, and presently in Long Beach, Washington. He has published six novels, four collections of poetry, and one collection of short stories with Dunecrest Press. His award-winning stories and poetry have appeared in regional, national, and international print and online anthologies. He has twice been honored with a Silver Certificate award from Writers of the Future and was awarded First Prize in the inaugural Edinburgh Festival Flash Fiction Contest. He is a regular contributor to* Frontier Tales *and* Saddlebag Dispatches.

He recalls moving from San Francisco to Logan, Utah, in 1979 and being both baffled and amused when he was asked, "What made you decide to move out West from California?"

In that moment, he learned that "the West" was not just a direction, but a cultural space infused with traditions and tales embracing a heritage of mountain men, pioneers, Native Peoples, cowboys, homesteaders, prospectors, ranchers, railroads, and a host of conflicts that stretched and expanded the United States into the country it is today.

His favorite corner of the West is the Sierra Nevada, where he has hiked and fly fished since he was old enough to walk.

WILL AMES

THE LAST RIDE OF RAFAEL VARGAS

A SHORT STORY

"Rafael?"

He straightened up from the gnarled stump and let the axe head dip to the hot sand. With a hand pressed to the small of his back, he squinted at the woman standing in the banded shade cast by the little adobe's *ramada*. "Luisa?"

A smile touched her lips. "They told me I might find you here," she said and dropped a burlap sack against one of the rough-cut cedar uprights. Scrawny chickens darted squawking past her long, faded skirt and scattered across the dry-baked sand as she came to stand by the spindly, split-rail corral.

Rafael leaned on the work-polished axe handle and frowned. "I have not used that name in many years. How did you find me?"

She smiled and he was surprised to see crow's feet dance around her eyes. "You do me an injustice to think I have forgotten your other names. You can hide from the world, *mi amor,* but not from me." She caught his eye and the smile widened "Do not worry. Your secret is safe." She glided up to him and fingered a ragged hole in his threadbare shirt. "Though how anyone could mistake you for the mighty Rafael Vargas is beyond me. Even I would not have recognized you had I not known what to look for. You are turning gray, *amor.*" She combed her fingers through his shaggy, uncut hair and shook her head. Then her hands slid down to his cheek hidden beneath a coarse beard and she tsked. "I still remember what they used to say about you. Faster than a striking rattlesnake and twice as deadly." Her smile came back. "And as handsome a *Californio* as ever rode."

He brushed her hand away. "Why are you here, Luisa? After all these years... Did my brother send you?"

Her eyes went back to the hole in his sleeve, and she began toying with the ragged edges, tracing the tear with a finger. "Emmanuel does not know."

"That does not answer my question," he said, trapping her hand beneath his.

Her hand lingered for a heartbeat, but then he felt pressure and let her go.

She frowned and looked up. "Can I not have come merely to see an old friend? Must I have a reason?"

"After five years, yes."

"Has it really been so long..." Her voice was quiet, and she turned away. "They said you had a small *rancho.*" She ran her hand along a cracked, sun-grayed rail, and the rawboned *grullo* in the corral raised its head and whickered. "But I had no idea..."

He folded his arms. "I manage. Has he left you again? Is that it?"

She paced along the corral away from him. "Do you ever miss the old days?"

He snorted and spread his hands. "When I do, I need only look where they got me."

She stopped and turned sidelong, the glimmer of dark beneath long lashes just visible. "We had good times. Even you must admit that." She spun suddenly and came striding back. "Every *don* in the territory lived in fear of the day the Chaparral Cock came riding onto their *estancia,*" she said, and there was a gleam in her eyes as she took him by the arm. "Even the *alcaldes* would not touch us! Have you forgotten what that power felt like?"

He grunted and looked away. "I have not forgotten." He stared at the stump he had been working on and sighed. The juniper had died hard, but the thick, knobby roots still fought him. He looked at his hands that had once been smooth and trim but were now rough, calloused things he no longer recognized and wondered if he would ever make a good *ranchero*. "Why do you think I told no one my real name? Those days are gone."

She scoffed. "They are only gone because you think that is how it must be. Look around you, Rafael." She flung an arm out and stared up at him. "Do not tell me this is how you want to live."

His eyes fell and he looked away.

"Open your eyes, *amor*." She clutched his arm. "They can be our times again. We can make this territory *tremble*."

Amor. It had been years since she had called him that. Her thin, vein-streaked hand was white-knuckled and clawlike on his arm; so different from the smooth mahogany that he still saw in his mind. Smoother even than the red silk sash he used to wear at his waist. He shook his head and ran a finger over the old scars that circled his wrists. "Three years in a *norteamericano* prison persuaded me there were easier lines of work."

"My Rafael would not say that."

"*Your* Rafael did not know San Quentin."

Her hand fell away and she turned from him, the stiffness gone from her shoulders.

He watched her for a moment and sighed. He sank the axe head deep into the stump with a grunt and went to her, and his hands fit the soft curve of her shoulders just as well as they did so long ago.

"Can I say nothing?" she murmured.

"You can tell me why you came," he said, looking at the sack resting in the *ramada's* shade. "It was not to talk about the old days, *querida*. I have not been your *amor* for many years." Her hair tickled his chin; raven-black hair that had once matched the fitted suits he'd worn in his vanity. Hair now streaked with coarse grays. "Has he left you?"

He felt her tremble. "He's in trouble."

"When is he not?"

"This time is different." She turned and the sun carved deep shadows in the faultlines crisscrossing her face. "They are saying he killed the son of some *norteamericano alcalde.*"

"They say?" Rafael's hands fell from her shoulders. "So I was right. You have not heard from him."

She folded her arms and looked away. "It has been two months. Some miners were talking at the *cantina* in El Dorado."

"Bastardo," he said and then grimaced. "So my brother has killed a grandee's son. So what? He has killed many and never been caught." He spread his hands and looked to the clear, sun-bright sky. His voice rose as he spoke. "For five years he has robbed miners, stolen horses, and killed sons across the breadth of the Californias, and what has come of it? Nothing. He has the luck of the devil."

"Because now there is a price on Emmanuel's head. A very big one. The *norteamericano* government has hired men to capture him. *Soldados* from the *Mexicano* war. They call themselves *Californio* Rangers, but I know what they really are."

"Cazarrecompensas." He turned away, but she caught his hand and locked eyes with him.

"You know what that means," she said. "You know how bounty men do these things."

Rafael rubbed his eyes with the heel of a hand. "Dead men cannot escape," he muttered.

Her eyes filled with tears, but her grip never lessened. "Please, Rafael."

He sighed and pulled away. "Tell me, *mi amor*. Tell me why I should risk my life for a brother who left me for dead. And for a woman who left me for him." He spread his hands and looked around. "What do I owe you? What do I owe either of you?"

She clutched at him and her grip was like iron. Her eyes wouldn't let his go. "He is family. Your *hermanito*. Your blood. And I am still your *querida*. Think, Rafael. All that we had before we can have again if only you will open your eyes."

Rafael laughed. "I was not the one to cut those bonds. Or have you forgotten?"

"There has never been a day I have not remembered," she said, and the smile died on his lips.

He dropped his eyes from her hard stare and found his gaze caught by a dull, pitted ring on her right hand. Five years ago, it had shone like gold fire.

His jaw tightened and he pulled away. He trudged to the *ramada* and snatched the dipper from the drinking gourd hanging on a cedar upright. The water was cool on his dry, cracked lips and he dashed the second dipperfull across his face. She had chosen Emmanuel, yet she still bore his ring... He stared through lank, dripping hair at his hands. His own work-scarred ring was barely recognizable as that smooth golden band he remembered so well. He twisted the fading memory around his finger.

Through wet strands of gray, he looked around the barren, sunburnt yard—the rickety corral, the rawboned animals, the crumbling adobe.

There has never been a day I have not remembered.

He glanced over his shoulder. "What makes you think I can still do this?"

"You are Rafael Vargas."

He blew out a breath. Footsteps crunched on the dry scree beside him, and there she was—part of her face lit by a streak of sunlight that lanced through the thin *ramada*. Her eyes were large and unblinking, one in shadow, the other lit, and she pushed the burlap sack into his hands.

He looked at her, brow raised, but she said nothing, simply stared back, half in, half out of the darkness. He peered in the mouth of the sack and felt his scalp tingle.

All that we had before we can have again.

He closed the burlap and sighed. "Just like the old days, eh?"

Her eyes bored into his.

"I was wonderin' when you'd show."

Rafael swung down and snubbed the rawboned *grullo* to the tongue of a partially dismantled buckboard. "Where is he, Morgan?"

The big man squinted up at him and went back to work greasing the axle shaft of a pot-bellied Concord, his bare back shining under the noon sun. He shook his head. "Whatever he did, I weren't part of it. My hands are clean." A few quick passes and the rag went into the bucket of grease between his feet and he stood. Wide hands smeared more grease on his black-crusted leather apron. He patted the faded red sideboard of the coach suspended on blocks beside him. Tall, iron-banded wheels leaned nearby in a corner of the adobe-walled courtyard. "La Grange ain't exactly high cotton, but at least I ain't gettin' shot at." He folded thick, hairy arms across his barrel chest and nodded at Rafael's waist. "Heard you was clean, too, but I guess I might'a' knowed better. You look like old times wearin' that damn fool red sash and those silvered shooters. Should'a figured she'd get her hooks back in you."

Rafael narrowed his eyes. "You knew?"

"Came through here 'bout a week ago huntin' you. Told her she didn't have no business with either of us, but I see I was wrong."

Rafael pinched the bridge of his nose and sighed. "I just need to know where I might find him, Morgan."

"No idea."

Rafael ground his teeth. "I know you were close with him. Before...." He looked away, staring at the bleach-brown adobe blocks that cut off the livery yard from the rest of town. "At the end he was keeping things from me. I thought perhaps...."

"No. I'm done with the Vargas boys. Y'all never brought me nothin' but trouble." He rubbed a big, puckered welt high on his arm. "Took this for him robbin' them miners up near Camanche. Damn near lost the arm and what'd he do? Took my horse and pistol, emptied my pockets and left me for dead."

"I am not asking you to make him a medal!" Rafael snapped. He pulled off his flat crowned hat and passed a hand across his face, staring up at the cloudless blue sky until his breathing evened. "Luisa said the bounty men were hunting him."

Morgan shook his head. "All these years and she still don't know she backed the wrong horse. And you're just as bad. Either one of you had a lick of sense you'd get shed of him and never look back."

Rafael looked away and spat, watching it wick away and disappear in the chiminea hot sand. "I need to find him before they do. Where does he run these days?"

"Don't know, but it can't be far enough to suit me."

Rafael ground his teeth and snatched up the grullo's reins. "I do not have time for this," he muttered and stepped into the stirrups.

"You mean you're really goin' back?" Morgan asked. "After everything?" He shook his head and spat into the dust, raising his voice. "Blood will out, huh? That it?"

Rafael stiffened but didn't answer, and as he pulled the gelding's head around, he felt a big hand on his leg. Before he knew it, a pistol was cocked and in his hand, shining silver-bright in the noon sun.

Morgan eyed the bright pistol and then squinted up at him from beneath the shade of a calloused hand. "You're a damn fool, Rafe," he said. "You know how this'll end. He ain't gonna change no matter how many times you pull his fat outta' the fire."

Rafael stared at Morgan and then at the pistol. The barrel was trembling slightly. He grimaced and eased the hammer down and tucked it back into his sash. "Where?" he asked, voice quiet, not looking at the big man.

Morgan sighed and removed his hand. He rubbed the ugly scar and nodded south. "Don't know for sure. Mostly keep my head down these days. But you might try the Cactus Blossom if you're feelin' your oats. I hear he still calls on her from time to time."

Rafael lifted an eyebrow. "I thought she was through with him."

Morgan snorted. "She sees them with money." He shrugged. "Way I hear it, business is slow. Maybe his is all she gets."

"Agua Fria?"

Morgan grinned and shook his head. "She got run out. They say she horsewhipped another gal bloody for poaching one of her regulars. I hear she keeps a room in Mariposa now, sparkin' the miners." His teeth were white against his skin's weather-brown. "Best watch yourself, you talk to her. 'Pears time ain't gentled her none."

Rafael sighed and gathered the reins.

"Rafe?" Morgan was there, still rubbing his arm. He looked up, grin gone, and shook his head. "He ain't worth it."

"How dare you!" An empty chamber pot crashed into the clapboard wall beside Rafael's head. "You son of a *puerco!*"

"Hello, Pilár," said Rafael, ducking to one side. "I see that my brother has been here already."

Her sharp face turned a deep shade of red and she looked around the tiny room for something else to throw. A bed with a small, worn steamer trunk at it's foot and a washstand were the only other furnishings. "Do not play the fool with me, Rafael," she snapped and stabbed a finger at him. "Where one Vargas goes, there is the other." She hefted the porcelain wash basin. "Where is the money he took from me?"

Rafael ducked behind his arms. "Peace, Pilár! I have not seen Emmanuel in five years!" The basin

AN EPIC JOURNEY OF RESILIENCE, HONOR, AND THE RELENTLESS PURSUIT OF JUSTICE.

As the trusted lieutenant of the infamous Geronimo, Chato's days are painted in the hues of raid and revolt until personal tragedy strikes when his family are taken into slavery in Mexico. Hoping to secure their release, Chato strikes a deal to aid the U.S. Army in maintaining peace with his people. But when Geronimo denounces him as a traitor and departs, all hope for Chato's family flees with him. Forsaken by his former brothers-in-arms, Chato vows to hunt down the renegades himself, becoming a beacon of the Chiricahua peace faction clinging to reservation life in the process.

WINNER OF THE 2024 WILL ROGERS MEDALLION AWARD SILVER MEDAL FOR TRADITIONAL WESTERN FICTION

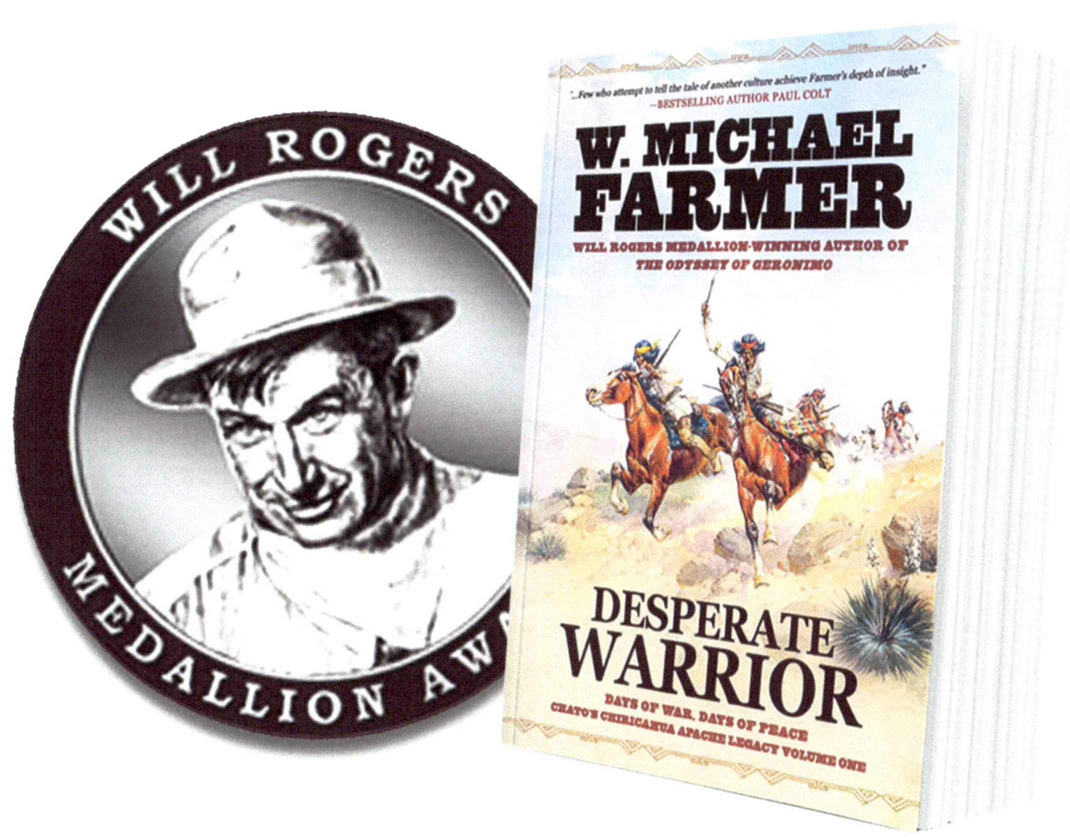

"... Few who attempt to tell the tale of another culture achieve Farmer's depth of insight."

—Bestselling Western author Paul Colt

faltered and he peeked around his arms. "I am looking for him as well. Morgan said you might know."

The basin lowered a fraction and she stared at him, eyes narrow.

"On the soul of my mother." He rasied a hand to the low ceiling. The mixture of perfume, cigarette smoke, and stale sweat that filled the small room stung his nostrils.

The porcelain thumped on the washstand and she flung her hand at the door. "Get out."

"Pilár," Rafael began.

"Get out!" She snatched the wash basin back up.

The silver pistol jumped to his palm, belly high and she pulled up like she'd been struck. Rafael fought to keep his hand and voice steady. "Do not, Pilár. I only need a word and you will be rid of me."

She sneered. "I am a whore, Rafael, not a fool. I know you. If I told you where he was, I would never see my money again."

Rafael rubbed his face. "What is this money nonsense you keep speaking of?"

She searched his face. "You really do not know?"

"Would I be here if I did?"

She cocked her head to one side, eyes partially closed, and then her lips twitched with the ghost of a smile. She set the wash basin aside. Hands smoothed her rumpled shift and she slouched onto the bed, where she leaned back on her arms and patted the thin, corn shuck mattress. "You must forgive my manners, Rafael. Please, sit down. You look like you have come a long way."

"I do not have time for your games, Pilár. Just tell me where to find him and I will go."

Her smile widened. "Emmanuel need not trouble your mind any longer."

Rafael narrowed his eyes. "What do you mean?"

She looked at her nails, a crooked smile on her lips. "I have sent a man," she said, and her eyes met his. "There is no need to go chasing after Emmanuel. You will see your *hermanito* soon enough. Or what is left of him." And then she batted her long lashes. "Perhaps we can find something to do while we wait, eh? Just like the old days?"

"You sent a man...." Rafael ground his teeth. He slipped the pistol away and rubbed his temples. He was so close, yet he could feel time slipping through his fingers. "All these years and you are still no better a judge of men...." he muttered. He looked up. "Did you ever stop to think, Pilár, about what your man will do when he hears about the thousand dòlar bounty the *norteamericanos* have put on Emmanuel's head?"

She sprang up, hand to her mouth. "A thousand dollars? *Dios no....*" she breathed. Her face went pale and bloodless behind the rouge.

"Where?" demanded Rafael.

She shook her head. "No. I do not trust you."

Rafael ground his teeth and thought. "How much money did he steal from you, Pilar? Eh? Just how much do you have to lose and your man gain?"

She stared at him and chewed her lip. Her fingers drummed on her bare arms and Rafael counted his heartbeats while the howling lobos began to close in on his brother.

"The arroyo," she spat finally.

"The one in the *Diablos?* The old *rancho?"* When she didn't answer he stepped in and shook her by the shoulders. "Pilár!"

Eyes wide with anger and fear bored into him, but she clenched her jaw and didn't answer. But it was enough. He spun and was halfway to the door before she realized what was happening.

"Rafael?" Her voice rose sharply. "What are you going to do?"

He ignored her. The thin floorboards creaked behind him as she sprang into motion, but he didn't slow. "Rafael? What about my money?" she screeched and stepped after him. *"Rafael!"*

He slammed the door shut.

Puffs of powder smoke drifted across the mountain basin like dirty clouds. He watched another volley shatter chunks from the crumbling adobe squatting in the rank bunch grass that grew along the arroyo. The roof had given way in one corner, taking part of the east wall with it, and he wondered how the old shack was still standing.

The thunder of an answering brace of shots echoed off the low *Diablos,* and smoke drifted skyward from the lone, eye-socket window facing him.

Emmanuel.

He shook his head. How many times before had it happened just like this?

Beneath him the *grullo* shifted, ears flicking back and forth with each gunshot. He wiped his palms on his thighs and brushed the heel of the revolver where it sat butt forward tucked into his sash. His palms never sweated in the old days. He licked dry lips and watched the gunsmoke blossom and drift away on the thin mountain air.

Suddenly something zipped by him, buzzing like a hornet. He swayed and clamped his heels tight to the startled gelding as it squealed and started crow hopping. A second shot kicked up a spray of dirt and gravel five paces away and he wrestled the plunging *grullo* down. He raked his heels back and the horse stumbled into a rough lope. As another shot whirred by, he found himself missing the smooth, easy strides of the big black that had carried him so many years before.

It took half a dozen jerking strides for the *grullo* to even out on the flats spread out before the crumbling adobe. Two more paces and his hat had gone to the wind. By ten he had the reins wrapped around his wrist, and by the next, almost without thinking, he had slid sideways along the heaving chest of the horse, pistol steady in his lower hand.

The *grullo* squealed and slewed to one side as Rafael's weight shifted, but it righted itself in another stride and pounded on. More shots were whizzing by now, but he focused on the pounding gallop. He ignored the blood pumping in his ears as he hung sideways like a burr and snapped off a brace of shots from under the *grullo's* sweat-flecked neck. Suddenly the gelding balked and swerved, and there was a tanned, rough-bearded face flashing by. He fired without thinking, and the face disappeared as the *grullo* swept past. And then they were clear, pounding toward the adobe.

Rafael pulled himself back into the saddle just as the horse flinched, missed a step, and then it's legs folded up underneath it. Time slowed as the gray head

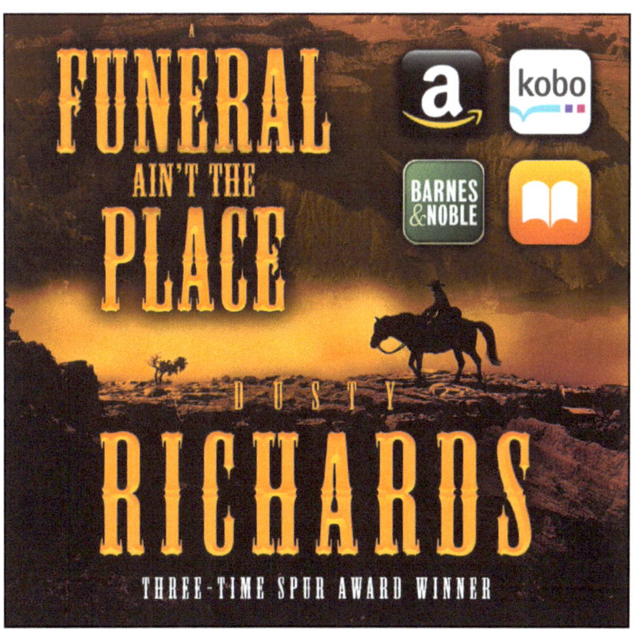

crashed into the hot sand, and he was catapulted forward into the scrub. Breathless and spitting sand, he staggered to his feet and dove through the gaping hole in the east wall with a brace of shots blasting chunks from the adobe as he went.

"I would have shot you from that sack of soap bones if I had not recognized that damned sash," growled a voice.

Rafael's head spun as he sat up, spitting grit and blood from a busted lip, and found himself staring into his brother's broad, broken-nosed face.

Emmanuel twisted and fired through the gaping window, glancing over his shoulder as Rafael scrambled up against the nearest wall. "What the hell are you doing here? I thought you had given up your *cajones* when you took up dirt farming...."

Rafael blew dirt from the cylinder of his revolver and scowled. "I knew I was a fool for trying to get you out of another mess." He spat more blood onto the buckled, rotting floorboards.

"Hah!" Emmanuel's bushy mustache twitched as he laughed. "The day I need help from an old woman like you to kill a few *norteamericanos* will be the day they lay me in the ground. Go back to your dirt farming."

Rafael flushed. He should never have come. Nothing had changed. Nor would it ever. He'd been a fool for listening to Luisa.

Shots tore into the shack, and Emmanuel ducked a flying chunk of shattered adobe. He half rose and poured fire from his two powder-blackened pistols. As the reports died away there was a sobbing moan from the distance. Emmanuel cackled. "You should have ducked, you son of a whore!" he crowed, and then hit the floor as a shower of lead rained crumbling adobe on top of him.

Rafael saw Emmanuel's shoulders shaking as he lay covered in debris and for a heartbeat, he thought his brother had been hit. And then he heard the laughter.

Emmanuel sat up, spitting grit between chuckles, his face deep red from laughing. He shook himself, dislodging bits of clay from his shaggy black hair and sarape that clattered to the floor.

"What is so funny?" Rafael growled. He peeked around a jagged-edged gap in the wall and fired at a mesquite thicket.

Emmanuel kicked away a large chunk of adobe, gouging a deep scar in the soft floorboards with his

spurs. He grabbed his fallen hat and began dusting off the concho-studded silver braid that wrapped it. "Truth be told, I never thought I would find myself in such a situation again." He set the hat aside and clicked through the cylinder of his pistol, then looked up and cackled again. "Just like the old times, eh, *hermano?*"

Rafael shook his head and looked around the tiny room. A rough-bearded *norteamericano* lay half in, half out of the doorway in a pool of blood, slack mouth open to the rotting roof thatch.

"Do not mind him," laughed Emmanuel. "The *bastardo* tried to get the drop on me. But he was too slow." He waggled the pistol back and forth.

Rafael watched flies buzzing around the norteamericanos' open, blood-filled mouth. Each time another shot rained powdered clay, they would scatter, only to alight once more within seconds of the dust settling.

"Come, *hermano,*" called Emmanuel. "Why aren't you shooting? Once we kill these *puercos*, we'll go down to Sonora and drink and whore the town dry, eh?" Without waiting for an answer, Emmanuel turned and fired again through the window hole. A shower of shots peppered the opening and he roared with laughter, emptying first one revolver and then the second.

Rafael looked at his brother's broad back and then at the pistol in his own hand. It was trembling again.

"Just like old times, eh?" he murmured. He let his head rest against the cool adobe and closed his eyes, breathing deep. Then he raised the pistol.

He grunted and sank the axe into the stubborn juniper, wincing as the bite jarred his arms. The chipped and splintered stump creaked as he worked the head back out and sank it again. Chips flew as he chopped faster and faster and harder.

"Rafael!" He froze midswing. Her slap snapped his head around.

"Bastardo!" Luisa's face was splotched red and streaked with tears. "You said you would save him!"

He worked his jaw, massaging the spot where she'd hit him, and looked at her. "I did, *querida*. The only way I could." He reached out a hand for her, but she turned away, sobbing.

He sighed and looked up at the sky, speckled with clouds. The scent of rain was sharp on the air, and he took a long, slow breath. Then he squared his shoulders and sank the axe deep into the stubborn juniper. This time the stump shivered.

THE AUTHOR

Blessed with an overactive imagination and an unrealistic grasp of time constraints, ***Will Ames*** *spends what little free time he has pursuing innumerable hobbies and dreaming far bigger dreams than he has time and money for. A tradesman on Alabama's Gulf Coast by day and a husband and father every other second, he gives thanks to God daily for the gift of sanity in a season of madness.*

LOVE & THE GOLD MINER

Luzena Stanley Wilson left her Missouri homestead with her family in search of a better future in California, embarking on a journey fraught with both peril and promise.

STORY BY

CHRIS ENSS

Luzena Stanley Wilson stood in the center of her empty, one-room, log home in Andrew County, Missouri, studying the opened trunk in front of her. All of her worldly possessions were tucked inside it: family Bibles, two quilts, one dress, a bonnet, a pair of shoes, and a few pieces of china. Mason Wilson, Luzena's husband of five years, marched into the house just as she closed the lid on the trunk and fastened it tightly. They exchanged a smile, and Mason picked up the trunk and carried it outside. Luzena took a deep breath and followed after him. In a few short moments they were off on a journey west to California. It was May 1, 1849, Luzena's birthday. She was thirty years old.

The Wilsons were farmers with two sons: Thomas, born in September 1845, and Jay, born in June 1848. Three payments had been made on the plot of land the Wilsons purchased in January 1847. Prior to news of the Gold Rush captivating Mason's imagination, the plan was to work the multi-acre homestead and pass the farm on to their children and their children's children.

Rumors that the mother lode awaited anyone who dared venture into California's Sierra Foothills prompted Mason to abandon the farm and travel to the rugged mountains beyond Sacramento. In addition to Luzena, her husband, sons, her brothers, and their wives had committed to travel to California as well. A train of five wagons was organized to transport the sojourners west. On the off-chance Mason never found a fortune in gold, the couple left behind funds with the justice of the peace to make another payment on their homestead. In the event the Wilsons were able to stake out a claim for themselves in the Gold Country, they would sell their Missouri home and use the proceeds to aide in their new life.

"It was the work of but a few days to collect our forces for the march," Luzena recorded in her journal shortly after they left on the first leg of their trip. *"We never gave a thought to selling our section [of land], but left it. I little realized then the task I had*

"The Road to Oregon," painting by W.H.D. Koerner (1933).

undertaken. If I had, I think I should have stayed in Andrew County." It would take five months for the Wilsons to reach their westward destination. Most of the belongings Luzena packed in their prairie schooner would be lost or left behind on the trail because they proved to be too burdensome to continue hauling.

Luzena described the long journey west in her memories as *"plodding, unvarying monotony, vexations, exhaustions, throbs of hope and depth of despair."* Dusty, short-tempered, always tired, and, with their patience as tattered as their clothing, the Wilson family and thousands like them plodded on and on. They were scorched by heat, enveloped in dust that reddened their eyes and parched their throats; they were bruised, scratched, and bitten by innumerable insects.

Luzena's Quaker upbringing in North Carolina had not prepared her for such a grueling endeavor. Her parents, Asa and Diane Hunt, had relocated from Piedmont, North Carolina, to Saint Louis in 1843, but the trip was comparatively easy. After the Hunts arrived in Missouri, they purchased a number of acres of land at a government auction. Luzena lived on the family farm until she and Mason wed on December 19, 1844.

The first day of the Wilson's journey to California was without incident. It wasn't until the sun began to slowly sink in the sky and Mason announced it was time to make camp that Luzena became terrified. *"Our first campfire was lighted in Indian Territory, which spread in one unbroken, unnamed waste from the Missouri River to the border line of California,"* she shared in her journal. *"Around us in every direction were groups of Indians sitting, standing, and on horseback, as many as two hundred in the camp. I had read and heard whole volumes of their bloody deeds, the massacre of harmless white men, torturing helpless women, carrying away captive children the most precious in the wide world, and I lived in an agony of dread that first night."*

Luzena noted in her memoirs that the Indians never posed any threat to her or her family. She admitted they were in more danger of the elements and terrain than any Native Americans they encountered along the way. Torrential downpours, swollen rivers, prairie fires, and knee-high snowdrifts impeded their progress and at times exhausted their resources. *"The winter rains and melting snow saturated the earth like a sponge, and the wagons sunk like lead in the sticky mud,"* Luzena wrote in her journal. *"Sometimes a whole day was consumed in going two or three miles, and one day we made camp but a quarter of a mile distance from the last. The last days were spent in digging out both animals and wagon, and the light of the campfire was utilized to mend broken bolts and braces. We built the fire at night close to the wagon, under which we slept. To add to the miseries of the trip it rained, and one night when the wagon was mired and we could not shelter under it, we slept with our feet pushed under it and an old cotton umbrella spread over our faces. Sometimes we went down the mountains, they were so steep we tied great trees behind to keep the wagon from falling over the oxen; and once when the whole surface of the mountain side was smooth, slippery rock, the oxen stiffened and their legs, and the wagon and all literally slid down a quarter of a mile. But the longest way has an end. At last we caught a glimpse of the miners' huts far down in the gulch and reached the end of our journey."*

In spite of the overwhelming challenges the Wilsons faced en route to California, many travelers before them considered them to be fortunate. Gravel markers lined the wagon trail west. Burials were common, especially when cholera struck. Some died in battles fought with Native Americans trying to protect their lands, but more succumbed to illness, accidents, and to violence among wagon train members. Women died during childbirth along the way, and their children fell before all manner of disease and fatal mishaps.

Luzena, Mason, and their children were among the more than twenty-five thousand people who came west in 1849. The journal she started at the beginning of their harrowing trip did not end when she arrived in California on October 1, 1849. Luzena wrote about her time at the immigrant campsite in Sacramento where the family initially settled. *"The population was about two thousand wood buildings, forty-five cloth and tent, three hundred campfires, etc., in the open air and under trees,"* Luzena recorded in her memoirs about the Gold Rush town.

Given the daily growth of the area, Luzena determined there was a great need for a boarding house. Mason agreed, and the two decided to go into the hospitality business. They sold their oxen for $600 and purchased a hotel called the Trumbow House. The majority of boarders at the Trumbow House were men. There were few women in Sacramento or the outlying gold mining camps. Luzena's homemaking skills were well received and in high demand. Guests were charged $17.50 a week for a clean room, laundry services, and savory meals. During the two months she operated the boarding house there was never a vacant room. Everyday more and more immigrants poured in from the plains or got off the steamers that brought them to California via the Isthmus of Panama—each one was eager to get to the mountains to hunt for gold. *"The world will never see the like again of those 'pioneers of 49,'* Luzena recalled in her journal. *"They were, as a rule, uptight, energetic, and hard-working, many of them men of education and*

Placerville, California, Ca. 1854.

culture whom the misfortune of poverty had forced into the ranks of labor in this strange country."

A major flood in Sacramento, combined with a flurry of excitement about gold nuggets lying in the streets of Nevada City, prompted Mason to uproot his family again and head for the hills in March 1850. Nevada City was sixty miles from Sacramento. The Wilsons lacked the funds to purchase a wagon and team to get to the boomtown. A miner with a vehicle and horse was on his way to Nevada City and offered to take Luzena, Mason, her boys, a stove, and two sacks of flour with him for $700. *"This looked hopeless, and I told him I guessed we wouldn't go as we had no money,"* she explained in her memoirs. *"I must have carried my honesty in my face, for he looked at me a minute and said, 'I'll take you, Ma'am, if you will assure me the money.' I promised him it should be paid, if I lived, and we made the money, So, pledged to a new master, Debt, we pressed forward on the road. It took twelve days to make it to the bustling mining camp. A row of canvas tents lined each of the two ravines leading to the tent city, and the gulches were crawling with men panning for gold. Donner Pass, a seven-thousand-foot barricade of naked rock lay beyond the camp."*

Mason was in a hurry to start his search for gold. After he built a crude shelter to help keep his wife and children warm and dry, he hurried off to stake out a claim. Luzena quickly went to work unpacking, making beds, and firing up her stove. As she worked, she contemplated how she was going to help make good on the cost it took to transport her family to the area. *"As always occurs to the mind of a woman, I thought of taking in boarders,"* she wrote in her journal. *"So, I bought two boards from a precious pile belonging to a man who was building the second wooden house in town. With my own hands I chopped stakes, drove them into the ground, and set up my table. I bought provisions from a neighboring store, and when my husband came back at night he found, mid the weird light of the pine torches, twenty miners eating at my table. Each man as he rose put a $1 in my hand and said I might count him as a permanent customer."*

Within six weeks of opening her business, Luzena had earned enough to pay the money owed to the miner who brought the Wilsons to Nevada. She also expanded and renovated the hotel and purchased a

Nevada City, California, Ca. 1856. Photo by Julia Ann Rudolph.

new stove. By the end of the summer in 1850, Luzena had an average seventy-five to two hundred boarders living at the establishment, each paying $25 a week.

She named her establishment El Dorado after the fabled kingdom in Spanish America supposedly rich in precious metals and jewels, which had lured sixteenth century explorers away from their homes. In addition to the clean accommodations offered at Luzena's were her biscuits. It was not uncommon for men who survived on a regular diet of beans and bacon to offer Luzena $5 for one biscuit. The hotel's reputation grew, attracting more and more customers. Late in 1850, Luzena expanded her commercial enterprise, hiring cooks and waiters.

It was clear to Luzena that the best way to strike it rich in a gold camp was to provide the necessities of life to the miners swinging pick axes and dumping dirt into rockers and gold pans. Mason agreed and abandoned his quest for a strike. Luzena then made him her business partner. The couple expanded their holdings. They built a mercantile and furnished it with all the supplies prospectors needed.

After six months of hard work, Luzena's El Dorado Hotel was estimated to be worth $10,000, and the stock of goods in the new store was worth even more. *"The buildings were of the roughest possible description,"* Luzena noted in her journal. *"They were to Nevada City what the Palace Hotel was to San Francisco."*

Not long after the Wilson's mercantile opened for business, Luzena recognized a need for a bank in the area and determined to provide for the growing community. *"There was no place of deposit for money,"* Luzena noted in her memoirs, *"and the men living in the house dropped into the habit of leaving their [gold] dust with me for safe keeping. At times I have had a larger amount of money in my charge than would furnish capital for a country bank."* Luzena did provide capital for Nevada City residents at ten percent interest on loans. Her kitchen was also her bank vault. *"Many a night have I shut my oven door on two milk-pans filled high with bags of gold dust,"* she wrote in her memoirs, *"and I have often slept with my mattress literally lined with the precious metal. And at one time I must have had more than $200,000 lying unprotected in my bedroom...."*

Luzena never worried about being robbed. According to her journal entries, *"lawbreakers were dealt with quickly and harshly."* On July 22, 1850,

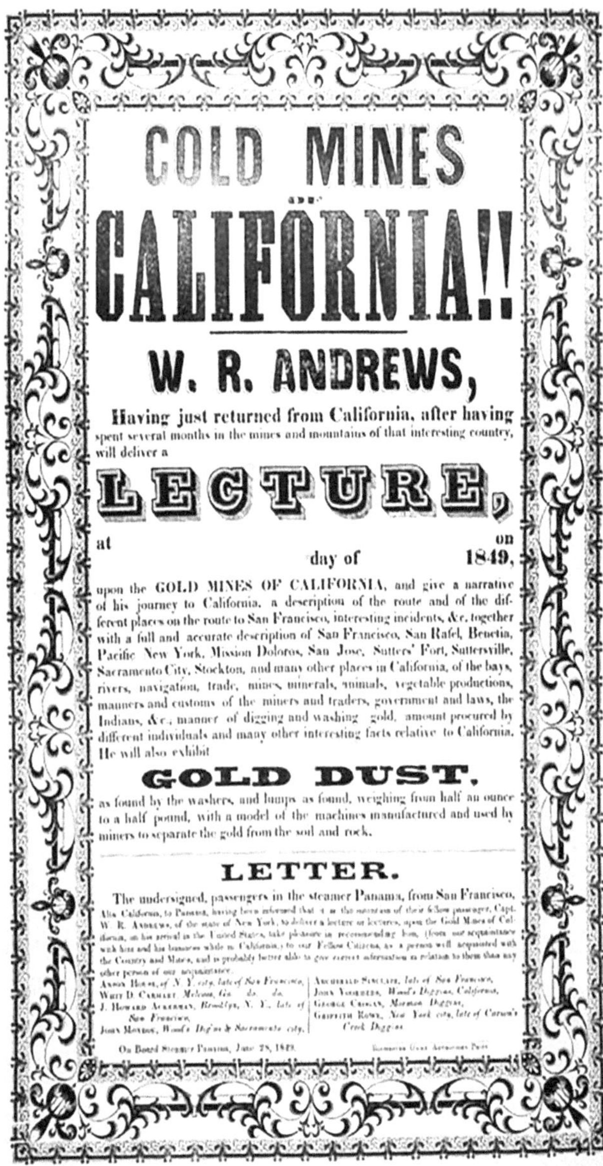

she witnessed the severe punishment inflicted upon a man who had stolen a mule. *"He did not travel far before he was overtaken and brought before a jury,"* the *Sacramento Transcript* newspaper reported on the scene. *"He was found guilty of theft, not only of the mule, but also the earnings of the young man who had placed confidence in him, [and who] gave him his bag of gold dust to take out.... The verdict of guilty was given...and his punishment twenty-five lashes on his bare back, and [he was] compelled to work at $5 per day...."*

Luzena enjoyed eighteen months of prosperity before she, Mason, and her sons, along with eight thousand other Nevada City residents, were left homeless and virtually destitute. *"Some careless hand had set fire to a pile of pine shavings lying at the side of the house in course of construction,"* Luzena recorded in her memoirs, *"and while we slept, unconscious of danger, the flames caught and spread, and in a short half hour the whole town was in a blaze."* The Wilsons lost nearly everything they owned. Mason had $500 in his pocket he had forgotten to place in the stove the night before. The couple used that money to make a new start for themselves.

Luzena found a few pieces of unburned canvas and some wooden planks; Mason pulled her stove from the ruins of the boarding house, and the pair set up another eatery. Once everything was in place, Luzena wasted no time returning to what she did best, which was cooking. Her culinary skills were popular during the rebuilding of the mining camp. She provided meals from dawn until dusk at prices she believed the struggling community could tolerate. In early July 1850, a prospector who appeared as though he could not afford anything gave Luzena a gold claim in exchange for one of her delicious dinners. The gold claim was a half a block from where her business stood before the fire. He told her he had removed $16,000 from the mine the day before. She eagerly agreed to the payment, imagining the mine would be a quick way to renew the fortune she had lost. Mason was opposed to the idea, however, and didn't want to work a claim. He felt the painstaking effort seldom resulted in a rich find and that the prospector had probably located all the gold to be had on that spot. Luzena sold the property for $100 to a miner. A few days prior to the Wilsons leaving the area to move back to Sacramento, the miner pulled $10,000 in gold out of the diggings.

Unlike the time it took for the Wilsons to travel to Nevada City, it was only a two-day journey returning to Sacramento. During their stay in Nevada City, the roads had been drastically improved.

Luzena and Mason purchased another boarding house in Sacramento. *"We took possession of a deserted hotel which stood on K Street,"* Luzena wrote in her memoirs. *"This hotel was tenanted only by rats that galloped madly over the floor and made journeys from room to room through openings they had gnawed in the panels.... At the time, Sacramento was infested with the horrible creatures."*

After three months, the Wilsons moved on to a valley north of Sacramento called Benicia. The beautiful area was ideal for the pair and their children.

Illustration of a boarding house in Sacramento, ca. 1850.

Their goal was to purchase land and stay there for the rest of their lives. *"We were again penniless, however, and felt that we must get to work,"* Luzena noted in her journal. *"Hay was selling in San Francisco at a $150 a ton, so my husband, leaving me to my own resources, set hard at work cutting and making hay; and I, as before, set up my stove and camp kettle and hung out my sign, printed with charred fire-brand on a piece of board, it read Wilson's Hotel."*

Within six months of opening, Luzena had earned a substantial amount of money, and the Wilson's Hotel had earned the reputation of being the best on the route from Sacramento to Benicia. Mason supplied the variety of meat Luzena served to her boarders. Elk, antelope, geese, pheasant, cattle, and bear were all on the menu at various times. On April 21, 1851, the Wilsons were able to purchase two hundred acres of land along Alamo Creek. Seven months later they bought three parcels in Vaca and another one hundred acres south of town.

Mason's hay business was as profitable as Luzena's boarding house. For a time, things were going very well for the pair and their sons, and then a heavy, substantial rain came and wiped out Mason's crops. Not long after that, government surveyors came to officially lay out the town of Benicia in Vaca Valley. They divided the valley including all the land the Wilsons had purchased. Immigrants quickly moved in and squatted on Luzena and Mason's property. *"My husband was furious,"* Luzena recalled in her memoirs. *"He swore that he would either have the land or kill every man who disputed his ownership. He left the house on an errand of ejectment, taking with him a witness, in case he should be killed or be forced to kill the squatters, many of whom knew and feared his reckless and determined purpose, would not have hesitated to dispose of him with a bullet."*

The courts were called upon to intercede and settle the matter; in the interim, the Wilsons moved from Benicia to Vaca Valley. Using the profits made from the Wilson Hotel, Luzena bought lumber and bricks to build the family's home and a new boarding house business. The wooden structure was the first one of its kind built in Vaca Valley. Luzena's new business was as successful as her previous one. Well-respected judges, such as Murray Morrison and Justice Serranus Clinton Hastings of the California Supreme Court, were frequent guests at the establishment.

In January 1855, Luzena and Mason welcomed

Three men panning for gold while a woman looks on during the California Gold Rush, ca. 1850.

a third son to their family, Mason Jr. In May 1857, the couple welcomed a daughter, Correnah. The Wilsons continued to invest the money made from Luzena's boarding house in real estate. By the end of 1859, Luzena and Mason owned a considerable portion of the Vaca Valley town site and more than five hundred acres of surrounding lands.

By 1858, the Wilsons had outgrown the small, temporary hotel they initially built in the area and decided to have a new one constructed at a cost of $14,000. The new business had two stories, a billiard room, and a large parlor. Mason became an agent for the Wells Fargo Company and operated the Wells Fargo office out of the hotel.

In December 1872, after twenty-eight years of marriage, Mason abandoned his wife and family to travel to Missouri and Texas. Luzena never saw Mason again. Rumors circulated during that time suggested that Mason might have been suffering from a mental illness. Other people insisted that he had simply become miserable living with Luzena. Willis Jepson, one of Mason's friends, wrote a letter to the Wilson's oldest son Jay explaining why he believed Mason chose to leave his home and family. *"Luzena, Forty-Niner, was a determined and strong-minded personage—a woman of the real pioneer type,"* Jepson noted. *"But even so her husband, your father, became wearied. He could stand Luzena no longer and went away from Vaca Valley. He put as much distance between himself and Luzena as well as he could."* Ten years after Mason left Luzena and California, word came from an attorney in Waco, Texas, that he had passed away.

In 1881, Luzena's daughter helped her compile her remembrances into a book entitled *Argonaut: A Woman's Reminiscences of Early Days.* Solano County historian Sabine Goerke-Shrode called Luzena's book *"an important historical source illustrating the Gold Rush from a woman's perspective."*

On July 11, 1902, Luzena died of thyroid cancer. She was eighty-three years old. According to her obituary, that ran in the July 12, 1902, edition of the *Woodland Daily Democrat* newspaper, Luzena's funeral service was held at her daughter's home. *"Mrs. Wilson was a respected pioneer of Solano County, and was for many years a resident of Vaca Valley,"* the notice informed readers. *"Mrs. Wilson was a noble woman and her death will be profoundly regretted."*

Chris Enss *is a* New York Times *bestselling author who has written about women of the Old West for more than thirty years. She's penned more than fifty books on the subject and been honored with nine Will Rogers Medallion Awards, two Elmer Kelton Book Awards, an Oklahoma Center for the Book Award, three* Foreword Review Magazine *Book Awards, and the Laura Downing Journalism Award.*

WWW.DUSTYRICHARDS.COM

BENJAMIN THOMAS

CANVAS SKY

A SHORT STORY

1848

That damned fly.

Bouncing off the stretched canvas again and again. Trapped, or so it thinks. Angry buzzing. Not smart enough to try a different route of escape. Just bounce, bounce, bounce, stop and rest for a spell, then bounce again. And all the time, buzzing. Annoying as all get out.

Although now that he thought about it, James admitted it provided something to stare at. Something besides the dirty gray canvas forming the roof of the wagon. Just frustrating that the fly refused to try any other direction.

Mayhap a metaphor for his own life. Always headed in the same direction... no matter how many times he failed.

And now he was dying.

Stubborn damned fly couldn't leave a man in peace. He continued to stare at it. Nothing much else to do. Lying helpless, flat on his back didn't leave him many options for entertainment. Anything to take his mind off the earthy stink of the wagon's canvas cover and the monotony of the never-ending trail.

A groan caught his attention until he realized it had come from deep within his own chest as the wagon rolled over a particularly large stone or clump of grass. Or maybe it was a wide crevasse or something. Made no matter. When a man lay gut-shot and feverish, any jolt in the wagon was bound to irritate.

After another ten minutes or so of incessant jolts and lurches, the wagon master called for a halt. Thank God. A respite from the jostling, no matter how short the break, was welcome indeed. But why the halt? Too early to stop for the day, unless he had passed out and it was now later than he'd thought. Hard to tell where the sun lay when their trail had them creeping in and out of the steep mountain passes of the Sangre de Christos. Must be an obstacle of some kind. No way they'd stop any sooner than necessary. Not after yesterday's massacre in Manco Burro Pass.

Yesterday? Or was it the day before?

Sounds of horses nickering and snorting mixed with orders shouted from the wagon master, Lucien Maxwell. His voice was calm, reassuring as it had been even back in the Pass, a fact that had probably saved some of their lives. Several minutes later, the canvas flaps parted at the rear of the wagon. A welcome puff of cool air caressed James's scarred cheeks. He tried to look down the length of his body to take a gander at his visitor, but he couldn't bend his neck. That was new.

Soft, whispering footsteps neared him. Not boots. Moccasins. Indian George, then.

"Checking on you." A man of few words was Indian George. He'd been the devoted servant of Charles Bent until the former New Mexico Territorial Governor's death in 1847. Then the Cherokee had transferred his allegiance to fur trapper and guide, Lucien Maxwell.

"I'm just dandy," James said. "Be up and at 'em shortly."

A grunt was the only reply. The Cherokee moved up closer so James could see him clearly. The ruddy, lined face was blank, but the eyes were deep pools of oily blackness. Clearly, he would not reply further.

James asked, "How's Maxwell doing anyhow? He caught an arrowhead or two, I know. Heard how you packed him on your back and carted him all the way out of the Pass. That's a good many miles."

The attempt at flattery seemed to have fallen on deaf ears. Indian George just gazed at him for a minute or two, those dark eyes looking deep into him. Delving into his future, probably. Finally, he said, "He will be good. He is not good now. You, also, are not good now."

"Sounds kinda like you think I won't be good later, either."

Another grunt. Then, just as swiftly as he had appeared, Indian George backed out of the wagon, leaving James alone with his thoughts.

An eternity passed but was probably more like half an hour. The canvas flaps parted once more. Had the Indian come back? Scuffling sounds came to his ears with that eerie sort of echo that always happened inside the wagon when it was covered. His visitor, evidently, was crawling over supplies in the wagon. Next came a bang, followed by a whispered curse, then a face entered James's range of vision. It was a pretty young woman's face this time, light brown hair tucked behind one ear, and a smile as big as Georgia. A crooked tooth at the top left just added to her charms.

Luisa.

"Hi, darlin'." Her voice was sweet as molasses and completely unconcerned.

Seemed like he hadn't seen her in a coon's age. He tried returning her smile but realized it was more like a grimace.

"Hi, yerself."

"How're you? Getting to lollygag back here in comfort instead of putting more miles on that old nag of yours." The gentle tones of her accent reminded him of his Mississippi home.

He knew what she was doing, of course. Taking his mind off things. Teasing him, like usual. He let his gaze roam across her features. Sharp cheekbones, dimpled chin, light freckles across her little pointy nose. The crooked tooth. And those eyes. He could fall in and drown in those emerald-green eyes.

She was waiting for his answer, so he tossed out a throwaway line about enjoying the view from under the canvas sky. But he couldn't just carry on like all was right with the world. He let his smile drop and then murmured, "I ain't gonna make it, honey. Not with this kind of belly shot."

"Oh, pshaw." She moved his blanket aside and tugged at the cloth that wrapped around his thick torso, as if examining his wound. The sound of a soft crackle puzzled him until he realized it was dried blood on the cloth, splitting as she moved it. She said, "Well, this don't look so bad."

He could tell she was lying.

A few more minutes passed while she took her look-see and then wrapped him up again. Then her face came back into view. "You've been in worse shape before. Remember back when we met? Now that right there was some serious wounds."

"Yep. It was May, wasn't it? About seven years ago? On the Trace."

"Natchez, yes. But it was eight years ago. May the 8th, 1840, to be exact. The day after the big tornado."

"The Great Natchez Tornado. That's what they call it now." He smiled at the thought of such a moniker but then sobered at the remembrance. Over three hundred folks were counted among the dead and another two hundred injured.

"Worst damn tornado in our country's history. So far, anyway."

"Yes, well, what I remember most is the pretty young gal that nursed me back to health." He was pleased to see the blush rise in her cheeks.

"Some nurse. All I did was clean you up and slap bandages across all your holes."

"Not all of 'em." He started to laugh but his belly cut that off in a hurry.

She made as if to slap him, but her heart wasn't in it. "You had so many sticks comin' out of you, I thought I was working on a porcupine. That wind turned tree branches into arrows."

"Good thing there weren't no fence posts. Would have been hard bandaging over that kinda hole."

She shook her head slowly, remembering.

His thoughts, too, returned to that hellish day in May. The night before the monster slammed into town, lightning had ripped through heavy clouds. More than three inches of rain fell throughout the area. Vidalia was his home, just a small town on the river. Its only claim to fame was the Jim Bowie sandbar fight thirteen years earlier—already a legend. But then the twister came. Nobody prepared.

Nobody expected anything more than a thunderstorm.

"I remember you were among the first to see what was coming," she said. "Least ways, that's what you boasted later."

"It's true. I'd been on the river working a flatboat when I realized it was more than just a thunderstorm. Most folks were eating, the dinner bells having rung earlier, and I'd hoped they would have had the sense to stay indoors."

It had come from the Southwest, following the river, crashing over fields and forests. The noise came first, a murderous riot of massive trees being uprooted, huge timbers cracking and splitting. James had moved toward the nearby riverbank, but no sooner had he reached it than the roar of the beast came upon him. He'd run for a hill, dived over it, then looked back. His eyes tried to take in the width of the thing, touching both sides of the shore as it did, but his brain couldn't register its massiveness. He had seen other men nearby, screaming, but he couldn't hear them over the cacophony of the tornado. Something had whacked him over the head, bringing him blessed relief from the oncoming tempest and plunging him into darkness.

He'd come to in a bed, a single lamp illuminating the dark interior of a house. A soft sheet covered him, and for a few minutes, that's all he could concentrate on. Then he made out the caress of the sheet and the soft glow from the lamp. It wasn't his own house, that much he knew, but there was nobody else around, so he might as well lay there and enjoy it.

A girl's face appeared above him—pretty, framed by light brown hair and featuring a delicate, dimpled chin. She frowned in concern, and her pretty green eyes reflected the same. He tried to speak to her but discovered he couldn't open his mouth. She had shushed him, ordering him to keep quiet. She went on to describe his injuries, including a broken arm, several cracked ribs, and assorted scrapes, cuts, and bruises. But the look in her eyes told him there was more. Something she hadn't the heart to tell him. Why couldn't he speak? Or even open his mouth? He remembered lowering his eyelids and staring at her hard, attempting to communicate to her that he wanted to know the rest. Finally, she relented.

It was a tree branch. A good sized one, maybe an inch across. It had speared him through his jaw, entering from below, missing his lower teeth and then exiting through the cheek just above his mouth. His upper front teeth were gone, and his tongue frayed. She hoped he would eventually heal, if the infection didn't take him, but he would be scarred for life. And it would be weeks before he could take solid food.

As the time passed, James grew stronger. The feared infection never materialized but the torn muscles in his face meant having to learn how to talk all over again. He went through periods of deep depression, wondering if it mattered whether he lived or died. Through it all, she was there, nursing him through the pain and urging him past his reluctance to go on living.

Luisa. And they fell in love.

He looked at her now, sensing the similarities with the day they'd met. Him lying flat on his back with a dreadful injury and her leaning over him, ready to nurse him back to health through prodding, urging, arguing, joking, and storytelling to distract him from the pain.

"Penny for your thoughts," Luisa said, her voice soft as a kitten's purr but still managing to penetrate his memories. "What's that you're smiling about?"

"Ahhh...you know." He let his smile grow a little wider. "How you could come to love a feller with a mug like I got. Truly a blessing."

"Your mug, as you call it, don't look half bad, you know. Once your beard grew in, nobody could see the scars on your jaw."

"They're still there, though. Got a large area that won't grow nothing, so I've got to comb it over and kinda blend it into the other parts." His smile turned to a smirk. "And no mustache at all. If I tried, I'd end up with half a lip full of hair and nary a whisker on the other half."

"Well, that would be... different." Another smile, but it was more on her lips and not so much in her eyes. And that too melted away, turning to sorrow.

He reached out and cupped her chin with one calloused hand. "My little angel of mercy."

Silence stretched between them for a minute or two, then Luisa took his big hand in her two little ones. "Tell me, sweetie. How do you keep yourself entertained while you're lollygagging back here in the wagon?"

"There's that lollygagging accusation again. I swear, I shoulda gotten gut shot days ago so's I could enjoy all the entertainments available to me back here under this stinky canvas. What with the bouncing and the creaking, I've just been riding along as peaceable as if I was swayin' in our porch swing back home." He realized his tone was beginning to show some irritation and immediately felt bad. She was just trying to keep his mind off his trouble. "Well, there was one funny thing that happened this morning." He chuckled, gently as he could to keep the pain in check.

"Oh?"

"Yeah, it was a bird situation. With Lee."

"A... bird situation?"

"Yeah, you know... a bird flew over and... dropped a load. Right on Lee's forehead. Big white splotch. You know how his hair's receded so far back and how he's kinda sensitive about it? Well, he'd just taken his hat off and was stooping down to look in the back of the wagon. Checking on me, I suppose. Folks do that now and again. Anyway, there he was, just peering in at me and... splat!"

Luisa laughed, rocking back and forth on her knees, eyes twinkling with delight. "A big target, was it? That forehead of his?" Her laugh almost bordered on a snort. It was infectious, and James started to join in. But his insides shouted at him to stop, agony streaming up through his chest and into the back of his neck. Like a white-hot branding iron pressing into him. It left him breathless and light-headed.

Luisa, bless her heart, waited patiently, still gripping his hand with the both of hers. She made soft shushing noises as he struggled to find a point of

equilibrium. More silence. But eventually, as if nothing had happened, she once again tried to take his mind off the pain. "Tell me about the time you first met Lee. When was it? And where? I don't believe I've ever heard tell of it."

"Oh, you remember, surely. Well, I guess maybe you wouldn't. Let's see, what can I tell you...." As he pondered how to start the story, a slight tickle in his throat threatened a coming cough. He fought it off, waging war against the very idea of an actual cough and the inevitable result.

Managing a deep swallow to clear his throat and satisfy the tickle, he said, "I guess everything changed there at Bent's Fort. We'd come all the way from St. Louis, you know, picking up the Santa Fe Trail there in Independence. Trying for that new start we'd always talked about after the tornado. You remember how it was. Tried farming here and store clerking there, working our way up the Mississippi until we finally landed in St. Louis. But I have to say, that didn't work out so well, either. Then we heard about that treaty. You know, the one from the Mexican War. Guadalupe-Hidalgo or some such name they gave it. Anyways, the government wanted all that new land populated. Didn't want the Mexicans to ever lay claim to it again. So, we set out for the territories hoping, for opportunities. Always headed in the same direction but never learning a thing from our mistakes."

Another pause. Gotta fight that tickle a little longer—at least until he could finish telling her the story.

"Anyway, the regular Cimarron cutoff route to Santa Fe was proving to be a problem for other wagon trains due to the Indian troubles, so Lucien decided we'd head to the Fort to get some ideas on different ways to get ourselves down to New Mexico. We picked up Lee there. Elliot Lee. He was always particular about making sure you knew his name was Elliot, but we all just call him Lee."

Luisa nodded, encouraging him to continue talking.

"We also picked up the young'uns there at the Fort. Mary and James Tharp. Pretty young they are, about six and four, I think. Their pa was a trader but was killed by Comanche some time ago. We promised to take them to Fort Union where they had an uncle waiting for 'em."

"An admirable notion."

"Well, it's just a bit north of Las Vegas, so it was

pretty much on our route anyways. So, we set out from Bent's on the sixteenth of June. I remember because it was the day after my birthday.Was a gloomy, cloudy morn. Made me wish we'd waited a day longer. Lookin' back, I wish we had."

A strange something was bubbling up from his stomach. Sort of like syrup except it tasted like an old horseshoe. Swallowing again, he tried to ignore it. "Fourteen folks and our horses, wagons, and of course the two little Tharp children. We headed straight up the Santa Fe trail, looking toward Raton Pass. See, that's still the preferred route if you skip the Cimmaron cutoff. But when we got down to the Purgatory River, we saw some Apache sign. Mister Town... well, he had told us of another way, just a little east of Raton, through the Manco Burro Pass. 'A perfectly easy route,' he called it. Better than the Raton route, anyway, as Colonel Kearny proved when he and his Army of the West came through in the summer of '46. Remember that? Uh... never mind. They left parts of wagons scattered all along the Raton passage. So, Lucien made the call, and Manco Burro was the way we went."

Luisa stared at him, lips tight, and eyes like pools of rain, ready to spill over.

James had to clear his throat again, but now the iron taste had turned to something more like vinegar. "At noon on the nineteenth, we reached the little valley up top at the pass. Lucien called a halt for the wagons so we could eat our lunch and let the horses graze a little ways away. Most of the grass in that area was dry as old hay but there was this one patch. Beautiful green grass it was. Young growth. Healthy looking, you know?

"Yes, I know just what you mean. Sweet grass, we used to call it back home."

"That's right." He smiled up at her and saw the edges of her face were a little blurry. The tears in his eyes, still unshed, made him blink rapidly for a second, then her face was back as it should be. "And then... then it was that we heard 'em. Jicarilla Apaches, they was. Thousands of 'em. Least ways, it seemed like that."

"Oh, James. Don't tell me no more. Not if it strains you so."

"No. I need to tell it. So's you know what happened. Let me tell it. It's important somehow. Please."

She was still for a moment, looking solid as a statue, brows worried together. Then she nodded.

"At first, we just heard their yellin' and whoopin'. Then we saw they was trying to run off our horses. As they passed us by, we fired on 'em but they was so far off that it weren't effective. After a few minutes, they came back. Surrounded our little camp. Set fire to the grass. The dry grass, anyways. But we kept our position. Held 'em off like King Arthur and his knights. Heh. Now there's an image for you. We needed to keep the wagons safe—the baggage, you see. Couldn't make it much further without the baggage. We fired at everything we could, but we were outnumbered. By a whole lot. We lasted a good long while though. Three or four hours, judging by the sun. By then, five of us was wounded and old Joe was killed dead." He lifted an arm, and shakily pointed at the canteen that lay nearby. "Some water, please. My throat."

"Of course." Luisa opened the canteen then trickled some water into his open mouth. It took some effort to swallow it, but he felt better.

"Anyhow, we couldn't hold out forever, so we tried to high tail it to the mountains. We weren't able to take much with us, but Indian George had gotten a couple of horses hitched up to a wagon by then. This wagon here, as a matter of fact. Not much in the way of supplies, but we got some stashed in here as we lit out. Mister Town was behind us all when I heard him cry out. Shot in the leg and couldn't walk no further. Couldn't get himself up to where the wagon was neither, so he got left behind. A Spaniard was also shot—through the kidneys—and fell by the wayside. Feel bad that I don't know his name, now I think on it. Lee took one in the thigh but could still amble along. I turned to help him, and that's when I got mine. Smack in the middle of my belly. Didn't seem too bad at first. Lots of blood, but I was able to get on for a while. That left eleven of us, counting the two children. Eight of us wounded. Lucien and Indian George stayed behind to draw their fire. Later I found out Lucien caught a couple of arrows, but Indian George carted him out on his back. Pretty amazing when you think about it." He paused a moment then added, "But still, we managed to escape."

He had to stop again, his chest heaving up and down as he tried to keep enough breath to finish the story. He wasn't certain he'd make it but knew deep down inside it was important he did.

"Night came on. We traveled along until we

come to water. We all huddled together, trying to rest and maybe get some sleep. I don't remember doing it, but I blacked out. Woke up here in the wagon. Somebody had taken off my shirt and used it to wrap up my gut like it is now. Holding me together, mostly. Anyways, it was still night, and we were moving on through the mountains. Lucien was afraid to travel in the day, see, and wanted to make sure we was far away from the Jicarilla. That was night before last. I think. I've not been out of this damned wagon since."

Luisa had taken a bit of her shawl, dribbled some canteen water on it and was busy wiping down his forehead. The familiar worry lines between her brows were deep as he'd ever seen. She seemed distracted somewhat, not certain his story was done. But then her eyes darted to his, her gaze softened, and she said, "And now you're headed to Fort Union, I suppose."

"Yep. Heard Lucien tell somebody he thought it was near ninety miles away still. Maybe we can get patched up there."

She wiped his brow some more, content to let the comfortable silence linger a while. He'd always enjoyed watching her and relished the opportunity to do it some more now. His thoughts traveled back through time, back once more to when they met after the tornado in Mississippi, their courting after he had recovered from his wounds, the wedding on the little pier jutting out into a calm bend in the river, and the jokes their friends had played on them during the so-called honeymoon. All of it was crystal clear in his memory. But her face, as he looked at her now, was blurry, his tears getting in the way.

No, he thought. It wasn't his tears. Something else. Just a little bit more time. Just a little bit longer to spend with her. Don't let it all fade away now.

The coolness of the damp cloth on his forehead soothed him, relaxed him.

She whispered to him, her voice soft as a light breeze among the trees. "Don't fret, my darling. We will be together again, very soon. And this time, we will never part."

He tried to see her, but all he could make out was that damned fly, bumping and buzzing up against the canvas.

Lucien Maxwell had called for wagons ready almost fifteen minutes earlier and now grew frustrated they hadn't yet departed. Break time was over. They should have been on the trail by now. There was only one wagon left, after all. Where was that Indian George? He would get 'em moving.

He turned, then his face flushed at his irritation. Indian George stood right behind him, face impassive as always. But there was something around his eyes, something that told Lucien not all was well.

"What is it?" Lucien said. "What's happened?"

"James." Indian George shook his head sadly. "We've lost another one."

Lucien bowed his head. It had been inevitable with such a wound, but the man had lasted much longer than he'd expected, so he'd held out some hope.

"Funny thing, though," said Indian George. "I overheard him talking. From the wagon. He was telling the story of our recent experiences with the Jicarilla."

"Telling it to...who?"

"His wife."

"His wife? Luisa?" The wagon master reached a hand to his jaw to scratch at his beard but stopped it halfway up. "But Luisa died three years ago. Cholera, I think it was."

Indian George nodded, his face just as stoic as always. But then a slight smile broke through.

"Sometimes we need a little help to make the final journey. It is, perhaps, for the best. They are together now."

THE AUTHOR

***Benjamin Thomas** is a retired US Air Force Medical Service Corps officer and former National Organ Transplant program officer for Veteran's Affairs. He has authored numerous short stories as well as a time travel novel and a historical whodunnit. Published works can be found in western anthologies published by the Western Fictioneers as well as Saddlebag Dispatches. Additionally, he is the author of the interconnected "Leland and Charlie" stories featuring a grandfather/granddaughter duo as they travel through Colorado in the 1850s collecting bounties by outconning the conmen. A native of New Mexico, Benjamin has always been a "westerner" at heart, currently enjoying life with his family in Colorado Springs at the foot of Pikes Peak.*

GAMBLING QUEEN OF THE GOLD RUSH

Born Simone Jules in Louisiana in 1829, Eleanor Dumont—better known by her cruel nickname, Madame Mustache—forged an extraordinary life as a professional gambler, brothel owner, and frontier legend.

STORY BY
TERRY ALEXANDER

She was often called "The Frenchwoman." She was born Simone Jules in Louisiana in 1829, to French Creole parents. In 1850, at twenty-one years she arrived in San Francisco, California at the height of the gold rush. At this time, the line of dark hair on her upper lip was barely noticeable. She called herself Eleanor Dumont, worked as a professional gambler, and dealt cards at the Bella Union Hotel. This was a privilege only afforded to women on the Las Vegas strip in 1971. She had a look that captivated the men in the gambling halls. She dressed in the finest clothes and had a quick mind with easy words to ensure her rapport with her customers. The men in San Francisco dressed in their finest clothes to spend time at her table.

After she was accused of cardsharping and fired from the Bella Union, she knew it was time to move on and decided to strike out on her own. In 1854, she arrived by stagecoach in the mining town of Nevada City, California. The local miners were hungry for female companionship, and they had deep pockets filled with gold nuggets. For four days after her arrival, she wandered up and down Broad Street, dressed in her best finery. She spent hours peering into the windows looking for the perfect spot to open her casino.

She eventually found the building she wanted and opened her casino. She named the business Vingt-et-Un (21 in French.) One local newspaper described it as the *"Best gambling emporium in northern California."* The grand gambling hall was fifty feet long and decorated with luxurious carpets, with gas-powered chandeliers, and modern plush furnishings. The finest wines and liquors were served while a small orchestra played in the background. It was the only casino in California at the time that had a dress code. The local miners had to bathe and wear their finest clothes before they were allowed inside her establishment.

Eleanor became romantically involved with a fellow professional gambler named David Tobin. She invited him to help manage the casino, and this al-

The Bella Union Hotel in San Francisco, California, ca. 1855, where Eleanor Dumont dealt cards in from 1850 to 1854.

lowed her to open a second venue, named Dumont's Place. It specialized in games not played at Vingt-et-Un, including keno, roulette, poker, chuck-a-luck (a game played with three dice,) and faro. When the prospectors moved on to new areas and towns, Dumont and Tobin followed. The arrangement soured, and Tobin returned to New York.

Eleanor relocated to Columbia, California, in 1857, and opened a casino in a hotel. Around 1860, she made a serious attempt at domestic life. With her savings, she bought a ranch in Carson City, Nevada. She didn't know anything about cattle and ranching. She met a well-dressed saloon keeper named Jack McKnight. She fell in love with Jack and within a few months they were married. Eleanor signed the ranch over to him so he could manage the property. A few months later, he had sold everything and skipped town, leaving her with a mound of debt. She had no choice but to return to the gambling tables.

The experience with McKnight soured Eleanor. She became a heavy drinker, and indulged in some of the harshest liquor, taking less care in her appearance. The fine hair above her lip became darker, and she became more cynical. She began carrying a gun wherever she went. Rumors said that she met up with McKnight later in life and killed him with a blast from a double-barreled shotgun. She was never charged with his murder, but admitted later in life that she did kill him for leaving her penniless. Eleanor followed the miners and traveled to Nevada Montana, Idaho, Arizona, and Utah.

One night she horse-whipped a man who was caught cheating at her gambling table at Fort Benton, Montana. In 1864, in Bannack, Montana, Eleanor opened a brothel to supplement her gambling earnings. One of her employees was a fifteen-year-old girl named Martha Jane Cannary, who would later bcome known as Calamity Jane. While in Bannack, she drummed up business by having her girls dress in their finest outfits and driving them around the town in open carriages, making special slow trips by the railroad construction camps. One night in Bannack, she was accosted by two men as she was leaving the gambling table. They demanded the money

Martha Jane Cannary, better known by her nickname of "Calamity Jane," worked at a brothel owned by Eleanor Dumont in Bannack, Montana in 1864.

she had won. She opened her purse on the pretense of giving the toughs the money, instead she pulled a pistol free and killed one of the would-be bandits. The other turned and fled.

In the late 1860's, she acquired the cruel nickname that would stay with her the rest of her life. A drunk miner once referred to her as "Madame Mustache." The moniker stuck, although no one would address her by that name to her face. As she aged, the fine hair on her upper lip darkened, and one day a disgruntled gambler threw the insult to her face. She swallowed the insult and kept chasing the miners.

In the 1870's, she traveled to several states and some places that were only territories. Rough places where a life wasn't worth much. She spent time in Boise City, in the Oklahoma Territory, Cheyenne, Wyoming, Blackfoot City, Idaho, Eureka, Nevada, Tombstone, Arizona., While she was in Arizona, she opened a gambling parlor and a house of ill repute that rivaled Blonde Marie's. She later ended up in Deadwood, South Dakota. She ran into an old acquaintance in Deadwood.

Martha Jane, now called herself Calamity Jane and worked part time as a muleskinner and a cavalry scout. The two became close friends and Eleanor tried to teach Jane how to be a successful gambler. Jane's ability with the pasteboards never improved. In 1878, Eleanor settled in Modesto for a week-long visit on her way to Bodie.

Eleanor arrived in Bodie in 1879, she began dealing Twenty-One at the Magnolia Saloon on Main Street. She was greeted warmly, and the miners swarmed her table, anxious to play. In September of that year, she had a run of bad luck and lost most of her money. She borrowed three hundred dollars from one of her friends and opened her table, hopeful to win enough money to repay the loan and give her a cushion to work from.

She lost all the money in a few hours. She excused herself and left the saloon. Eleanor walked down the Bridgeport Road, after she had traveled approximately a mile, she left the dirt road and ventured into the grass and weeds off the roadside. She drank a mixture of wine and Morphine.

A sheepherder found her body on September 8th. She left a note addressed to the public administrator of Bodie. She stated she had grown tired of life and wanted to be buried next to a newspaper editor in San Francisco. Her last request was denied, and she was interred in Bodie, California. She was placed with the outcasts and the sinners outside the fence. The miners collected enough money for her to have a first-rate funeral. Two special carriages arrived from Sacramento for the service. Although she had a headstone, it vanished over time and the location of her grave is now unknown.

Terry Alexander *and his wife, Phyllis, live on a small farm near Porum, Oklahoma. They have three children, thirteen grandchildren, and four great grandchildren. If you see him at a conference, though, don't let him convince you to take part in one of his trivia games–he'll stump you every time.*

we shoot life.

not just posing for pretty pictures.

Porch Pig Productions

Candid

Event photography

patricia@porchpigproductions.com

www.porchpigproductions.org

THOM BRUCIE

LEGEND OF THE LAURELWOOD TIE

A SHORT STORY

On Monday, the tenth day of May, in the year 1869, Governor Leland Stanford of California drove a gold spike into the ceremonial laurelwood tie at Promontory Summit, Utah, thereby joining the burgeoning East Coast cities with the Wild West pioneers of the Pacific. Governor Stanford did not actually drive the spike. Having begun the celebration of the joining of the rails the night before, he awoke that morning with a hangover. The noise of celebratory activity hammered in his ears like the dense echo of a train whistle inside a long tunnel. Such inebriation derailed his hand-eye coordination, and he hit the rail instead of the spike. The hammer ricocheted, leaving the gold spike sticking in the bore-hole. One of the laborers tapped the spike home before Mr. Andrew J. Russell snapped his famous picture of the event.

The jubilant mishap did not discourage Mr. Michael Strahle, the carpenter in San Francisco who crafted the laurelwood tie. In fact, at the same instant the spike settled into the laurelwood, Mr. Strahle's eyesight returned.

The occurrence of young Mr. Strahle's regenerated eyesight remains a mysterious and relatively unknown piece of the legend of the laurelwood tie.

As the completion of the inter-continental railway drew near, plans for the artifacts intended to memorialize the occasion included a special tie made from California laurel. Laurel, since ancient times, has represented greatness in achievement. Accordingly, Mr. West Evans, the tie contractor for the Central Pacific Railroad, enlisted the craftsmen at Strahle and Hughes, a manufacturer of quality billiard tables, and a company known to have used, on occasion, the rare laurel.

When word got around to the shop that Strahle and Hughes won the tie contract, Michael Strahle, the owner's son, went to his father's office.

"I want to make the tie," Michael said.

"You? Why?"

"We're going to have our name on it. It should be me to find the tree and make the tie."

"This task is both delicate and dangerous, Michael. I prefer a more seasoned hand."

"Surely, I'm seasoned enough."

"The laurel is a mysterious wood, and any laurel that grows into a tree is a rarity."

"I know," Michael said. "And I know its names. Pepperwood. Spicebush. Balm of Heaven."

"Yes, it has a strong aroma. Yet, it carries another name as well. Headache Tree. Do you know why it carries this name, son?"

"No, sir."

"The cutting of such beauty carries a price. The beauty of nature is all about us, and when we find extraordinary beauty, such beauty must be shared."

"What do you mean?"

"If you find a laurel tree, you must kill it to make the tie. Nature does not complain that men take of her beauty. But when you destroy a gift of beauty, to amend, you must create a gift of beauty. If you choose this responsibility, you will be bound to it."

"You have taught me to love the wood, and I do. If I am to carry the company after you, I must be the one."

Strahle paused, considering Michael's attitude and perhaps his maturity for this task.

"All right, then," he conceded. "But I will name Steward Franklin as your guide. The wilds are full of danger, and the search will test you. Listen to him."

Just past mid-day of their first day into the denseness of forest altitude, Michael and Franklin stopped at the top of a ridge. Michael drank from his canteen. "Invigorating up here."

Franklin nodded.

Michael pointed north. "Think we can reach that valley and make camp before sundown?"

Franklin looked with a practiced eye. "Might make a safe descent off to the right. Then back to the left into the valley."

Michael nodded agreement.

By the time the men found the valley floor, the sun reached the far horizon and provoked an orange sky and pink-tinted clouds. They strung a rope and tethered the horses and pack mule. This way, the animals acted as lookouts, alert to any nighttime dangers. Franklin shot a short-eared rabbit. After he cleaned it, they ate it with beans.

"We made a good first day," Michael said.

"It'll take time, Michael. No guarantees, you know."

"I know. But, still, it was a good first day."

They searched two more days. They let the horses travel with an easy gait through the ancient forest, and the land, though accessible and beautiful, remained alien.

Near noon of the third day, Franklin suddenly reined his horse.

"Will you look at that?"

Michael raised his head, uncertain what to look for.

Franklin walked his pony to a strange-looking tree. From the sturdy branch of a yew, near eye level, another tree, a sycamore, grew straight up—a rare twinning of trees.

"It's a double-tree," Franklin said.

"What's a double-tree?"

"The Chilula tribe hereabouts tells of them. They say they're magic. Claim good luck in a hunt to any who come upon one."

"Is that so?"

"I ain't never seen one before today, but if it's true, Michael, you may just find your laurel after all."

"Well, I should take a leaf for good luck."He reached up and grabbed a leafy twig from the sycamore.

"No, Michael," Steward cautioned. "Wait. They also tell that any man who harms one will suffer."

Michael snapped the small branch and cinched it in his belt.

"I will accept the good luck and the bad, as I must. But I will call for the good."

Franklin stared at Michael as if seeing him for the first time. The young man did not seem deterred by omens.

They continued on. The deep, shadowy solitude of dense redwood growth enclosed them. Within the confines of two-thousand-year-old giants, even the rattle of a woodpecker and the rustling of wind became components of the landscape. Lost in the power of their surroundings, they meandered into a sunlit meadow, in the center of which stood a laurel. The umbrella spread forty feet across, and from treetop to ground it measured sixty feet. Three thick branches grew upward like a fan from a single trunk, which itself measured more than two feet across.

Michael dismounted and walked to the tree. He spread his fingers and pressed his palms against its bark. "The bark is strong, gray-green, slightly moist. The heartwood will be rich."

When they camped, the pepper-sweet scent of the laurel enveloped them. They drank dark coffee and took their evening pipes in silence. The moon rose, and the clarity of its brightness portended a calm night before a new dawn.

The next morning, Franklin left early to hunt meat.

Michael planned the cut. He wanted to drop the tree in an area where he and Franklin could work easily and where the fall would do the least damage to other trees. The plateau lay generally flat with a slight declining grade, more pronounced to the left. Michael walked off a distance he felt equaled the overall height of the tree. Plenty of room. Satisfied, he organized their equipment—two double-headed axes, two short ways, a two-man saw, chain, rope, and a steel cant hook.

"Ready," he said.

Franklin returned carrying a buck. "Meat enough now." He insisted, though, they hang the deer away from camp.

"Cougar might take it," Michael said. "Too far away, unguarded."

"And she's welcome," Franklin said. "Cougar ain't likely to raid the camp. A grizzly, they're more fickle. I seen scat up east. I don't want to offer no invite."

They hung the carcass two hundred yards from camp and tied the guy rope to a sapling. As they walked back toward camp, Michael explained his plan. "It's a sizable tree. We'll cut the fan branches, then the base. I want the heartwood. The rest we'll harvest next spring."

"Would not one of the branches do?" Franklin asked. "It is only a railroad tie."

"No," Michael answered. "The tie must come from the heartwood. Nothing less. Do you not sense its importance? We have strapped machine power to the back of an untamed continent and united this nation. A civil war ended. A wilderness mastered. God's hand on our efforts. No, Franklin, our luck goes well beyond just making a rail tie."

"Still, the thicker the log, the more difficult our task getting it down the mountain."

"But history, Franklin. Surely you understand that."

"History ain't nothin' to me," Franklin explained. "A man lives, a man dies. None escape that history."

The following morning, the men began the careful cutting of the laurel. The rhythm of the axes echoed into the deep woods. When the tree fell, the crash reverberated against the hillside like the sound of flood water.

After the tree's collapse, the men enjoyed a leisurely pipe before they began the arduous process of claiming the section of tree trunk they would use to make the laurel tie. They measured a sixteen foot length, and with the two-man saw, they end-cut each side at a twenty-two degree angle. This slight bevel would reduce drag as the pack mule skidded the log through the woods.

Franklin went to check on the stock and start the evening fire. Michael remained to seal the end cuts. He laid out a new hog's-hair brush, mixing can, ladle, jar of terpene, and tub of tar pitch. He mixed the ingredients, one ladle of terpene to two scoops of tar pitch. He stirred slowly, taking care not to splash any. This sealer would keep the tree sap intact, and it would prevent rain and atmospheric moisture from seeping into the trunk. This preservative also helped prevent cracks and discoloration. He painted each end. He covered all the raw wood, and he over-painted onto the bark as further precaution. He applied a second coat in order to insure a complete seal.

At the campsite, Franklin watered the horses and the mule. The animals pulled at their ropes and struggled to break away. Franklin feared their discomfort meant trouble. He looked around, and on the side of the hill, he spotted the grizzly. He grabbed his Remington.

"Michael," he called. "Bear!"

Michael turned in the direction of Franklin's voice.

At the same time, Franklin shot in front of the great, brown paws of the beast, spewing dirt near its eyes. The bear turned and ran, for the crack of the gunshot and the dust ghost were enough to scare it off. He calmed the horses, and they relaxed.

But the shot had startled Michael, and he tripped on a branch. As he fell, he dropped the container. Some of the sealer splattered on his face and seeped into his eyes.

"Franklin, help me!" he cried.

Michael's hands covered his face. Franklin grabbed Michael's wrists and pulled his hands away.

"Do not rub," Franklin ordered.

Michael nodded, but he clenched his jaw in pain.

"I'll get water."

Franklin washed Michael's face and flushed his eyes, but the heat of the chemicals had already scarred the tender surface of Michael's pupils. He was blind.

"I'll take you down. Come back for the wood."

"No," Michael insisted. "Nothing can be done about my eyes that can't wait. You lead the mule pulling the log. My horse will follow. He'll take care, and I will be fine."

A craftsman understands the connection between the maker, the wood, and the object of creation. Although Franklin did not comprehend this expression of life through craft, he had witnessed it enough to trust it.

Franklin knew how to care for Michael and how to manage the animals in order to guide them with their loads safely through difficult terrain. Nevertheless, they made the descent with caution. Though

less strenuous than the climb, it took two days and one intervening night of watchful riding and little conversation. Finally, they reached the great cascade of the Sacramento River and the sudden, salt-sting of the iron-gray San Francisco Bay. Near sunset, the men arrived at the warehouse of the Strahle and Hughes Company.

When Franklin went to Michael to assist him from the horse, several of the dock hands rushed to help.

"What's happened, Michael?"

Michael, tentative and unsteady, did not answer.

"What's happened here, Franklin?" Tenneyson demanded.

When news of an injury to his son reached Jacob Strahle, he rushed to the warehouse. "We must get you to the doctor." Mr. Strahle helped Michael into his carriage, then the driver hurried to the office of Dr. James Dryer.

"It's common enough," Dr. Dryer said. "I see it some with gunpowder."

He returned his magnifying glass to its case.

"You done right washing it with water, Michael. If you do ever see again, that'll be the cause."

"Franklin did it. Insisted, in fact. I wanted to rub. It burned. He held my arms."

"He done you a favor, son." The doctor sat and spoke to both men. "There is some surface damage, but the eye is a queer critter. Sometimes it will remake the cells, and sometimes it won't. There ain't no way to guess which way yours will turn."

"What can we do?" Mr. Strahle asked.

"Best thing is rinse them with water morning and night. Pat a towel around them to dry your face, but do not rub. Real important not to rub."

"Nothing else?" Mr. Strahle asked.

"Lord's hands now, Jacob. Only so much we humans can do."

"I want to make the tie," Franklin told Mr. Strahle.

"You, Franklin? You're a field hand."

"For Michael, sir."

"Oh?"

"On the pack down the mountain, well... blind he was. But he kept to the reins and the stirrup, and he held his horse. Trusted me. Never complained. Not once."

The old man nodded.

"At evening camp on the way down the mountain,

he told me the tie and him was connected. 'It ain't made yet,' I said. 'Sure it is,' he told me. 'Here. In my head.' He visioned it. And in that firelit night, his blind eyes shining, I seen it too. Seen the tie. And I seen his face in it."

As work progressed, Franklin described each day's activity to Michael.

"The log's squared and ready for the first rough cut."

"Do not cut it," Michael said. "Dry the log first."

"We never dry a full log, Michael. You know that," Tenneyson said.

"I know. But to deliver the tie on time, we cannot wait eight months to dry the piece and still have the possibility it will warp or split. Instead, we will quick dry the entire timber."

"What do you mean by quick dry?"

"Set up a drying tent. Leave one end of the tent open. Build a five inch deep water trough, three feet wide, and two feet longer than the trunk. Weld a grated table to fit over it. Make a gas bar and keep a constant flame below the water. The fire must burn low, and it must not go out. Set the laurel on the grated table to dry. The moist heat will make steam that will dry the wood slowly from the inside."

"I never heard of that, and it won't work. You dry it too fast like that and the piece will twist."

"Yes. Maybe even crack. Once done, though," Michael explained, "we can remove a section from the center for the tie, and it will hold."

They kept the log in the tent for twenty-eight days. Then they soaked it in water for eight hours and steam-dried it again for another month. This second drying not only cured the great log, but also, the process deepened the lime, yellow, and bronze highlights in the grain.

When they finally made the first rough cut, Michael touched the edges and the surface texture of each face. He touched the corners with his thumb and forefinger, testing for square. He felt it for possible imperfections. And he felt it to know it.

"It's coming along," he said.

On May 1, 1869, Leland Stanford left Sacramento, riding the connecting line from California to Utah. The trip took three days and two nights. When they reached the high plateau of Utah, Stanford called for

Blanchard Noirson to meet him in his walnut-paneled lounge car. Stanford looked out the window at the gathering of men and events that would conclude the great adventure.

"When that last tie is set, Noirson, those men will release years of pent up energies."

"Your return engine is already in place on the secondary line. We'll be gone before the fireworks begin."

"And the tie?"

"All set. Me and three trusted men. We will replace the laurelwood with the pine replica."

"Take care that no damage comes to it. No bruises. No scratches."

"I will see to it, sir. It will make a fine display at Mrs. Stanford's Museum."

The two steam locomotives, the Central Pacific #60 from the West and the Union Pacific #119 from the East, were polished and drawn up face to face, ready to meet. News men mingled with saloon girls, both occupations temporarily idle, anticipating the big event. Western Union electricians would hook a wire to the final steel rail so that the sounds of the silver-plated maul clanking the last spike would signal completion in telegraph offices across the country.

The ceremony was scheduled for May 8. Man, machine, technology, news, and a united nation stood at the ready. However, the morning eased the black night aside with a gray, uninviting sky. A harsh wind carrying sandy gravel stung the skin, and thunder rumbling across that high, desolate prairie foretold a bitter rain.

This rail line experienced many great delays and hundreds of small ones in its seven years of construction, so a short delay of its ceremonial conclusion did not much spoil enthusiasm. However, when the second day of weather misery began, and the effects of its gloomy rain and stinging wind added to the sourness of the day prior, equipment, animals, men, and anticipation all dampened.

Stanford met with Mr. Thomas Durant, the Vice-President of the Union Pacific Rails.

"The men are restless," Durant said.

"The country is restless," Stanford countered. "We cannot delay much longer."

"You control much, Leland, but you cannot yet control the weather."

"Not for lack of desire," Stanford said.

Both men peered out the windows into the unbroken gloom.

"Perhaps we should provide some diversion," Durant suggested.

"You're right," Stanford agreed.

The spirits of the men who were gathered to make history needed attention, and Stanford released a boxcar of whiskey cases to help ease their anxiety. By evening, the elevated spirits of inebriation released into that somber and rain-soaked Utah plateau setting loose song, gunfire, and passions nearly fit enough for the original date of setting the final tie.

Even Stanford and Durant drank enough that they found themselves staring at the dizzying pattern of a star-gorged horizon.

"Think there's life out there?" Stanford asked.

"Yes, sir, I don't mind if I do," Durant replied.

"I'd like to go there someday. Maybe we can build a celestial railroad and charge a fee."

"I feel rather free myself," Durant admitted, although he could not hold his glass steady as he attempted to pour another drink.

When the sun rose on the morning of May 10, the signal bell rang loud enough to awaken magistrates and workers alike. Everyone knew they must take advantage of the break in weather to finally set the last rail with the last spike to the last tie of the trans-American railway.

Except for the men of the Twenty-First Infantry from Camp Douglas in Salt Lake City, most of the 1,500 on-lookers arrived intoxicated or severely hung over. Two of the reasonably sober laborers set the laurelwood tie over a cowhand's tarpaulin and slightly below grade to insure the last rails did not mar its rich, lacquered surface.

The memorial silver plaque, secured in the center of the laurel tie, was inscribed with these words:

The last tie laid on completion of the
Pacific Railroad, May 8, 1869.

The plaque also listed the officers and Directors of the Central Pacific, and below their names, Mr. Michael Strahle, the blinded wood-artist who crafted the tie.

Mr. Stanford held the memorial, silver-plated spike maul. He and Mr. Durant would drive the final gold spike. The spike measured 5 5/8 inches in length, and it was fashioned from 23 twenty-dollar gold pieces. On its top, the foundry stamped the words:

The Last Spike.

At this same moment, Mr. Michael Strahle rose from his bed in San Francisco. He had heard the news of the weather delay, but he was unaware the ceremony in Utah had begun. Still sightless, he grabbed the dark purple robe from the wing-back chair stationed next to his bed, shoved his arms into the sleeves, then cinched the cloth tie. Next he sat, slid his feet into the slippers, then felt the warmth of the morning rays ease through the glass of the bedroom window.

Mr. Stanford stepped to the rail. The golden spike rested in the bore-hole. He lifted the maul to set the spike, a gesture that would enshrine him to immortal greatness. He did not need to hit the spike with force. The prepared hole would allow easy insertion and removal of the spike, with no damage to it or to the tie.

Mr. Stanford's hangover persisted so that he swung with the efficiency of a one-handed cymbal player, and when he hit the rail instead of the spike, the maul ricocheted and struck the laurelwood tie, leaving a quarter-moon dimple on its heretofore unblemished surface.

Mr. Durant took his turn to tap the spike into place. However, Mr. Durant remained completely inebriated. When he swung the maul, he missed the spike and the rail and hit instead the tie. The maul left a circular, teacup-sized indentation adjacent to Mr. Stanford's smaller and somewhat less adroit blemish.

The two men were helped away, then one of the workers dutifully tapped the gold spike home.

At the precise moment the gold spike settled into place, Michael Strahle's skin tingled. He felt a jolt, like jumping into a frigid mountain stream. The startle response quickened his blood-flow, and he squeezed his eyes shut in surprised reaction. When he opened his eyes, he saw the light of the morning sun.

"Father!" he called.

The engineers at Promontory Summit eased the #119 and the #60 locomotives toward one another. As their cowcatchers touched, signaling the official conclusion of the ceremony, Mr. Strahle brought Michael to Dr. Dryer's office in San Francisco.

"Well?" Mr. Strahle asked.

"It appears his eyesight has returned," Dr. Dryer confirmed. "You say it just happened?"

Michael nodded.

"James, we know he can see," Mr. Strahle said. "Is it permanent? How did it happen?"

"As I told you at the first, Jacob, we do not know all the mysteries of the human body. I have heard of cases of sight recovered. It happens. That's all I can tell you for explanation."

"Is it permanent, then? Can you state that?"

His old friend looked at him, knowing he already understood no such guarantee existed for anything.

"Is it not enough that his sight has returned?"

Mr. Strahle looked at his son. Michael returned the glance.

"Yes," Mr. Strahle said. "It is enough."

Michael Strahle became the young leader of Strahle and Hughes, and Steward Franklin abandoned his semi-wild life to become Michael's assistant. Under their guidance, the firm became the most renowned wood-artists in the American west.

In the interval between the ceremony at Promontory Summit, Utah, and the early spring of 1906, no further historical significance regarding the laurelwood tie exists outside of its prominence as one of the main reasons for the early reputation of the Stanford Museum.

In the early days of April, 1906, the weather along the northern California coast lessened its firm seventy-degree ambience and its crisp ocean-enervated winds, and citizens of the rapidly growing bay area enjoyed soft breezes and unusually mellow humidity. It felt as if nature had become passive. Commerce slowed, neighbors lingered in conversation, and sunsets displayed a vast horizon of gold and scarlet which lingered into the early springtime evenings.

Then, at 5:12 a.m., on Wednesday, the eighteenth day of April, 1906, the earth rumbled. Twenty-two seconds later—beneath the becalmed surface, the substructure that in its elastic history spewed forth the mountainous seascape and the five thunderous rivers that empty into the turbulent Bay—this same violent architecture of earthly geology released enough pent-up energy to reshuffle the positions of the mountains, the rivers, and the sea.

In its unrestrained roiling, the San Francisco earthquake of 1906 crumbled buildings, cracked bridges, and uplifted roadways. The dreadful rumblings traveled all the way from Oregon, south along the coast, beyond the precinct of Los Angeles, and inland as far east as Winnemucca, Nevada. No one is certain of the actual number of dead.

In the explosive uplift of the aftershocks, water lines cracked, sewer lines spewed, and gas lines split with the result that the fires after the quake did as much damage as the shifting plates. Smoke billowed and fire roared for miles as San Francisco and all the foundling communities around the Bay burned—San Mateo, Mill Valley, San Leandro, all of them, including that little township named Stanford, after its founder, and the location of the Stanford Museum.

The flames spread, unrelenting, day and night, and they spread to the Stanford Museum where they reached the laurelwood tie. The fire engulfed the tie. It stripped the delicate edges along the corners, and when it burst forth from within the heart of the wood, the eroding process of wood to dust began.

Michael Strahle ran to the shop, struggling against the violent upheaval of the wave-like buckling of the seismic wobble. Inside, he found the building on its way to total ruination—an overturned lathe, scattered pieces of exotic wood, broken glass, interior walls collapsing.

Suddenly, at the same instant the laurelwood tie burst forth into consummate flame, Michael fell to the floor, as if consumed by exhaustion. As the tie burned and the substance of the laurelwood released into smoke, Michael's energy abated. Gradually, as the tie flamed, Michael's sight left him. His breaths grew more and more shallow, and as the last of the laurelwood ember fell to dead ash, Michael Strahle exhaled his last breath.

When they discovered his body, everyone concluded the quake caused Michael's death. City records indicate he died of a heart attack. Now, only legend survives, offering a hint of the unity of life and spirit and art, that triad of purpose which yokes one man's brief spark of momentary vitality to the transient history of human time.

THE AUTHOR

Thom Brucie's *novel,* Children of Slate, *won the 2023 bronze medal Illumination Award for excellence in Catholic literature. His novel,* Obsidian Mirth, *won the American Writing Award in fiction (2022) and was short-listed for the Hawthorne Prize. His poetry chapbook,* Apprentice Lessons, *earned the 2024 Miriam Chaikin Award in Poetry. His chapbook* Moments Around The Campfire with A Vietnam Vet *was named the best chapbook of 2010 and is a finalist for the American Legacy Award in Poetry, 2024. He has been nominated twice for the Pushcart Prize, and his short stories and poems have appeared in a variety of journals including* The San Joaquin Review, Cappers, The Southwestern Review, Pacific Review, Wilderness House Literary Review, North Atlantic Review, *and many others.*

Dr. Brucie is retired Professor of English and Professional Writing at South Georgia State College.

THE SUMMONING

POETRY BY SCOTT M. BRENTS

A STARRY SATURDAY NIGHT
AFTER A SADDLEBAG SUN
HAD BEATEN US ALL DAY LIKE LEATHER
HORSES ON THE RUN
CATCHING OUR BREATH IN PHOENIX
AS THE OWLS HOOTED OUR DEATH
WE DREAMT OF GOLD AND WOMEN
AS SHOOTING STARS STOLE OUR BREATH
IT'S NOT A GOOD JOURNEY TO TAKE
EATING DUST ON THE PLAIN
BUT THE PROMISE OF GREAT RICHES ADDS
SWEETNESS TO THE PAIN
NEXT DAY WE DEPARTED, THE SUN
ON OUR BACKS FIERCE AND MEAN
WE SOLD OUR SOULS FOR HIDDEN GOLD
THAT MIGHT NEVER BE SEEN

TALKING WESTERNS

Terry Alexander
ENTERTAINMENT EDITOR

California Gold Rush on Screen

Three Unique Hollywood Takes on the 1849 Phenomenon

The California Gold Rush began on January 24th, 1848, when James W. Marshall discovered gold at Sutter's Mill in Coloma, California. The landowner Johann August Sutter was a German/Swiss citizen, who immigrated to California in 1834. He came in search of land and riches. He changed his first name to John when he arrived in the new land.

The gold rush had disastrous effects on the Native American population in the area. Many died from disease, starvation, and the California Genocide. Thousands of people from Latin America, Europe, Australia, China, Mexico, and the United States poured into the area seeking their fortune. San Francisco went from a small settlement of two hundred people to a boomtown of over thirty-six thousand souls in less than two years. At this time, California wasn't a state, and no one had any property rights beyond their own will.

Several movies and one TV show have been made about California during this wild time. This article is about three of them.

The Californians was a half hour black and white TV show that ran on NBC from September 24, 1957, to August 27, 1959. The show originally told the tale of the gold rush before statehood. Sam Brennon (Herbert Rudley) owned one of the local newspapers. Dion Patrick (Adam Kennedy) worked as a reporter during the day. At night Patrick sought to maintain order with a group of vigilantes headed by storekeeper Jack McGivern (Sean McClory),

The sponsors grew uneasy about glorifying vigilantism. They met with the producers, changed the premise, cast of the show, and introduced new characters. On March 4th, 1958, in the episode titled "The Gentleman from Philadelphia," Matthew Wayne (Richard Coogan) was added to the cast. The original cast members were gradually phased out in preference to the new additions.

Wayne arrived in San Francisco and bought a saloon. He was accused of murder in his debut and had to be cleared by McGivern and his vigilantes. Wayne was then elected sheriff of San Francisco and became the main character. In the second season, Wayne was now City Marshall with a police department of fifty people. The second season also saw the introduction of Wilma Fansler (Carole Matthews), a widow,who owned one of the local gambling houses and became the romantic interest for Wayne. Attorney Jeremy Pitt (Art Fleming), sometime friend, sometime foil, was also introduced.

The theme song, "I've Come to California," was performed by the Ken Darby Singers. He also did the background music for the show. It received an Emmy nomination for Best Art Direction in a weekly program in 1959. During its short run, it had episodes that focused on the plight of the Chinese miner who worked in a strange land. It tended to avoid any shows dealing with the Native American population.

Sutter's Gold was a 1936 western film, directed by James Cruze for Universal Pictures. Carl Laemmie, the president of Universal Pictures, wanted a big outdoor western spectacle. He acquired the rights to the 1925 French novel *"l'OR"*, by Blaise Cendrars, and the stage play based on the novel written by Bruno Frank. Cruze had directed over a hundred silent movies in the twenties, his epic western *The Covered Wagon,* made in 1923, won the Kinema Junpo Award for Best Entertainment Film in Tokyo, Japan, in 1925. He had also directed several talkies in the thirties. He hired character actors to star in the picture, avoiding the more well-known actors, thinking they would detract from his epic. Edward Arnold was signed to play John Sutter. Binnie Barnes, Katherine Alexander, Lee Tracy, and Montague Love, with Harry Carey as Kit Carson made up the main cast. Laemmie gave Cruze *carte blanche* on the film, and he spent lavishly. The film cost two million dollars to make, at the time the average Universal film was approximately one hundred thousand dollars. The preview trailer alone was ten minutes long.

The movie proved to be a box office disaster that cost Laemmie his position as president of the studio and resulted in Cruze being blackballed by most of the studios in Hollywood, he made four movies for Republic Pictures, one in 1937, and three in 1938. Cruze had an alcohol problem that only worsened after *Sutter's Gold* failed to find an audience. He committed suicide on August 3rd, 1942. He was cremated and his remains are buried at Hollywood Forever Cemetery. In 1960, Cruze was awarded a star on the Hollywood Walk of Fame.

Der Kaiser Von Kalifornien, translated to *The Emperor of California,* was another 1936 western film loosely based on the novel *"l'OR"*. This movie was funded by Nazi Germany and told the story of Johann August Sutter. The movie was written, directed by, and starred Luis Trenker as Sutter. The film was also the acting debut of Vikitoria Von Ballasko, the final film for Marcella Albani, and also starred Werner Kunig. In the early days of the Nazi empire, they used everything at their disposal as propaganda, including movies. Josef Goebbels viewed himself a Patron of German Film, and he valued films as a propaganda tool. In the 1930's, the Nazi party had so much influence on American cinema, they could order films critical of the movement censored and controlled the release of news shorts.

No movie based on a true incident ever completely tells the truth, poetic license won't allow things like that to happen and in a movie the story must move quickly. A German born Swiss citizen emigrated to America in search of a better life and making a fortune. In this version California had previously been admitted to the United States, before the discovery of gold. John Sutter, gold rush pioneer and the founder of Sacramento, never changed his name from Johann, maintaining the German spelling to remain close to his roots. The film focused on his German heritage and brought his beliefs closer in line to the Nazi beliefs.

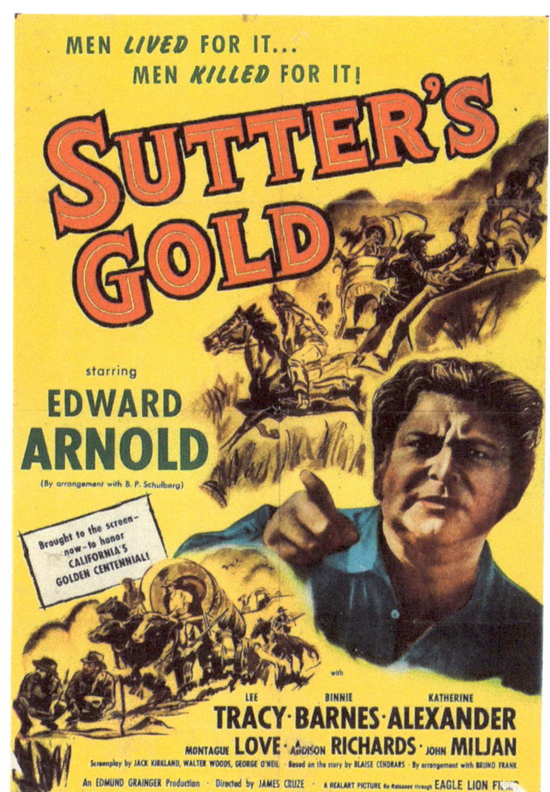

All the honest people in the film are of German descent. They are shown to have honored their agreements with the Native Americans depicted in the film. In one scene, a swastika was visible on the side of a teepee. The crooks are the Americans in the motion picture. They are dishonest and always out for a quick dollar and more than willing to swindle anyone. The Chinese and Black people in the movie are looked upon as subhuman.

Friedrech Gnab, one of the actors in the movie, made disparaging remarks about Adolf Hitler while he was drunk, during the trip back to Germany. Some reports even stated that he threatened Hitler's life. He was arrested and detained upon his arrival in the fatherland. He was placed in jail for two years and his part in the film was edited out and any scenes that had to be included in the picture were refilmed with another actor. There is a gap in his filmography from 1935 to 1938.

Some of the exterior scenes were filmed at Sedona, Arizona, and at the Grand Canyon. Scenes from Death Valley in California were also included in the picture. Adolf Hitler attended the premiere in Germany, and stated how much he enjoyed the film. It was the winner of the Mussolini Cup as Best Foreign Film in 1936, at the Venice Film Festival. The film was well reviewed by various movie critics in the United States. In 1961, Luis Trenker wrote a novel of the same name.

The movie ended with Johann Sutter, a broken penniless man getting a vision of the future and seeing the tall buildings and advances of 1936 California.

Terry Alexander *and his wife, Phyllis, live on a small farm near Porum, Oklahoma. They have three children, thirteen grandchildren, and four great grandchildren. If you see him at a conference, though, don't let him convince you to take part in one of his trivia games—he'll stump you every time.*

TRIBAL PASSAGES

Regina McLemore
FEATURES WRITER

The Evans-Cherokee Party

The Dark Legacy of the California Gold Rush

If Native Californians viewed their existence under Spanish rule as bleak, they undoubtedly considered it to be paradise compared to the hell the Americans brought on them when they claimed the land for themselves in 1848. Editors Clifford E. Trafzer and Joel R. Hyder give a harrowing account of the events that transpired in *Exterminate Them, Written Accounts of the Murder, Rape, and Enslavement of Native Americans during the California Gold Rush.*

It began when John Sutter decided to erect a sawmill on the South fork of the American River. His partner, James Marshall, was led by a Maidu Native to a possible site for the mill near the Maidu village of Coloma. Later, while the Maidu were digging a mill race on January 24, 1848, one of them discovered gold.

When this discovery was announced, white landowners, such as Charles Weber and William Daylor, hired Natives to accompany them to the Sierra Mountain foothills to search for gold. By August of 1848, approximately three thousand Indians labored in the gold fields, including men, women, and children. Much of this mining was done through the back-breaking method of panning for placer gold. White employers often paid the Native workers with goods, charging exorbitant prices for blankets, coffee, clothing, meat, sugar, and other necessities.

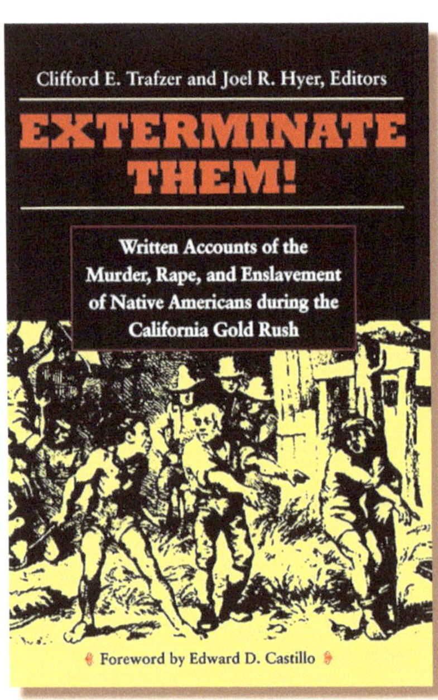

In 1849, with this claim came the river of newcomers, drawn by the elusive promise of striking it rich. Thousands of newcomers flooded California, not just Americans, but people from all over the globe. Some of these newcomers were not content to simply cheat the Natives, they sought to destroy them. In March 1849, a party of prospectors from Oregon attacked a Maidu village on the American River. The Native women were sexually assaulted, and the men who attempted to defend them were shot and killed. The Maidu sought revenge by attacking a party of Oregon miners, prospecting on the middle fork of the American River, and killing five of them. A mob of twenty men from Oregon retaliated by storming a village on Weber's Creek, killing at least twelve and imprisoning many. An angry James Marshall demanded their release since several were his employees. He backed down when the prospectors threatened his life. Between 1849 and 1850, the attacks and murders of Native Americans continued to rise until the Native Californians, who had been working in the minefields, realized their perilous position, and fled the fields.

When all this turmoil and violence was happening in California, across the country, in Indian Territory, a group of Cherokee caught a case of gold fever. The January 14, 1848, *Cherokee Advocate* advertised for *"all young men in the Nation who may wish to try their fortunes in the gold regions of California... wishing further information with regard to the "tramp" can obtain it by applying to the undersigned, Tahlequah, Cherokee Nation..."*

Within the article were listed requirements for participants: a good rifle, plenty of ammunition, and rations for the journey, consisting of 100 pounds of bacon and 180 pounds of flour, to be transported in wagons drawn by horses, mules, or oxen. The company planned to leave the first of April.

Luckily, quite a bit is known about this party's "tramp" to California, largely in part to the preservation of journals that various party members kept of their

"When Trails Were Dim," painting by Charles Marion Russell.

journey. These journals, and other documentation, have been collected by authors Patricia K.A. Fletcher, Dr. Jack Earl Fletcher, and Lee Whitely who included them in their publication, *Cherokee Trail Diaries*. Much of the following information is derived from this valuable source.

James Vann, the editor of the *Cherokee Advocate,* couldn't resist putting his own spin on the expedition in the February 1849 edition. First, he extended an invitation to persons in Arkansas and Missouri "to go with us." Next, he pointed out the great advantage of going with a Cherokee group, "the Cherokee are on the most friendly terms with all the Indian tribes of the prairies—consequently there will be no danger of attacks from our red brethren." Evidently, Vann sold himself on the idea of the trip because he resigned his position as Editor of the *Cherokee Advocate* to join up.

On April 21, 1849, a company from Fayetteville, Arkansas, met the Cherokee group at the "Sulphur Spring" at the Grand Saline in the Cherokee Nation, near what would become Salina, Oklahoma. They carried a flag that had been given them by a group of ladies from Fayetteville. Lewis Ross, brother of Chief John Ross, owned a saltworks there, and people had been gathering there for days, waiting for the start of the expedition. Several others had arrived from Arkansas, including one married couple, Isaac and Carolyn Hale, and sisters Barbara and Herminia, accompanied by their brothers, Edward, Christian, and Henry Freyschlag. They soon organized their company and called it the Evans-Cherokee Company, naming it after the man elected as Captain, Lewis Evans of Evansville, Arkansas. James Vann was elected as Secretary.

Several of the travelers kept journals or wrote letters home. Company member, James Sawyer Crawford, who had served as a Captain of the Washington County Militia in Arkansas, kept a diary of the company's proceedings. He wrote: *"We have in our company 128 (written over 128 is 129) persons 40 waggons 304 oxen 41 mules 65 Horses and 31 cows, making in all the Stock 441 head."*

The company traveled northeast from the Grand Saline, blazing a new trail, which would become known as the Evans-Cherokee Trail. On April 28, at Redbud Creek, northwest of Nowata, Oklahoma, they encountered a group of Osage. Crawford wrote: *"The Osages tell us we will have to fight the Pawnies, and Camanchees before we git Through the mountain, but I think it is uncertain...the osage Indians are coming to our camp every night, they are quite filthy but verry sivil; they made a big dance last night for the amusement of our company."*

A letter was dispatched to the *Cherokee Advocate,* written on April 29, 1849, and published as an update on the company on May 7, 1849. It was obviously written by an educated Cherokee and was signed OO-CHA-LOO-TA: *"I have snatched a few moments from camp duties to announce the safe progress of 90 miles from Tahlequah... we are all together."*

He ended his letter by affirming that for the Cherokee... *"the fire of patriotic love burns with continued intensity of fervor for the future welfare, progress and onward destiny of their country."*

On Tuesday, May 2, 1849, the company crossed the boundary line between Oklahoma and Kansas. Two days later, on May 4, someone recorded "Fish camp", which seems to indicate that some of the company caught fish in a nearby creek, believed to be Otter Creek, east of Sedan, Chautauqua County, Kansas.

By the end of May and during the month of June, home folks, hearing nothing from the company, were worried. Matters weren't helped by sixteen or eighteen of the company's oxen being found, wandering on the Verdigris River.

On May 12, 1849, the group arrived at the Santa Fe Trail and created their own post office, making a sign announcing the news of their arrival placing it under one of the few large rocks they could find. They also placed a large rock in the fork of the road and engraved it with: *"To Fayetteville, Ark., 300 miles—Capt. Evans' Cal. 'Com'y, May 12, 1849."* In addition, they wrote a letter describing their journey and informing readers they were heading to Bent's Fort near present day Pueblo, Colorado.

"Wagon Boss," painting by Charles Marion Russell.

The letter was carried by traders to the *Daily Missouri Republican,* where it was published on

July 4. It later appeared in the *Cherokee Advocate* on July 30.

A conflict arose at Pueblo, which divided the company. Cherokee Daniel Gunter wrote home about it on June 22. *"...some trapers told (us) that it was impossible ...to cross the mountains...with wagons, which caused thirty men to dispose of their wagons and what provisions they could not carry, to some trapper...."*

Another correspondent, Hiram Davis, was concerned about these men. *"...having exchanged their wagons for mules and ponies and will go through on packs. I entertain serious concerns for their safety—they have 1200 miles to pack from this place to California."*

The pack company wisely hired an experienced guide, Dick Owens. This decision, undoubtedly, saved them time and some hardships. They were also fortunate to be joined by Lt. Pleasanton and an escort of ten men from Company H, 2nd Dragoons, who were on their way to California.

James Vann, who joined the packers, wrote *"...we passed over Laramie Plains to the headwaters of Yampah River...to the Vermillion mountains, across said mountains to Brown Hole, from thence to Bridgers (Fort Bridger)."*

Another group broke away. Four wagons of men decided to turn back home. They carried letters back to Fayetteville, Arkansas, for those who remained.

The wagon group was soon joined by travelers from Helena, Arkansas. On June 22, the Evans-Cherokee Company left Pueblo.

On the way from Brown Hole, the combined packer group encountered disaster on the Green River. Using a "skin" raft to transport some of their packs across the river, an ill James Garvin was also put on the raft. Before reaching the west shore, the packs and Garvin went down. The party continued on to Fort Bridger without Garvin and some of their supplies.

Correspondent Cherokee C.W. Keys described their arrival at the "City of the Salt Lake" on July 24, 1849. Here they were welcomed by five or six thousand Mormons, who were gathered to celebrate their second anniversary in the valley. After speaking, singing, and parading, the Mormons invited them to a much-appreciated dinner.

The packer party had completed the trek from Pueblo to Salt Lake in a month, but it took the guideless Evans/Cherokee wagon group almost twice as long. They were building their own wagon roads over a different route. They left Pueblo on the Trapper's or Divide Trail, beginning a gradual ascent from 4,660 feet elevation to the 7,520 feet watershed Divide between the Arkansas and the Platte Rivers.

On June 28, they camped in the remains of the abandoned Fort St. Vrain. The industrious company constructed a ferry boat out of the plank from the fort. It took them four days to build it and cross their wagons over the South Platte River. After they crossed, they left the boat for the "benefit of the next who should come along this road."

Dissension and disease struck the party. Some of the men wanted to turn from their westward direction, which would lead them to a desert, and turn north instead. On July 18, blacksmith and correspondent, John Pyeatte, related that J.M. Mathews got lost from the train and lay out in the snowy mountains until he was found. He had severe sickness and had to stay in a wagon. Several others joined him in sickness, including Pyeatte's son. One of the sick Cherokee called the disease "Mountain Fever."

The decision had been made to continue the western route across the Great Divide Basin. Several cattle and oxen were lost from drinking too much salty water, and several men suffered from the same cause. On July 24, Pyeatte reported that the animals spent one night entirely without water and were almost famished. Soon, most of the men had no water and set out hunting for it. Finally, one man found a place where a heavy shower had fallen two days earlier. This rainwater saved the company.

With August came the first death in the company. Crawford wrote: *"one Mr. Tharp died with what the doctors call Diabetus."*

On August 8, Pyeatte reported that some of the Cherokee and *"Fayetteville trash...all together 12 wagons ...came on to bridgers fort...and many of them got drunk on whiskey...and cut up tall shines."* This group left the company and went on their own.

After receiving a warm reception by the Mormons, the Evans-Cherokee Company left Salt Lake on August 17. On August 24, Crawford wrote about *"a miserable Desert Where in many places we could not see the least vestages of vegiation of any Kind for many miles round us...a good many Cattle gave out and we had to leave our Waggons and go to water and grass...."*

Only the strongest animals were taken with four of the lightest wagons. Each man could only take

1850's Illustration of a wagon train on the trail.

his blankets, one change of clothes, his gun, and only enough food that the company could carry.

Leaving behind what was deemed unnecessary continued during the month of September and all the way to California. They had been counselled that they must reach the Truckee Pass by October 1, in order to cross the California Mountains in safety. It was nearly October 1, and they were still east of the last desert. They rose early and traveled as far as possible each day. Even so, they arrived at the Humboldt Desert with little water and food. They were forced to slaughter several oxen for food.

Meanwhile, the packing company arrived in California on September 17, and were working on the Stanislaus River diggings.

Freezing rain began on October 30, turning to snow by the following morning. The Evans-Cherokee wagon company and the breakaway group were both caught by the snow. There were no reports of anyone dying, but many animals were lost. The Evans-Cherokee group built winter cabins and hunted deer. Pyeatte said they also dug 35 ounces of gold and sold venison to the Indians.

In 1850, fifty more Cherokee completed the journey to California, along with groups from Arkansas and other states. For the most part, they followed the route blazed by the Evans-Cherokee Company. They experienced more deaths due to sickness, including cholera.

Most of the 1849 and 1850 adventurers soon returned home. Some came home better off than most. The *Cherokee Advocate* on June 3, 1851 states, *"They managed to get enough of the precious stuff to bring them home, and how much more is not said."*

It became obvious that some of the gold seekers did quite well. Many returning Cherokee and Arkansans soon purchased land and built valuable homes and farms.

Some made California their permanent home. Christian Freyschlag, and perhaps his sisters, Barbara and Hermina, stayed, even after their rich brother Edward returned to Fayetteville.

Some chose to stay for a time, like Cherokee Dennis Bushyhead, who came in 1849, and stayed nearly twenty years in California as a partner in the San Diego Union newspaper. He returned to Tahlequah in 1868, and was elected as Cherokee Nation's Treasurer. In 1879, he was elected as Principal Chief, an office he held until 1887.

Many lives, Native and White, were changed forever because of the California Gold Rush.

Regina McLemore *is a Will Rogers Medallion Award-winning author and retired educator of Cherokee heritage. Her great, great grandmother, Susie Christie Clay, survived the Trail of Tears in 1839. Regina's Young Adult Trilogy, Cherokee Passages, is a fictional retelling of her family's history from the Trail of Tears down through the modern day.*

www.ingramcontent.com/pod-product-compliance
Lightning Source LLC
LaVergne TN
LVHW071132190826
846010LV00028B/112

9798892990165